ABOUT THE AUTHORS

Amy McGavin is the pen name of a Scottish wife-and-husband writing team whose real names are . . . Amy and Gavin.

The couple's contemporary romance novels are set in the Highlands. Each story is crafted with humour and heart, with a wee bit of heat thrown in.

The pair live in Glasgow with their daughter and very lively cocker spaniel. When they're not writing, they enjoy exploring Scotland's breathtaking hills, glens, and beaches, then treating themselves to coffee and cake afterwards.

To keep up to date with all their publishing news, and gain access to exclusive bonus content, join their newsletter by visiting amymcgavin.com.

Newsletter

BY THE SAME AUTHORS

The Scottish Single Dads Series

Captain of My Heart

Built for Love

Catching Feelings

The True Scotsman Series

The Highland Kiss

The Highland Fling

The Highland Crush

The Highland Game

The Highland Bad Boy

The
HIGHLAND
BAD BOY

The True Scotsman Series

AMY McGAVIN

GRUMPY GROUSE
PRESS

ISBN 978-1-916734-09-8

Published by Grumpy Grouse Press

The
HIGHLAND
BAD BOY

CHAPTER ONE

ROBBIE

Seven years ago

Fights like this don't end with handshakes—they end with blood, broken bones, or worse. My fists are up, chest bare and shoulders taut, feet planted wide. Each breath tears out of me, harsh and uneven in the damp air of this crumbling warehouse. Sweat trickles down my spine, slick and cold against my skin.

My opponent stalks me in a slow circle, his eyes never leaving mine. He's bigger than me—most aren't—but I've got the reach. Our makeshift ring is nothing more than a chalk circle scrawled on the gritty floor, hemmed in by a heaving wall of bodies. The crowd stomp their feet and howl like they're at some ancient gladiator battle. The place reeks of stale beer and cigarettes.

He lunges, and I duck. It's instinct now, years of muscle memory that fires faster than thought. The world shrinks to only this: me, him, and the intoxicating simplicity of hit or be hit.

I feint left to draw him off balance then pivot sharply right. My fist shoots out—fast and clean—connecting with his ribs just below his guard. He grunts, stumbling back a step.

"Finish him, MacDonald!" someone yells at me, the voice cutting through the haze of my focus.

"Twenty quid says Big Cal drops in the next minute!" another shouts.

My focus tunnels back to Big Cal. He charges again, swinging wildly, but I step aside and his strike slices through air.

I shift my weight onto the balls of my feet, every muscle coiled tight. My joggers hang low on my hips, my skin gleaming under the harsh overhead lights that are rigged to a generator in the corner.

When Big Cal's next punch comes—a hook aimed square at my jaw—I'm half a second too slow slipping it. His knuckles connect with my mouth hard enough to split my lip wide open. Pain blooms hot and sharp for an instant, but then adrenaline numbs it to a dull throb.

"That all you got?" I taunt through bloodied teeth before spitting a mouthful of crimson onto the floor.

His eyes narrow. Good. Angry fighters make mistakes.

The crush of bodies presses in on us, like a noose pulling tighter and tighter. There's no official referee, just a burly man who occasionally barks out reminders to keep it clean. No hitting a man when he's down. No weapons. Everything else is fair game.

Big Cal comes at me again, throwing a flurry of combinations I mostly slip or block. One catches me in the ribs, and I let out a low growl, absorbing the impact. I counter with a hook that glances off his jaw. Not enough.

He grins, thinking he's got me. I let him think it.

Above us, heavy rain pounds the corrugated metal roof in a relentless drumbeat, a soundtrack to this brutal dance. My gaze locks on Big Cal's, watching for my opening.

When he winds up for another bone-breaking swing from

hell, I spot it. His right hand drops just a fraction lower than it should. Rookie mistake. Doesn't matter how big you are if you leave your chin unguarded.

I duck under his punch and come up with everything I've got, my fist connecting with his jaw in a perfect uppercut, the impact jolting up my arm. His head snaps back, then he crumples to the floor like his strings have been cut.

A sudden silence falls over the crowd. No one moves. No one breathes. The only sounds are the rain and the angry hum of the generator. Fighting is one thing, manslaughter is another. We're all thinking the same thing: *Get up, you bastard.*

Long seconds stretch out unbearably before finally Big Cal groans, his massive frame twitching on the grimy floor. His eyes blink open—unfocused, glassy, but alive. A collective exhale rushes through the warehouse. Someone hauls him upright, propping him into a dazed sitting position. He shakes his head like he's trying to remember where he is.

And then, as if someone has flipped a switch, the quiet shatters into a cacophony of cheers and groans. Money changes hands with greedy smirks or defeated grumbles. A meaty hand claps my back hard enough to jar my aching ribs.

"Fucking hell, MacDonald. For a second there, I thought you'd killed him!"

I swipe at my split lip with the back of my hand, wincing when the sting flares anew, but a cocky grin tugs at my battered mouth anyway. My knuckles are raw, my ribs throb like someone has taken a hammer to them—not far from the truth—but the noise in my head is quiet for once.

I'm aware there's nothing glamorous about this—bare-knuckle brawls in abandoned buildings, men betting money they can't afford to lose, every second loaded with the chance that blue lights will flicker outside and we'll scatter like rats into the night.

But winning? Winning just tastes so bloody good.

For a few fleeting minutes, I'm not Robbie MacDonald, Bannock's resident screw-up and walking disappointment, the man most folk have long since written off. Here and now I'm something better. Stronger.

I'm a winner, for once in my bloody life.

CHAPTER TWO

ROBBIE

Now

Scotland isn't built for weather like this, and neither am I. This far north we're more about drizzle, wellies, and complaining about how cold it is. Today, though? It's an absolute scorcher. The mid-August heat shimmers over the manicured lawns of the Glen Garve Resort.

It's a perfect afternoon for lying in the shade with an ice-cold beer, but instead I'm crouched over a wooden bench that's in need of some serious TLC. Hammer in hand, sweat dripping down my back, I drive in another nail with a loud crack. It's kind of satisfying, although given the long list of shit I've got to get through today, one measly nail is a bit like pissing in the sea.

Around me, the resort stretches out, a picture-postcard blend of fairytale charm and corporate polish. There's the castle-like main building, the golf course rolling off into the distance, the flower gardens bright enough to give you a headache—all set against the jaw-dropping backdrop of Highland hills. It's the kind of beauty that feels almost too perfect, like it was designed to be ogled at rather than lived in.

I'm on one of the resort's garden paths, tucked between rows of ornamental cherry trees and borders overflowing with roses and lilies. It's meant to be peaceful—a spot for guests to take lazy strolls and pretend a walk is enough to burn off their hearty Scottish breakfast. But if peace is what you're after, a bloke with a hammer is guaranteed to ruin it. That probably explains why the couple approaching me look as thrilled to see me as they would an overflowing bin.

Even from thirty paces, I can tell they're the type who booked into a five-star resort expecting the world to rearrange itself around their every whim. Him in golf-ready chinos and a yellow jumper far too heavy for this heat. Her in floaty linen trousers and sunglasses so oversized they're practically a visor. Their matching expressions of mild disdain suggest that neither has ever had to do anything more taxing than lift a wine glass.

Trailing behind them is their daughter—a definite upgrade on her parents. She must be in her late twenties, a few years younger than my own thirty-one. Her blonde hair falls in those artfully effortless waves rich girls seem to be born with, and she's wearing a flowy dress that screams "expensive" even though there's barely enough fabric to call it an outfit. Her gaze lingers on me as I crouch by the bench, her eyes sweeping over my broad shoulders and the navy polo shirt clinging to my skin in this relentless heat. A bead of sweat rolls down my temple, catching her attention before she zeroes in on the tattoo running up my right arm: a tangle of Celtic knots inked in black. She tilts her head like she's trying to unravel their meaning. Good luck with that, sweetheart.

Her parents are completely oblivious to her interest in me.

They're too busy radiating irritation. They haven't said a word yet, but I can see it coming a mile off: they've got a complaint lined up, and I'm to be on the receiving end of it. With a sharp crack of the hammer, I drive another nail into the bench, a wee bit harder than necessary.

Before either of them addresses me, the wife leans towards her husband and mutters in a stage whisper about as subtle as a bagpipe, "Why on earth can't they schedule this sort of thing for when guests aren't around?" She flicks a pointed glance at my tools, as if their mere presence is a personal insult.

When exactly would you suggest? I want to ask her. Because I doubt she'd appreciate me hammering away at three in the morning. Things need to be maintained. If they weren't, can you guess who'd be the first to moan about it? That's right, these two.

"Excuse me," the man says, his sharp tone carrying the entitled edge of someone who's used to getting his way without delay or argument.

I straighten up, all six foot five of me towering over him, hammer still clutched in my hand. "Aye? Can I help you?" The fake politeness in my voice has been hammered into shape over time. When you work in hospitality—even just in maintenance—it's a survival skill.

"Is it really necessary to make such a racket? We're trying to enjoy a peaceful walk."

I bite back what I want to say and plaster on a smile. "Sorry for disturbing you. I'll hold fire till you're well out of earshot." Because of course I've got time to add *Standing around doing bugger all for five minutes* to my schedule. It's not like I've got half a dozen other jobs to finish before the sun melts me into a puddle.

But if it wasn't this, they'd find something else to whinge

about. The roses aren't red enough. The hills are too hilly. The air smells too much like nature and not enough like whatever over-priced candles they burn at home. But hey, the customer's always right. Even when they're absolutely not.

With all the facilities on offer, you'd think these folk would be happy. Swimming pool, sauna, steam room, bubble pool. Eighteen-hole golf course. Massages in the spa. A cocktail bar and fine-dining restaurant to keep anyone's taste buds thoroughly spoiled. A fully equipped gym and yoga classes. And the sun is even out—they literally couldn't have picked a better time to come. How could you *not* be happy on a day like this?

But no. Despite all the indulgent possibilities they could be losing themselves in, they're here, moaning at me. Because, apparently, nothing beats finding something trivial to get angry about.

The couple move past me, and I offer them a tight-lipped nod as they go, though they don't acknowledge it. They do, however, mutter away to each other that tattoos are hardly the image they'd expect of an employee of the Glen Garve Resort.

"And an eyebrow piercing!" The woman tuts and shakes her head. "Honestly!"

All I can do is grit my teeth and bear it. I can't even get on with my hammering to drown them out.

"Maybe you could have a word with management about standards, darling," she adds.

Good luck with that, I think. The general manager of the Glen Garve Resort just so happens to be Craig MacDonald, my father. And trust me, he's heard it all before, and I've heard it all from him. But still I've got this job because, one, I'm good at it—very good, in fact—and two, despite all his fatherly failings, I don't think he's got the heart to let me go.

Even so, the couple's snide muttering gets under my skin, and one hand curls into a fist at my side, tension coiling in my muscles. I used to have a very effective outlet for my frustrations—one that also brought in a nice wee bit of money, even if it came with a guarantee of regular cuts and bruises. But I've not fought anyone for seven years. Not since . . .

I shake the thought away. Besides, right now there's something—or rather, *someone*—demanding my attention.

The daughter, still trailing behind her parents by several paces, pauses as she passes me. Her eyes sweep over me in lazy appraisal, lingering shamelessly on my arms. Then she looks up at me through thick lashes, her lush lips curving into a slow, deliberate smile that holds just enough cheekiness to make my pulse kick up a notch.

There's mischief in her expression. And heat. An unspoken invitation written plain across her pretty face.

Well, well. I may not fight anymore, but there are other ways to burn off some energy. Judging by the way this rich lassie is looking at me, she's thinking the same thing.

◆ ◆ ◆

I tug my polo shirt back on over my head, the cotton sticking to my sweat-slicked skin. The air conditioning in the room hums quietly, fighting a losing battle against the heat seeping through the half-open balcony door. Behind me, the daughter—Melissa? Melanie? I didn't catch her name and it doesn't really matter—lounges on Egyptian cotton sheets so crisp and smooth they practically whisper "indulgence".

She watches me through half-lidded eyes, a lazy, satisfied smile playing on her lips. Her blonde hair is splayed across the pillow, and the sheet is draped artfully across her naked body.

"Leaving already?" she purrs, stretching like a contented cat.

"Aye, time for me to head home." I buckle my belt. "That was my reward for surviving today's to-do list."

The suite around us is all tasteful opulence—crystal glasses on the minibar, plush carpet underfoot, and a bathroom gleaming with marble surfaces.

She props herself up on one elbow. "Will I see you again before I leave?"

"Depends on how many more benches need fixed near your parents' walking route."

This makes her laugh, a sound that's genuinely warm despite the silver spoon she was clearly born with. "God, they were awful to you. I'm sorry about that."

I shrug. "Don't worry about it. I've had worse."

Besides, I think to myself, there's a certain satisfaction in knowing that while her parents were looking down their noses at the tattooed maintenance man, their precious daughter was mentally undressing him. And then actually undressing him a few hours later.

"Well, thanks for . . ." She gestures at the rumpled bed. "Everything."

"My pleasure." I give her a sly wink. "Literally."

I smooth down my messed-up hair then glance into the corridor to make sure it's clear. There's no sign of her parents, so I slip out then head downstairs. With a tap of my keycard, I access the staff-only area, with its no-frills decor. The transition is always jarring—from soft lighting and artwork to fluorescent bulbs and noticeboards plastered with health and safety reminders.

I'm heading for the guys' locker room when Drew, another member of the maintenance team, emerges from it. He stops short when he sees me. "Robbie! Thought your shift ended an hour ago." His nose twitches. "Christ, mate, you reek of perfume. Wait, don't tell me you've been—"

"Just pleasing a guest," I cut in with a shrug. "Hospitality is all about going above and beyond, after all."

He lets out a low whistle. "You sneaky bugger. Was it that blonde in the sundress? The one you said was eye-fucking you earlier?"

I don't confirm or deny this, but my smirk is all the answer he needs.

"Unbelievable." Drew claps my shoulder. "How do you do it? Seriously, mate. Is it some secret module in manager training? Or just the appeal of the bad boy?"

I shoot him a grin. I'm not big on corporate hierarchy, but technically Drew reports to me. Not that it matters. We work well together because we don't take any of that superior–subordinate bollocks seriously. Truth is, he's one of the few blokes here I like. Most of the time, I keep to myself—I've always preferred doing my own thing—but Drew's all right. Easy-going, sharp enough to have some decent banter, and he doesn't act like a knob.

"Well, are you going to give me some tips on pulling or not?" Drew presses.

"Step one: look like this." I gesture to myself with mock seriousness. "Step two . . . there is no step two."

Drew snorts, loudly enough to make us both laugh, which is why we miss the approaching click of sensible heels. Samantha, the head of housekeeping, rounds the corner. As always, she's immaculately put together, not a hair out of place in her tight bun, uniform pressed to military precision, and make-up that could withstand a Highland storm. She fixes me with her signature glare.

Unfortunately, Drew—who has his back to her and hasn't yet

noticed her—picks this moment to say, "Honestly, mate, only you would have the balls to hook up with a guest."

It's only when my expression shifts—probably into something resembling *oh shite*—that Drew clocks Samantha. His grin falters.

Samantha's eyes narrow like she's about to deduct points from Gryffindor. "Well, well, Robbie. I'm sure your father would be *very* interested to hear about your unique . . . customer service approach."

I plaster on my best "innocent until proven guilty" smile. "Now, Samantha, you know me. I'm just here to keep the benches sturdy and the lightbulbs glowing. Anything else is pure speculation."

She holds my gaze, trying to rattle me, but it won't work. I've been standing my ground against authority figures since my teens. It's second nature to me.

She must realise she's not going to win our wee staring contest because she huffs under her breath then marches off down the hallway without another word. Only once she's out of sight do I let out a slow exhale.

"That woman's always had it in for me."

"Can't imagine why," Drew says deadpan. "You're such a delight to work with."

"Piss off," I fire back good-naturedly. Although I don't say it, I happen to know Samantha isn't quite as squeaky clean as her pressed uniform might suggest. "Anyway, I'm out of here. Try not to break anything before tomorrow."

"No promises!"

I push open the door to the locker room, grab my leather jacket, and shrug it on, even though I'm aware it'll roast me alive out there. But sweat is preferable to peeling half my skin off if I skid on loose gravel.

Out in the car park, my Triumph Bonneville Speedmaster sits waiting for me, its black and chrome finish catching the sunlight. This bike has been through hell with me—through storms, breakdowns, miles of unforgiving roads—and it hasn't failed me yet. That's more than most people can boast about their relationships.

I pull on my helmet, then my gloves, the movements practised and precise. As always, there's something oddly calming about the ritual. I swing my leg over, settle into the familiar contours of the seat, then kick up the stand. A turn of the key, a twist of the throttle, and the engine growls awake beneath me, sending vibrations buzzing through every nerve ending.

And just like that, freedom roars to life.

The bike eats up tarmac as I pull away from the resort—past manicured lawns trimmed within an inch of their lives, past carefully cultivated flowerbeds designed only to impress—and onto country roads that couldn't be less polished if they tried.

The Highlands unfold around me: emerald hills patched with untamed forest, fields scattered with woolly sheep. Hot air rushes against me, carrying the scent of sun-baked heather and pine.

Out here, there are no entitled guests, no haughty colleagues. Out here, I'm free.

CHAPTER THREE

CAT

"This is my new home!" I announce with a dramatic flourish, throwing open the front door like I'm unveiling some grand Highland castle instead of a modest flat above the Otter's Holt gift shop on Bannock's Main Street.

My three older brothers file into the narrow hallway, their broad shoulders practically brushing the walls. When they spill into the living room, their combined bulk makes the already modest space feel decidedly cramped. Each of them has the same chestnut hair and imposing height, but Ally is the rock, Lewis the gentle giant, and Jamie the wildcard who keeps us all on our toes.

"Well?" I prompt, rolling back on my heels and struggling to contain my grin. "What do you think?"

Ally, the eldest, runs a hand over a long crack in the wall with a sceptical frown. Lewis narrows his eyes at the peeling floral wallpaper like it's personally offended him. And Jamie, who at twenty-five is just one year my senior, prods at an ominous dark stain on the worn carpet with the toe of his trainer.

Okay, so maybe—just maybe—the fact I could afford this place has something to do with it being a bit of a fixer-upper.

Lewis is the first to speak. "Is the hotel really so bad that you'd rather live here?"

He's referring to the Bannock Hotel, just down the road, where all four of us grew up. After Maw and Da died seven years ago, Ally took over the running of it, but his heart was never in it. Two years back, Lewis, who's always loved the place, became manager instead, and it's flourished under his care.

"Wow, Lewis, don't try to spare my feelings or anything." I fold my arms.

He shrugs unapologetically. "I'm just saying."

"I was happy spending weekends at the hotel when I came back to visit, but now that I've moved back for good? I need my own space."

I've been away for six years. Five of those were spent in Glasgow, soaking up city life while earning my English degree and doing my postgrad in teaching. Then came my probationary teaching year in Wick, a remote town clinging to the northern edge of the mainland. It's a bonny enough spot, but let's just say it's not what you'd call *buzzing*. Not ideal for someone like me who thrives on a bit of excitement. Still, every cloud has a silver lining: without a whole lot there to spend my money on, I was able to save enough to put down a deposit on this place.

Moving back under the same roof as one of my brothers would have been suffocating, even if I do love all three of them (well, most of the time anyway). Besides, I'm young, single, and ready to mingle. The last thing I need is hotel guests overhearing my . . . extracurricular activities. Like Wick, Bannock is small, but at least it's only a drive away from Inverness, the Highlands' one and only city. Which means I'll be looking to make up for lost time after a year of near celibacy.

"Is it just me," Ally says, his nose wrinkling, "or is there a weird smell?"

Wow. That's the first thing he says? Nothing about the original fireplace or the gorgeous cornicing?

"You're right," Jamie chimes in, straight-faced. "It *is* you, Ally. You do smell. Always have. Glad we've finally got that out in the open."

Ally doesn't even dignify this with a response. He just levels Jamie with one of his trademark glowers.

"It is a bit stale in here," Lewis says, eyeing the carpet and the shabby sofa with suspicion.

"Och, it's nothing a bit of airing won't sort out," I say breezily. "Let me give you the grand tour."

In truth, it's less of a grand tour and more of a single-file shuffle down the hallway. I show them the bathroom (functional but dated, with a dripping tap), the bedroom (yellowing wallpaper and faded curtains), and finally the kitchen, which hasn't seen much love since the nineties.

Jamie flicks the light switch. The fluorescent tube buzzes and flickers like it's communicating in Morse code. "I think this light is having a seizure."

I roll my eyes. "It just needs replaced."

Ally crouches near one corner where cracked linoleum curls upwards. When he touches it, a piece breaks off in his hand. He straightens up with a sigh. "As does the lino."

"But I'd suggest you deal with that first." Lewis nods at a damp patch on the ceiling.

Jamie tugs open a kitchen drawer, only for it to come right out and dangle at an awkward angle. He smirks at me before shoving it back into place, although it remains defiantly crooked. "Very retro."

Ally exhales sharply, his face settling into that classic "sucking a lime" expression. Uh oh, I can feel a lecture coming.

"I can't believe you bought this place without checking with us," he says sternly. "I would have definitely talked you out of it."

And that's exactly why I didn't check with him. For someone who runs an outdoor adventure business, Ally can be surprisingly risk-averse. Also, I'm an adult! I don't *need* to check anything with my brothers.

"You're all being so negative," I say, my voice losing some of its earlier bounce. "It's nothing a bit of hard work and elbow grease can't sort out."

Jamie sniggers. "Hard work and elbow grease? Didn't know those words were even in your vocabulary."

"That's rich coming from you," I shoot back.

"I run a successful beer garden. That's hard graft."

"Aye, and you've been grafting at that for . . . what? Two whole months? Hardly makes up for all the years you spent doing hee-haw before that, does it?"

He cocks his head like he's going to argue, but then he shrugs. "That's fair."

We fall quiet for a while, my brothers continuing to survey my tired new abode. Right. I square my shoulders and lift my chin. So what if this place needs a wee bit of TLC? There are three strapping lads right here.

Turning on the charm with a dimple-popping grin, I meet each of their eyes in turn. "I know it's going to take some work. But maybe—"

"Oh no!" Lewis says.

"What?"

"That look!" Jamie waves at my face.

"What look?"

"The 'my brothers will do it for me' look," Jamie clarifies, his tone accusatory.

I press a hand to my chest in mock outrage. "I have no idea what you're talking about. Having said that, if you *did* want to pitch in . . ."

I look to Ally first. He scratches his jaw, the expression on his face already telling me what I don't want to hear.

"Cat, you know I've always done what I can for you, but Bannock Adventures operates seven days a week over the summer, and when I'm not working, I've got a sixteen-month-old and a very pregnant wife to look after. It's not that I don't want to help—it's that I physically can't."

"Oh," I say. Surprised and more than a little crestfallen, I turn to Lewis.

"Don't look at me!" he protests, his hands raised. "It's tourist season, by far the busiest time at the hotel. And my second-in-command is about to go on maternity leave. I'm stretched thinner than ever."

Lewis's second-in-command and Ally's very pregnant wife are one and the same person—Emily, my sister-in-law.

Desperate, I turn to Jamie, my last hope. "I can't believe I'm asking this, Jamie, but are you free to help?"

Jamie pulls a regretful face. "I'd love to, but I've got video games to play."

I glare at him.

"Joke! Actually, the new beer garden is keeping me busy, plus Maisie and I are trying to figure out how to make our businesses work *with* each other instead of against each other. You couldn't have picked a worse time. In winter? Perfect. Now? No chance."

"You'll just have to get a handyman in to do the work," Ally suggests.

I sigh. "Maybe when my bank account is looking a little healthier." The deposit just about cleaned me out.

This is the first place I've ever owned, and it's dawning on me what that really means. When I was renting, if a tap leaked or a light fixture went wonky, I'd just call the landlord and—*poof!*—problem solved. Now? Every creaky floorboard and peeling bit of wallpaper is officially my responsibility.

"Anyway," I say brightly, trying to brush off my disappointment, "loads of people learn how to do this stuff themselves. YouTube tutorials exist for a reason."

Jamie bursts into laughter. "Ha! Good one, sis. You and DIY."

I grit my teeth. I wasn't joking. What choice do I have?

"The new school term is starting soon," I say. "If any teenagers give me grief, I can come home and hit some nails with a hammer. It'll be therapeutic."

"Just don't hit your thumb," Lewis warns. "Or turn this place into more of a disaster zone than it already is."

"Thanks for the vote of confidence."

Ally places a hand on my shoulder. "We're not trying to rain on your parade, Cat. This place has potential but it needs a lot of work, and none of us has time right now."

"I get it," I say. And I do. They've all moved into new stages of their lives while I'm still trying to figure mine out.

I like to think of myself as independent, but the truth is, with three older brothers, I've never really had to be. They've always looked out for me, even Jamie. But now? Now they've all got partners and businesses, and suddenly rescuing me from my self-made disasters isn't top of their priority lists the way it once was.

"Anyway, I best head off," Jamie says. "Good luck, Bob the Builder." Smirking, he ruffles my hair, apparently oblivious to the existential crisis bubbling away behind my forced smile. "If you somehow manage to make this place livable, I'll bring booze for your flat-warming party." He fires me a wink then heads for the door.

Ally and Lewis make their excuses too. All three promise to check in soon, then the door clicks shut behind them.

"Well," I say to my empty flat, "looks like it's just you and me now."

Time to figure out how the hell I'm going to do up this place on my own.

CHAPTER FOUR

CAT

Sunlight filters through the forest canopy, dappling Bracken's smooth chestnut coat as she moves steadily beneath me. After last night's DIY disaster, a leisurely ride is the perfect therapy.

"This is more like it, eh, girl?" I give the mare a light nudge with my heels to keep her moving along the winding woodland path. "You and me, out here in the fresh air like old times. This is a whole lot better than wrestling with that bloody kitchen drawer."

Bracken snorts softly, which I choose to take as agreement.

The drawer in question is currently lying in disgrace on my tatty linoleum floor after a late-night attempt to fix its wobbly runners went spectacularly awry. No amount of fiddling, Googling, or swearing could coax it back into place. Turns out those smug YouTubers who make DIY look easy are liars.

Still, despite my ongoing efforts to reassure myself that buying my flat was not, in fact, a colossal error of judgement, it *is* nice to be back in Bannock. Those six years away were great, but there's something comforting about coming home, like pulling on an old jumper that still smells faintly of childhood memories.

And the best part? Once again living on the same street as Iona and Maisie, my best friends since, well, forever. It's brilliant—or at least, it should be. In practice? Not so much, given they barely have time to hang out these days on account of being surgically attached to their boyfriends, who just so happen to be my brothers.

It was weird enough when Iona started dating Lewis—even though, to be fair, he's basically been in love with her since dinosaurs roamed the earth. But then Maisie had to go and fall for Jamie!

Then, just when I thought things couldn't get any weirder, Lewis and Iona announced a few days ago that they're no longer boyfriend and girlfriend. No, they're now fiancé and fiancée.

Which is lovely news, of course. Really. Heart-warming and very romantic. But I expect it means even fewer opportunities for girls' nights.

Hmm. Seeing as everyone else has a man, I should probably pop into Inverness soon and find myself one. Not for romance, mind. Nah, just for a good shag.

Sorry, but it was a *long* year in Wick, okay?

A bead of sweat trickles down my neck, the August heat finding me even in the cool shade of the woods. I adjust my helmet then lean forwards to pat Bracken's neck, only for my hand to come away damp.

"Whoa, girl, you're as sweaty as I am."

I should've thought to bring water, for both of us. Rookie mistake. The River Garve runs through these woods—it would be the perfect spot to let Bracken cool down and take a drink. But where's the access point from here? If only I had a better sense of direction. I've only ever stuck to the well-trodden paths.

I glance around for any hint that might tell me which way the river is when something catches my eye: a glimpse of a stone wall through the trees. Oh! That must be Robbie MacDonald's place. His cottage—which is more or less in the middle of nowhere— sits right at the forest's edge, connected to the main road only by a dirt track.

At one point Aidan, Ally's best friend and Iona's big brother, thought about buying the cottage, but Robbie snapped it up. Ironic, really, given how much Ally and Aidan loathed Robbie back in the day. Not that their feelings towards him have changed much over the years.

Robbie isn't exactly what you'd call "neighbourly", which I suppose goes without saying, given he lives in a cottage so remote it might as well have a DO NOT DISTURB sign nailed to the front door. He's not really a fan of people in general, more of a "leave me alone so I can brood in peace" kind of guy. But surely even he wouldn't begrudge me and my thirsty horse some water on a day like this? He can't be *completely* heartless. Right?

"Come on, then," I say, nudging Bracken towards the clearing. "Let's see if Bannock's Big Bad Wolf is home."

As soon as we break through the line of trees and into full sunlight, I pull Bracken to an abrupt halt. Because there he is.

Robbie MacDonald stands near a neat stack of firewood, shirtless, his skin gleaming under the afternoon sun. His shoulders ripple with muscle as he lifts an axe high above his head before swinging it down in one powerful arc, wood splitting cleanly beneath its sharp blade with a satisfying *crack*.

My mouth goes desert-dry, and it's got nothing to do with thirst.

Robbie tosses the logs onto his pile, his jet-black hair clinging damply to his forehead, sunlight catching on the silver barbell in his left eyebrow. Tattoos wind their way across his chest and arms like intricate maps of a life lived boldly. All, I'm sure, have a story to tell.

Swallowing hard against what feels suspiciously like nerves (which is strange, as I'm usually confident around men), I clear my throat and call out scratchily, "Hiya, Robbie!"

His icy-blue eyes snap to me. No nod of acknowledgment, no polite "hiya" back, not even a twitch of his mouth that could be mistaken for a smile. Nothing.

"Er . . . would you mind if I nabbed some water for Bracken? She's parched."

After a pause, he jerks his chin towards a brass tap that protrudes from the wall of his cottage. Then he sets up another log on the chopping block. His silence is both captivating and maddening. The axe descends again, slicing through the log with ruthless efficiency.

Determined not to let his broody indifference get to me, I slide down from Bracken, unclip my helmet, and shake out my auburn braid. "Cracking day, eh?"

Robbie doesn't look up, just makes a noncommittal grunt then adds another pair of split logs to his collection.

Unperturbed—mostly—I wander over to the tap and twist it on. Water gushes into the battered bucket below. I glance over my shoulder at Robbie, but he's still ignoring me. It's as though I don't exist.

No, no, no. This won't do. I can't stand being ignored. If he thinks he can out-stubborn me, he's got another thing coming.

"Must take a lot of strength to chop wood like that," I remark as the bucket fills. "It certainly *looks* like hot and sweaty work."

Thwack! Another log splits, but otherwise, no reaction.

Leaning down, I take a sip from the tap then swipe at my mouth with the back of my hand. When I glance his way again, I'm annoyed to see he's *still* not looking at me. Seriously? I happen to know these snug tan jodhpurs showcase my arse beautifully, thank you very much. I'm kind of insulted he didn't even sneak a peek.

Well, since I'm apparently invisible, I might as well use this superpower for some uninterrupted ogling, right?

Turning off the tap, I lift the heavy bucket and set it beside Bracken, who plunges straight in, drinking noisily, her tail swishing lazily behind her. Meanwhile, I let my eyes roam over Robbie, observing the fluid shifts of muscle as he moves, the tattoos twisting their way over his forearms and shoulders like living artwork. A sprawling Celtic knot winds up his right forearm before melting into some sort of mythical beast across his biceps. On his chest, shapes and symbols shift in the sunlight, fascinating me.

To be honest, I think Robbie MacDonald has always fascinated me. When I was a kid, his name was practically a byword for trouble. He was constantly scrapping (mostly with Ally), smashing things up, even shoplifting. He kept the local police busier than anyone else in town, racking up multiple warnings and even landing a suspended sentence for his antics.

In a bigger place, his actions might have been dismissed as ordinary teenage rebellion, but in a small and otherwise idyllic town like Bannock? His defiant and unpredictable behaviour set him apart.

Most small-town rebels grow out of it eventually, but Robbie never shed his shadows completely, or at least not in the eyes of Bannock's rumour mill. Even now, years later, something simmers beneath his exterior, something raw and untamed.

"Why not take a picture?" The sound of his voice hits me like a slap. It's low, rough, and laced with sarcasm. "It'll last longer."

Well, hello to you too. I cross my arms loosely over my chest. "I'm not the one who decided to chop wood shirtless in public."

Those blue eyes meet mine once more, the intensity of his stare sending a shiver down my spine. "Except . . . it's hardly 'public', is it? This place isn't easy to stumble across. You have to purposely leave the footpath."

Leaning his axe against the chopping block, he pulls a rag from his back pocket and rubs it over his shoulders—and then across his pecs—in lazy sweeps.

Oh. My. God.

And then I see it: a glint of silver in the sunlight. A piercing through his right nipple. Not a straight barbell like the one in his eyebrow, but circular. How did I miss that before? And who gave him permission to throw *that* into the mix? Tattoos, muscles, brooding bad-boy energy, *and* a nipple ring? It's a wonder I don't drop dead on the spot.

Right, this is too much for me. Needing a distraction, I spin on my heel and make a big show of inspecting his cottage.

When Aidan considered buying it a few years back, it was run-down, but it's now neat and well cared for. Through the spotless French windows, I spy a warm rustic kitchen with wooden cabinets and a sturdy oak table.

"Your place is looking great," I call over my shoulder. "Who did you hire to do the renovations?"

Grunt. Thwack. Apparently, he's gone back to chopping wood. "Did it myself."

Considering Robbie has worked in maintenance at the Glen Garve Resort for years, I suppose it's no shock he's skilled, but even so, the work he's done here is downright impressive.

I let out a low whistle. "You're good with your hands. I like that in a man."

A sharp breath escapes his nose, not quite a laugh, but close enough to make me wonder if that was his way of suppressing one. Wow, am I getting somewhere with him? And yet, when I glance back, his features are as cold as ever. Damn.

"I actually just bought a fixer-upper on Main Street."

Genuine interest lights up those frosty eyes for half a second before his default blank expression slams back into place. "Oh aye?" It comes out almost grudgingly, like he can't help but be curious even though he resents it. And honestly, I don't know whether to feel triumphant or insulted that *this*—not me bending over and giving him an excellent view of my arse, but *this*—is what finally gets his attention.

"Aye. I'll be doing it up, just like you did this place up."

"*You'll* be doing it up?"

"Yes." I fire back my most saccharine smile. "*I'll* be doing it up."

"You experienced when it comes to DIY, then?" He leans casually against the axe handle.

"Well . . ." I wave a hand breezily. "I wouldn't say *experienced*, exactly." Total novice, more like. "But anything I don't know, I'm sure I'll pick up in no time. I've been bingeing videos from home-improvement gurus on social media."

His lips twitch—just the barest hint of a smirk—as though he finds this deeply entertaining. "Right."

"They all swear if you've got the will, you can build pretty much anything," I add, as though last night's drawer debacle didn't nearly end me. Fake it till you make it, right?

Robbie releases a low huff of sound and shakes his head. "Well, good luck with that."

His tone is dismissive enough to make my blood simmer. Before I can decide whether to give him a piece of my mind or swallow my pride like an adult, he nods towards Bracken, who's now contentedly munching on grass—*his* grass.

"Your horse is finished its water. And I've got jobs to be getting on with."

Its? *Its?* Bracken's a *her*, obviously. Anyway, it's a clear dismissal. He might as well have said, *You've got what you came for, now off you trot. Literally.*

Heat creeps up my neck, not from embarrassment but from sheer indignation. I grab my helmet and gather Bracken's reins. Fine!

I swing myself gracefully into the saddle then nudge Bracken forwards without sparing Robbie another glance, even though every fibre of my body is screaming at me to steal one last ogle at those muscles gleaming in the sunlight.

My resolve crumbles when we're almost past him. The faint smell of pine shavings reaches my nose, mixed with the salty tang of his skin, and before I can stop myself, I call brightly, "Cheers for the water!" And then, because apparently some part of me refuses to leave with my dignity intact, I add with a cheeky wink, "And the show!"

◆ ◆ ◆

"There you go, girl. Go see your friends." I give Bracken's rump a light pat, and she trots past me into the field. Her coat gleams, fresh from a well-deserved rubdown. I latch the gate behind her and lean against it, watching her wander over to join the others under the shade of an old oak. She dips her head to graze, completely at ease.

Bannock Stables has always felt like a home away from home. When I was thirteen, the owner, Janice, struck a deal with me— free lessons or a trek in exchange for mucking out stalls and helping with the younger riders. It was hard work but I loved every second of it. Now that I'm back for good, we've struck up a similar arrangement, one that'll work around my teaching schedule.

A sharp whinny cuts through the quiet. I glance across the yard and spot Janice standing by the gate to the indoor arena, peering inside with her arms folded.

"Hey, Janice!" I head over.

She turns at the sound of my voice, her long greying ponytail swinging behind her. "Cat! How was your ride?"

"Brilliant. Bracken was a good girl, as sweet as she's always been. Some things never change. But who's this beauty?"

I nod towards the horse being worked in the arena, a sleek black stallion whose coat gleams like obsidian. His powerful frame tenses, and he jerks sideways on the lunge line, tossing his head in clear defiance.

Janice's face, etched with years of working in the elements, softens into a smile. "That's Midnight. We're looking after him for a private client."

"He's magnificent."

Midnight prances to the side again, wild energy radiating from every taut sinew in his body.

"Aye, but he's a fair handful. Barely three years old and already he thinks he rules the world."

Billy, who's in his late fifties and is one of the stable's most senior instructors, lets the line slide just enough through his gloved hands, giving Midnight the room to widen his circle.

Something about the stallion—his barely contained power, his untamed spirit—reminds me of a certain topless woodcutter.

I was thinking of venturing into Inverness to find myself a man, but maybe that's not necessary. Not when Bannock has its own brand of fun, specifically tall, tattooed, and broody Robbie MacDonald.

Aye, he's one stallion I'd *very* much like to ride.

CHAPTER FIVE

ROBBIE

"Christ, Drew, not like that." I reach over and take the trowel from his hand. "This whole section will collapse if you keep at it that way."

Drew steps back and wipes sweat from his brow with his forearm. "Didn't realise there was a wrong way to slap mortar on a wall."

"There's a wrong way to do everything." I demonstrate the proper technique.

It's another scorching day, and the sun beats down mercilessly as we work on repairing a section of the low stone wall that borders the main pathway leading to the resort entrance. It's the kind of heat that makes your clothes stick to your skin and your patience wear thin. But at least the sprawling branches of a nearby sycamore cast enough shade to keep us from roasting alive.

"Sorry we can't all be master craftsmen," Drew mutters, but there's no real annoyance in his voice. He watches as I smooth the mortar with practised strokes. "Where'd you learn all this stuff anyway?"

I shrug. "Here and there. Picked things up."

The truth is, I've always been good with my hands. Even as a kid, I could take things apart and put them back together again. It's the one thing my da has never complained about—my ability to fix what's broken. Everything else about me, though? Fair game for criticism.

"Well, you're bloody good at it." Drew accepts the trowel back. "No wonder Craig keeps you around despite your . . . extracurricular activities."

I snort. "You make it sound like I'm running a drug ring, not occasionally shagging a guest."

"Speaking of which . . ." Drew grins and his eyes gleam with mischief. "Any new prospects on your radar?"

"Nah." I shake my head and lift another stone into place. "I try not to make a habit of it, but sometimes it's hard to resist."

Even as I speak, my mind flashes to yesterday, to Cat McIntyre appearing out of nowhere astride that chestnut mare. Her auburn hair escaping from her braid . . . her hazel eyes sparkling in the sunlight . . . and those jodhpurs hugging every curve of her arse and legs.

I had to look away when she bent over to drink from the tap, the fabric stretching tight across her backside. And, oh man, the way those dimples flashed when she smiled, the light catching the tiny stud in her nose . . .

Fuck.

Cat McIntyre is off limits for about a dozen different reasons, starting with her being Alasdair McIntyre's wee sister. Pretty sure he'd murder me if he so much as caught me looking at her sideways.

"You've gone quiet." Drew nudges me with his elbow. "That means you're thinking about someone."

"I'm thinking about how this wall won't fix itself while you stand there yapping."

Drew rolls his shoulders, loosening them up. "All right, forget guests for a moment. Have you ever thought about dipping your pen in the company ink?"

I raise an eyebrow. "Not my style. Too messy. The thing about guests is they check out. Other staff members? That's a whole other story."

Drew chuckles. "C'mon, are you really telling me you've never looked at someone here and thought, 'Aye, I'd give that a go?'"

I shrug, focusing on my task. "Nope. Don't shit where you eat, Drew."

He smirks, clearly enjoying himself. "What about Samantha? She's always giving you the stink eye. Maybe she's just mad because she wants you. Ever thought about that?"

I consider the head of housekeeping—always immaculately dressed, not a hair out of place, lips perpetually pursed like she's just tasted something sour. "Samantha? No way. Not if she were the last woman on earth."

"Why, she too old for you?"

"It's not that." Sure, she's in her forties, but age has never been a factor for me. I've been with women older than Samantha.

"Why then?"

"She's too stuck-up for my taste," I say, tamping down a stone.

"Fair enough. She does have that whole 'I'm better than you' vibe going on." Drew pauses, a strange little smile playing at his lips. "Still, I bet she's got a wild side under all that starch."

"Wouldn't surprise me."

"And she was divorced recently. Got to let all those emotions out somehow, right?"

I'm about to respond when I spot Johnny walking across the lawn towards us, his usual easy smile nowhere to be seen. My younger brother is dressed in the resort's front-of-house uniform—crisp white shirt, dark green waistcoat with the Glen Garve Resort logo, perfectly pressed tartan trousers, and a matching tartan tie. His dark hair is neatly tucked behind his ears, though a few strands have escaped to fall across his forehead. Compared to him, I must look like something the cat dragged in—covered in dust and mortar, sweat-stained and dishevelled.

"Robbie," he says, his voice tight. "Da wants to see you."

I straighten and wipe my hands on my already filthy trousers. "Now? I'm kind of in the middle of something here."

"Now," Johnny confirms. He glances at Drew. "Sorry to interrupt."

Drew shrugs. "No worries. I can handle this. Try not to get fired, aye?"

"As if," I scoff, though something about Johnny's expression gives me pause. I know my wee brother well, and right now he's wound tighter than a spring.

I cast a doubtful glance at the wall, wondering if it'll still be standing when I get back, then fall into step beside Johnny as we cross the manicured lawn towards the main building. The silence between us is unusual. Normally, Johnny fills the air with stories about guests or gossip from the break room.

"So," I say, trying to keep things light, "how's David? You two do anything fun last weekend?"

Johnny blinks, like he's having to drag his mind back from somewhere else. "What? Oh, aye. We, er, went to that new restaurant in Inverness. The Italian one."

"Any good?"

"Aye, it was . . . David wore that bright orange shirt, you know the one. Said he wanted to make sure the waiter could spot us in a crowd."

I chuckle. That sounds like David all right. Johnny's boyfriend has never met a colour he didn't want to wear, preferably all at once. "Subtle as ever, then."

Johnny attempts a smile but it doesn't reach his eyes.

We're halfway to the main building now, and his unease is starting to get to me. "All right, are you going to tell me what's going on? Has word got to Da that I slept with a guest?"

Johnny's eyes widen. "You did *what*?"

"Oh, so it's not that, then? I figured Samantha might have gone running to Da about it. She overheard Drew and me talking the other day."

Johnny pinches the bridge of his nose. "Nope, it's not that. And Robbie, as I really don't want you getting into any more trouble, maybe *don't* go into this meeting offering Da a list of other transgressions." He gives me a pointed look. "I didn't know you'd slept with a guest, and I'm immediately going to forget about it. For your sake."

"Well, if it's not that, what is it?"

Johnny stops walking and turns to face me, his blue eyes troubled. "It's serious, Robbie. I don't know all the details, but . . ." He pauses, searching my face. "I hope it's not true." He looks even harder into my eyes. "No, I *know* it's not true."

Before I can ask what the hell he's talking about, Johnny steps forwards and pulls me into a tight hug. As a matter of principle, I never let other guys hug me, but my wee brother? That's the one exception.

I awkwardly pat his back. "Relax! Whatever it is, I'll sort it. I always do." Pulling away, I clap him on the shoulder.

"Hmm." Johnny doesn't look convinced. "I hope so."

We enter the main building through the staff entrance, the cool air a blessed relief after the scorching heat outside. The corridor to my da's office feels longer than usual, each step bringing me closer to whatever storm is brewing.

Da has been the general manager of the Glen Garve Resort for as long as I can remember, and he's always been more devoted to this place than to his family. While other fathers were teaching their sons to fish or taking them to football matches, mine was here, making sure the resort ran like clockwork. Not that I'm bitter or anything.

When we reach Da's office door, Johnny takes a deep breath. "Just . . . stay calm, all right? Because losing your cool isn't going to make things any better."

"You worry too much. I'll be fine."

Johnny isn't reassured, but he nods and leaves me standing there, the weight of his concern settling on my shoulders like a physical thing.

I knock twice then enter without waiting for a response, a small act of defiance I can't seem to shake, even after all these years. "You wanted to see me?"

"Yes. Take a seat."

Like Johnny, Da wears a serious expression, though in his case it's his default setting, so nothing new there. At fifty-eight, his hair is more grey than black now, but his jawline is still sharp, his posture impeccable. He has the same piercing blue eyes he passed down to both his sons, although the years of responsibility have etched permanent lines around them, and there's a rigid set to his shoulders that comes from decades of maintaining standards at a five-star resort. Even his tie sits perfectly centred, so neat I wouldn't be surprised if he measures it with a ruler every morning.

Da *does* know how to laugh and smile. He does it when he's schmoozing with rich guests. It's just not a side of him I often get to see.

I lower myself into the chair opposite him, a familiar tension settling between us. His office, as always, is spotless: polished mahogany desk, awards and certificates displayed on the walls, not a paper out of place. Everything about the room screams control, just like the man himself.

"Well." Da folds his hands on the desk. "Let's get to it, then." He pauses for a few moments, studying me. "You'll remember that ten days ago Mr Ashford reported a watch missing."

Of course I remember—the damn thing was supposedly worth twenty-five grand. Not exactly pocket change. An older gent from London, Mr Ashford *believed* he locked it in his room safe but admitted he wasn't entirely certain. After tearing apart his luggage and scouring the room, he reported it missing to the front desk the next day. We were all told to keep an eye out for it, but there's been no sign of it.

"Did someone find it?"

Da shakes his head. "But three days ago there was . . . another incident."

I arch a brow, my curiosity piqued. This is news to me.

"A Ms Laurent in room 207 reported a pair of diamond stud earrings missing, and she was adamant she put them in her safe. Their value is, apparently, around ten thousand pounds."

I blow out a breath. "Jesus."

This kind of thing doesn't happen here. The Glen Garve Resort prides itself on its security and discretion, especially given the calibre of guests we host. In all my years working here, I've never heard of anything like this. And it's not exactly easy for some random chancer to waltz into a guest's room, let alone crack their safe.

"As you're aware," Da continues, his voice taking on the rehearsed quality he uses when addressing staff meetings, "the resort's reputation is paramount. If word gets out that guests' valuables are . . . disappearing, it could devastate business. I managed—just barely—to dissuade Ms Laurent from contacting the police immediately. I offered her compensation and promised an internal investigation. But she made it very clear: if nothing comes of my investigation, she'll be calling the police."

There's tension in his shoulders as he speaks, a stiffness that reminds me how much he thrives on control, and how much he hates even the slightest hint of disorder.

"As it turns out, she won't need to make that call—because this morning there was a third incident." He pauses, letting the weight of his words sink in. "A Mr Harrington in room 203 reported a signet ring and two thousand pounds in cash missing from *his* safe."

My stomach tightens. Three incidents? What the hell is going on?

Da watches me closely, like he's studying my every twitch and breath.

"Well, shit," I say, because what else is there to say?

Da nods grimly. "It's clear I have no choice now but to involve the police and hand over my findings. But first I wanted to have a quick chat with you."

The way he says it makes my skin prickle. I straighten in my chair. "Why?" When he doesn't respond straight away, the penny drops. *Crap.* "You don't seriously think I did this, do you? Bloody hell, Da!"

His gaze hardens. "It wouldn't be the first time you've stolen something."

The words hit me like a physical blow. "Christ." My laugh is bitter and humourless. "It doesn't matter how many years pass, does it? You're never going to let me live down the things I did as a teenager. I'm thirty-one now!" I shake my head, fury rising hot and fast in my chest. "So that's it? Items go missing from guests' rooms, and your first thought is it must be your own son? That's why you summoned me here? Jesus. You really do have a low opinion of me, don't you?"

I'm on my feet now, though I don't remember standing. My hands are clenched at my sides, my pulse hammering in my throat.

Da holds up a hand like he's silencing a child then fixes me with a look so cold it could freeze fire. "Sit down, Robbie. And I can assure you I was hoping beyond hope that you had nothing to do with this. You can imagine my disappointment, then, when I discovered evidence connecting you to each of the thefts."

For a moment it feels like all the oxygen has been sucked from the room. Evidence? What bloody evidence? I didn't steal anything!

CHAPTER SIX

ROBBIE

"Evidence?" The word scorches through me, my skin tingling as though I've been dragged too near an open flame. Did he actually just say that? *Evidence?*

I lean forwards, my knuckles pressing into the polished surface of his desk, hard enough that I half expect it to splinter beneath my fists. "What fucking evidence?" My voice comes out louder than I mean it to, but I don't care. "There can't be any evidence because I didn't do this, Da. I didn't take anything!"

Da sighs, weariness etched across his face. "That temper of yours. Could you *try* to rein it in? And for the second time, Robbie, sit down."

"Bloody hell, you're accusing me of stealing from guests! Getting upset is a pretty natural reaction."

"I wanted to speak with you directly before calling the police, to give you a chance to explain." His voice is maddeningly calm, as if this is all just a bit of admin he has to sort out before lunch. "But I'm only willing to talk with you if you make an effort to control yourself. So can we discuss this like adults, or should I go ahead and make that call now?"

My hands itch to break something, anything. Instead I force myself to take three deep breaths, the way Johnny always tells me to when I'm about to lose it. The rage doesn't disappear, but it simmers down enough for me to drop back into the chair.

"Okay, then," I say through gritted teeth. "Let's talk and maybe we can sort this mess out."

Da presses his fingertips together. "As I mentioned, I've been conducting my own investigation and . . . well." He fixes me with that piercing stare of his. "Unfortunately, Robbie, your keycard was used to access Mr Ashford's room the day his watch went missing . . . to access Ms Laurent's room the day her earrings disappeared . . . and last night to access Mr Harrington's room."

"What?" My voice is flat at first—quiet disbelief—but then it spikes. "Are you serious? This is bollocks! Someone must have—"

"According to the maintenance logbook," he continues, cutting me off, "you didn't perform repairs in any of those rooms on those dates." He leans forwards, his gaze never wavering from mine. "So tell me, if you weren't working in those rooms, what exactly *were* you doing in them?"

"I wasn't in the rooms!" My chest is tight now, each breath coming shorter than the last as both fury and panic set in. "Someone is stitching me up. You have to believe me, Da."

But I can see it in his eyes—that familiar look of disappointment and suspicion.

"Fucking hell." I rub my hand over my face. "I swear I didn't do this."

He watches me carefully, his expression giving nothing away. "Your words might hold more weight if you hadn't said the exact same thing to me on multiple occasions as a young man, only for it to emerge later that you were guilty as sin."

The old resentment flares hot in my chest. "C'mon, Da, what

is this, the boy who cried wolf? I'm thirty-one years old, not fifteen. I'm telling you, I didn't do this."

He taps his fingers against the edge of his desk in a slow, deliberate rhythm, like he's counting down to something I'm not going to like. "And I truly hope that's the case. But at this stage I have no choice but to contact the police, and I have to pass on to them what I've uncovered so far. If you're as innocent as you say, the truth will come to light."

I shake my head, a hollow laugh escaping me. "For fuck's sake." It's like a knife to the heart that my own father won't believe me. After all these years, after everything I've done to straighten myself out, he still sees me as that troublemaking kid.

"Furthermore," he says, his tone sliding into the clipped, formal cadence he uses for staff disciplinary issues, "in line with policy, I'm going to have to suspend you until the police have concluded their investigation. If your name is cleared, you'll of course be reinstated to your position."

I huff out a breath. He's not just accusing me—he's suspending me. My own father. "You know what? Let's make this easier for both of us." I push to my feet, the chair scraping loudly over the polished floor. "I quit."

"Robbie—"

"Nope. This is bullshit, Da. You don't believe me? Fine. But I don't need to stand here and take this crap from you." I turn and stride towards the door.

"Wait!"

I pause, gripping the handle but refusing to look back.

"There's something else that needs to be addressed."

Reluctantly I turn back to him. "What?"

He clears his throat, still pretending like this is some official HR meeting instead of a father accusing his son of being a thief.

"As you're currently under suspicion, I can't allow you to wander around the resort unattended."

"You can't be serious. You honestly think I'm going to nick someone's Rolex on my way out?"

"It's policy," he replies firmly, stony-faced even as colour rises in his cheeks.

"Policy? Right. Because heaven forbid we ever bend a single rule at the Glen Garve Resort."

Ignoring me, he says, "Johnny will escort you to your locker so you can collect your belongings. Once you leave today, you aren't permitted back on the premises without prior agreement from me."

So my own brother is to escort me out of here like I'm a common crook? You couldn't make this up.

"It's not personal," Da adds. "It's just procedure, son."

Son. The word sounds hollow, a formality rather than a bond. I stare at him, this man who shares my blood but has never really understood me. I wonder if he ever will.

"Fine," I grit out. "Let's get this over with."

Johnny's waiting outside, his face a picture of misery. He falls into step beside me as we head down the staff corridor towards the locker room, his shoulders hunched like he's carrying the weight of this whole mess. The silence between us is thick enough to cut with a knife.

I hate seeing my wee brother like this. It takes the edge off my anger, just a bit. I've spent my whole life trying to shield Johnny from the worst of things, and here he is, caught in the middle of this shitshow.

"Hey." I nudge his arm. "Relax. I'll be fine."

He shoots me a look that's somewhere between exasperation and concern. "I should be the one reassuring you, Robbie, not the other way around."

I shrug. "I've got thick skin."

"I warned you to keep your cool in there." He glances around to make sure no one is within earshot. "I was right outside, and you weren't exactly being quiet. I know it's not fair, but Da was only going to suspend you while the police investigate. Did you really have to quit?"

I exhale sharply through my nose. "You weren't in the room, Johnny. You didn't see the way he looked at me. He'd already decided I was guilty."

"That's not tr—"

"It is," I cut him off. "And we both know it."

We reach the locker room, and I'm grateful to find it empty. The last thing I need is an audience. I spin the combination on my locker, open it, and pull out my leather jacket, which is stuffed in a heap at the bottom. As I do, something clatters to the floor between us.

A ring.

A signet ring, to be precise. Gold with some sort of crest on it.

For a beat, neither of us moves. The ring just sits there on the floor like it's mocking me. My brain stutters, trying to make sense of what I'm seeing.

"What the fuck?" The words come out low and sharp, my pulse pounding in my ears. I glance at Johnny, whose face has gone as white as the resort's overpriced bedsheets.

He swallows hard, his Adam's apple bobbing like he's choking something down. "Is that—"

"The ring that was reported missing this morning? I think so." My heart thuds harder. "Johnny, I swear to God, I've never seen it before in my life."

His eyes dart between me and the ring like he's waiting for someone to yell, "Surprise!"

"Robbie . . ."

"I didn't put it there," I bite out, shoving a hand through my hair. "Seriously, if I'd nicked it, do you think I'd chuck it in my bloody locker? Only for it to then fall out right in front of you?"

I crouch down and scoop it up. "Here." I thrust it towards him. "Take it. Say you found it somewhere else—outside maybe, or on a table or something. I don't care. But if the police find out this was in my locker, then between that and those keycard logs, I'm done for. We're talking jail time, Johnny. Someone is framing me, I swear."

He doesn't move to take it. Just stares at the ring, then at me, his expression torn. "You want me to lie . . . to the police? And to Da?"

I can see the conflict in his eyes, the weight of what I'm asking him to do pressing down on him. Johnny's always been the good son—honest, reliable, the one who follows the rules. Asking him to lie goes against everything he is.

"Johnny, you know me." I step closer to him, lowering my voice even though we're alone. "If I was guilty, I wouldn't drag you into this with me. I've always looked out for you, haven't I?"

He hesitates, his features shifting like he's at war with himself. "Aye," he says softly. "You have."

"This is something I need you to do for me." I hate how it sounds like begging, but right now my pride is the least of my concerns. "Please."

He's quiet for what feels like forever, his gaze dropping back to the ring in my outstretched hand. Finally he takes it and slips it into his pocket. "Aye, I'll . . . come up with something. A story about where I found it."

The look on his face twists something deep inside me. He doesn't like this—lying for me—but he's agreeing all the same, which makes the guilt churn hotter in my stomach.

"Thank you. Seriously."

He doesn't respond, just gives me a slight nod as I shrug into my leather jacket. Usually, the worn weight of it feels grounding, comforting. Not today.

We head out, Johnny leading me towards the exit like I'm a dodgy punter being shown the door after causing too much trouble at the pub. The sound of our footsteps echoes off the corridor walls, every step grating on my nerves. We pass Samantha coming out of her office, and her lips curl into a satisfied smile. Being the head of housekeeping, she'll know all about the thefts—and, no doubt, about me being the number-one suspect.

"Bad day, Robbie?" Her voice drips with false sympathy.

I stop in my tracks, ready to give her a piece of my mind and wipe that gloating expression off her face, but Johnny places a hand on my shoulder and urges me forwards. "Not worth it," he murmurs.

And he's right. Losing my temper now wouldn't solve anything. It'd only give people another excuse to call me trouble.

Outside, the summer sun is still blazing down. Clearly, it hasn't got the memo that my life is crumbling to pieces. My bike gleams in its usual spot. Johnny stops a few paces from it, his mouth set in a grim line.

"Da . . . has asked me to keep my distance from you while the police investigate."

Another blow, right when I thought things couldn't get worse.

"He says we can't risk it looking like we're meddling, given we're your family. We've got to let the police do their job without getting in their way."

"I get it," I admit, although that doesn't mean it stings any less.

"I don't *want* to keep my distance. Now is when you need your family the most." The emotion in his voice threatens to crack my composure, but I refuse to let it.

"I'll be fine," I assure him, feigning a confidence I don't feel. "This'll all blow over once the police realise none of it holds up."

Johnny nods but doesn't look convinced. He pulls me into another hug.

When he lets me go, I swing my leg over my bike, settle into the seat, and turn the key in the ignition. The engine roars to life beneath me. Usually, this is the moment when everything else falls away—when it's just me, my bike, and the open road.

Not today. Today the engine's rumble can't drown out the chaos in my head.

As I pull away from the resort, I catch a glimpse of Johnny in my mirror, still standing there, watching me go. It hits me all over again that this isn't just happening to me. It's happening to him too, caught between his brother and his father, between loyalty and doing what's right.

And me? I'm completely and utterly screwed. Because someone has gone to a lot of trouble to set me up, and I've no idea why. All I know is that I'm on my own, and the evidence against me is stacking up by the minute.

This entire situation is a mess.

CHAPTER SEVEN

CAT

"Easy, boy. That's it."

I keep my voice low and even as I edge closer to Midnight, who's standing in the middle of Farmer Murray's south field looking like he owns the place. The stallion's ears flick back and forth, alert but not pinned in aggression. His obsidian coat gleams in the early evening light.

"You've caused quite the commotion, you know that?" I slowly reach into my pocket where I've stashed a handful of oats. The lead rope is looped over my shoulder, the halter dangling from my other hand. "Everyone is out looking for you."

When Janice called to say Midnight had kicked through a weak section of fencing and bolted, she was crystal clear: "If you spot him, call me immediately. Do *not* approach him yourself. He's unpredictable."

But where's the fun in that?

Besides, I've always had a way with horses. Even the difficult ones. And from the moment I first saw him being trained in the arena, something about this magnificent beast spoke to me.

Midnight tosses his head, nostrils flaring. His powerful muscles tense, and for a moment I think he might bolt again.

"I'm not here to hurt you." I take another careful step. I'm about fifteen feet away now, close enough to see the whites of his eyes. "I've got something tasty, though."

I extend my hand, palm flat with the oats nestled in the centre. Midnight's ears prick forwards with interest, but he doesn't move. He's too smart for such an obvious ploy.

"Playing hard to get, are we?" I return the oats to my pocket then pull out my secret weapon—a shiny red apple. "What about this, then?"

His attention sharpens. I take a slow breath, calculating my next move. This is the tricky part. I need to get close enough to slip the halter on without spooking him, but not so close that I can't dodge if he decides to kick.

"You remind me of someone, you know," I continue conversationally, inching forwards. "Bit of a rebel. Doesn't like being told what to do."

Midnight snorts, as if to say, *Damn right*.

I'm ten feet away now. Eight. Six. Close enough to see the powerful rise and fall of his chest with each breath. Close enough for danger.

Suddenly a bird takes flight nearby, startling him, and he rears up, front hooves pawing at the air. My heart leaps into my throat, but instead of retreating, I stand my ground, keeping my posture relaxed even as my pulse races.

"It's all right," I say firmly when his hooves return to earth. "You're fine."

The moment stretches between us like a taut thread. Then, slowly, his posture softens. I take a careful step closer, then another, the apple extended like a peace offering.

Finally, temptation wins over caution. Midnight stretches his neck, his velvety muzzle reaching for the treat.

"That's it," I murmur, daring to stroke his neck while he's distracted with his prize. His coat feels like warm silk beneath my fingertips. "You're a handsome devil, aren't you? Even if you are naughty."

While he munches, I ease the halter over his nose then up behind his ears, securing it with practised movements. He twitches but doesn't pull away, too focused on the last bits of apple.

"Gotcha," I whisper, clipping the lead rope to the halter. "See? That wasn't so terrible."

The thrill of success bubbles up inside me, that little rush I've always loved when I take a risk and it pays off.

"Come on, then." I give the lead a gentle tug. "Let's get you home before Janice has a heart attack."

◆ ◆ ◆

"Good boy." I reach over the door to give Midnight's neck a pat. A faint scent of hay and leather fills the stable, mingling with the comforting rustle of horses shifting in their stalls. "You'll behave now, won't you?"

He snorts. I choose to interpret this response as agreement rather than mockery.

"Catriona McIntyre!" Janice's voice cuts through the stable like a whip. I turn to find her marching towards me, her face a storm cloud of worry and exasperation. "What part of 'do not approach him yourself' was unclear to you?"

I offer my most winning smile. "He's fine! Look, not a scratch on him."

"That's not the point." She folds her arms across her chest. "If he'd reared or kicked while you were alone with him—"

"But he didn't," I say, a white lie. "We had a moment, me and him. Sometimes you just have to trust your instincts."

Janice sighs. "You're lucky you've got a way with them," she says eventually. She looks at Midnight, who's now calmly munching hay, and her gaze softens. "And I am grateful that he's back safe."

She gives him a pat and a half-hearted scolding then we head out of the stable together. Outside, a rhythmic hammering sound draws my attention to the far end of the paddock, where a tall figure is working on the broken fence. Even from this distance, there's no mistaking those broad shoulders or the black hair.

"Is that . . . ?"

"Robbie MacDonald," Janice confirms, following my gaze. "Talk about good timing. He called the other day to say if I ever needed help with odd jobs around the place, he's available. When Midnight busted through the fence, I rang him, and he was here within the hour."

"Interesting." I watch Robbie drive another nail into the post. The word around Bannock is he left his role at the resort a few days ago, but no one seems to know why. It's all very hush-hush, though that hasn't stopped the rumour mill from churning out wild theories. Someone even suggested the police were involved. Whatever went down, as far as I'm concerned, it's only added another layer to his bad-boy mystique. And if he's looking for work . . .

"I should go thank him," I announce, already moving towards the paddock. "For fixing the fence."

"Cat," Janice calls after me, a note of warning in her voice. "Don't go stirring up trouble."

I turn, walking backwards and flashing her my most innocent smile. "Me? Never."

I approach Robbie with the same fearless confidence I used with Midnight earlier. He doesn't look up as I near, too focused on measuring a replacement rail against the gap in the fence.

"Fancy seeing you here," I say brightly.

His shoulders tense, the only indication he's heard me. Then he reaches for another nail from the pouch at his belt.

"I'm the one who found Midnight," I continue, undeterred by his silence. "The black stallion? Janice told me to keep my distance, but let's just say he's not the first stubborn male I've won over."

Robbie drives the nail in with one sharp blow that almost sinks it completely, then finishes it off with another for good measure. "Sounds . . . reckless." His deep voice sends a shiver down my spine.

"Or brave," I counter. "Depending on how you look at it."

He glances up, those icy-blue eyes meeting mine for a brief moment before returning to his work. "Hmm. There's a fine line between bravery and stupidity."

"So I've been told." I lean against the fence post next to him, close enough to catch his scent—sawdust and sweat and something distinctly masculine. "Do you like horses?" I watch as he reaches for another rail then positions the wood. His hands are large and capable, with calluses that speak of years of physical work.

"Don't have much of an opinion one way or the other."

"Really? No opinion on creatures that are strong, wild, and impossible to ignore?" I look him up and down. "Thought they'd be right up your alley."

His grip on the hammer tightens. "Did you need something?"

"Just making conversation." I shift closer to him, watching as he lines up another nail. "So, what's the deal with you not working at the resort anymore?"

The hammer freezes mid-swing, and the temperature between us seems to drop several degrees.

"Not something I'm discussing." His tone is low and controlled but with an edge to it.

Retreating, however, has never been my style, especially when it comes to things—or people—that set my pulse skittering.

"I'm just curious. Must be weird, leaving a place your own father manages."

The hammer comes down with enough force to make me jump. Robbie straightens to his full height, towering over me.

"Unless there's something I can help you with," he says tightly, "I'd rather push on with this in silence."

Perfect opening.

"Actually, there *is* something you could help me with. As I told you the other day, my flat is in need of renovation, and I hear you're looking for work at the moment. Perfect timing, eh?"

He raises a sceptical eyebrow, his silver piercing catching the light. "Oh aye? And what would your eldest brother think about me hanging around your flat?"

The question triggers a flash of memory. Fifteen-year-old Ally stumbling through the front door of the hotel, blood streaming from his nose. Maw fussing over him with an ice pack while he cursed Robbie MacDonald. The two of them were always at each other's throats back then.

"He needn't know," I say with a coy smile. If anything, the thought of Ally's disapproval only makes the idea more appealing. After all, the forbidden fruit always looks sweeter . . . especially when it comes with tattoos. "Besides, I'm a grown woman. I can hire whoever I want."

Robbie studies me for a long moment, his expression unreadable. "Would you talk to me as much as you are now? Because if so, I'd need to double my rate."

"Humph!" I place my hands on my hips, feigning offence. "I actually have a job to go to. I'm an English teacher at the high school, and the new term starts tomorrow. So I'll be leaving you in peace most of the time."

He considers, his eyes scanning my face as if searching for some hidden catch. "I can swing round tomorrow evening," he offers eventually. "See what needs to be done and give you a quote?"

"Oh, I'm actually going to the Pheasant after work tomorrow for the pub quiz. How about Tuesday?"

"That works for me. What's the address?"

I give it to him. "It's above the Otter's Holt gift shop."

"Right." He nods then turns back to the fence. Apparently, our conversation is over.

"Great! I'll see you Tuesday, then. Looking forward to it."

Robbie just grunts.

I head back to the stables, smiling to myself like an idiot. True, I don't have a great deal of money in my bank account at the moment, but there's no harm in getting a quote, right? And if it means having Robbie MacDonald in my flat—with those muscles and tattoos and that delicious grumpiness—well, that's just a bonus.

Besides, maybe I'll even find out what really happened at the resort. There's definitely a story there, and if there's one thing I love almost as much as a well-built man with a nipple piercing, it's a good mystery.

CHAPTER EIGHT

ROBBIE

I pack my tools into the saddlebags of my motorcycle then fasten the buckles. I was lucky the stables had the wood I needed for the repair job, but this setup isn't going to work long-term. If I'm serious about making a go of being a self-employed tradesman, I'll need something bigger than my bike to haul equipment around. A van, most likely.

Not that I've got the cash for one. Especially not now I've quit my job at the resort.

I get on my Speedmaster, the evening sun beating down on my shoulders. Still, that was a nice wee bit of work. Janice was pleased with the fence repair, and the payment will definitely come in handy. Small mercies.

The engine rumbles to life beneath me, the familiar vibration humming through my body. Time to head home, crack open a cold beer, then let loose on the punchbag hanging in my garage. I've been hitting it a lot these past few days.

The police have already paid me a visit. DS Sinclair even made a joke about it having been a few years since we "hung out".

There was a time when we saw rather a lot of each other, back when I was Bannock's resident teenage troublemaker.

I haven't been arrested—yet—but I suspect the cops are building up a case against me. It's only a matter of time. And the waiting? It's fucking torture.

Movement catches my eye. It's Cat, leading that chestnut horse—Bracken, was it?—towards one of the fields. She's got her riding gear on again, those tight jodhpurs hugging her arse.

I allow myself a moment to look because, well, I'm only human. Cat McIntyre is undeniably beautiful—and not just her arse. I especially like the way those delicate features of hers somehow manage to look both innocent and mischievous at the same time. She's got this energy about her, like she's constantly buzzing with life.

But . . . she's way too shiny and sweet for the likes of me. Too untarnished. Too McIntyre.

And yet, Christ is she forward! She didn't even attempt to be subtle earlier when she compared me to that stallion. What was it she said? "Strong, wild, and impossible to ignore"? Cheeky! Oh, and let's not forget the way she eyed me up the other day when I was chopping wood. She might as well have licked her lips.

I watch her for a little longer, admiring the way she moves with such easy confidence.

She looks like her mother did.

The thought hits me out of nowhere, and suddenly I'm seeing it again—lashing rain, crumpled metal, blood. Death.

My heart rate spikes. I grip the handlebars tighter, forcing the image away. Not now. Not ever, if I can help it.

I pull my visor down, kick off, and navigate out of the stables' grounds. As I do, I spot Cat again. She's mounted now and in a field that runs parallel to the exit road.

When she sees me, a wide grin splits her face. She says something to Bracken, and suddenly they're picking up speed, galloping alongside the fence line.

Jesus, she can go fast on that thing. My pulse quickens as I watch her urge the horse faster still, her body moving in perfect rhythm with the animal.

She pulls ahead of me and throws a challenging look over her shoulder. I could easily overtake her—my bike is capable of much more than this leisurely pace—but I'm enjoying the view too much to rush.

Cat crouches forwards, her arse slightly raised off the saddle, those jodhpurs hiding absolutely nothing. Every curve, every line of her body is on display. She glances back at me again, a knowing smirk playing on her lips.

Damn, maybe she's not quite as sweet as I thought.

From this angle, I can see the way her thighs grip the saddle, the subtle flex of her calves with every stride, and that tantalising gap between her body and the leather that sends my thoughts spiralling into dangerous territory. She leans even further forwards, urging the horse faster, and the shift in position offers an even better view—a glimpse of pure temptation that makes my breath catch.

For a moment I'm entranced. So entranced I nearly veer off the side of the road and have to jerk the handlebars to right myself.

Fucking hell, MacDonald. Eyes on where you're going.

I shoot Cat one final glance then turn off the single-track road and onto the main road, acutely aware that my jeans are feeling suspiciously snug in certain areas. When I get home, I *definitely* need to have a go at my punchbag. Now, as well as being falsely accused of theft, there's something else I need to work off.

CHAPTER NINE

CAT

"And at the end of that round, the Bannock Brainiacs are *still* in the lead, now with twenty-four points!" Jamie announces into the mic, his voice carrying across the packed pub. "As for the rest of you, remember, it's not about the winning or the losing, it's about . . . oh, who am I kidding? It's totally about the winning. Step up your game!"

I roll my eyes and take another sip of my wine. My brother will always find ways to stir the pot.

From a corner of the room, Scott—who used to teach me maths at Bannock High but as of today is now a colleague of mine—calls out, "We all know *you'll* do anything to win, Jamie, but some of us have a wee thing called dignity!"

Laughter fills the Pheasant.

"You don't have to tell us its name, Scott, or that it's wee—just keep it in your trousers, please!" Jamie fires back, not missing a beat.

The pub erupts, and even I can't help but laugh. As irritating as Jamie can be, I have to admit he's handling this quiz night like he was born for it.

"I've missed this," I say, turning to Iona, who's perched on the barstool beside mine. "Just us girls, hanging out."

"Me too," Iona agrees. She's wearing one of her signature animal-print blouses, this one covered in tiny owls with spectacles. "Sorry I've been so busy lately."

"It's fine." I wave it off. "I get it. You've got Lewis, and Maisie's got Jamie. I'm just glad we're getting some girl time tonight."

It's strange, seeing my two best friends coupled up with my brothers. For a few years, Iona and I shared a tiny flat down in Glasgow, where we'd spend hours dissecting our dates and hook-ups over cheap wine and takeaway. Back then, Iona was always searching for "the one", poring over romance novels and sighing dramatically about finding her own hero. Meanwhile, I wasn't looking for the one but rather the fun—the flirting, the banter, the tumble between the sheets.

Funny how she ended up finding her perfect match in Lewis, who was right under her nose all along. I mean, Iona literally grew up in the building opposite me and my brothers.

"Check out the way she's looking at him." Iona nods at Maisie, who's behind the bar and gazing at Jamie with undisguised adoration.

"Aye, she's absolutely smitten."

Apparently overhearing us, Maisie turns to me and plants both hands flat on the counter. "If *you* had a man who can go three rounds in one night and still have the energy to make you breakfast in the morning, you'd be smitten too."

I've just taken a sip of wine, and I choke on it. "Jesus Christ, Maisie! That's my brother!"

"What? Making breakfast is a very attractive quality."

"That wasn't the bit I objected to, and you know it."

Before Maisie can torment me with further details of my brother's bedroom prowess—details I absolutely do not need to know—Jamie speaks into the microphone again.

"Before the next round, I have a few important announcements. If I could have everyone's attention, please."

The pub hushes, and all eyes turn to Jamie.

"First off, look at this, eh?" He holds one arm out wide. "Me, hosting quiz night at the Pheasant! Who'd have thought it? Especially after the rumours that Maisie and I were set to start World War Three with our competitiveness. But here we are, working together! And this is just the beginning of a more collaborative approach between the Bannock Hotel and the Pheasant."

People murmur their approval, and a few break into applause.

"Next up," Jamie continues, "I regret to say I've actually had a number of complaints tonight. About you, Iona Stewart."

Everyone turns to Iona, who blinks. "Er . . . you have?"

"Aye," Jamie confirms. "If you could *please* stop waving around that sparkly engagement ring quite so smugly, then people might be able to concentrate on my questions. Thank you."

The room bursts into laughter again, and Iona holds her hand aloft and gives her fingers a proud wee wiggle, the diamond catching the light.

I shake my head but laugh all the same. Iona's been on cloud nine since getting engaged.

"Remind me," I say quietly, nudging her with my elbow, "how *did* Lewis propose?"

Her cheeks flush pink. "Why do you keep asking me that? I've already told you. We were on a lovely walk one evening, and he just went down on one knee."

"We keep asking," Maisie says, leaning across the bar with a sly grin, "because every time we do, you blush. Which makes us think there's more to the story than you're letting on."

"There isn't!" she protests.

Before Maisie or I can press her further, Jamie continues. "And in other news, Ally and Emily welcomed their second child—another wee boy—into the world just yesterday. Baby and mother are both doing great, and Ally is . . . well, still Ally. So, I hope you all have a drink to hand—and if not, stop being a cheapskate and go order something off Maisie! This is a pub, people! *Anyway*, I'd like to ask you all to raise a glass to wee Ciaran."

There's a round of chuckles, and drinks are raised. "To Ciaran!" we all say.

I heard the good news last night as I was finishing up at the stables, and I popped by Ally and Emily's house after work today. Ciaran is perfect—all pink and wrinkly with a tuft of chestnut hair, just like his big brother, Ru. Emily looked exhausted but delighted, and Ally was practically bursting with pride, even though he tried to play it cool.

"One last thing," Jamie says. "Can we please all take a moment to appreciate how stunning Maisie looks tonight? That lilac hair suits her perfectly—not that there's any colour she couldn't pull off."

The whole room goes, "Aww!"

Maisie tosses her hair and gives the pub a jokey regal wave.

"Of course, there are a lot of people around the world who adore Maisie's videos," Jamie adds, "but let's not forget, she was ours first!"

The room answers with more awws and a smattering of cheers. Bryce, Maisie's da, bellows, "Damn right!"

Jamie shoots Maisie a wink then dives back into his quiz-master routine.

"I *still* can't believe you're with Jamie," I say to Maisie as he reads the next question. "I'm happy for you. I just . . . can't wrap my head around the appeal."

Growing up, Jamie was the bane of my existence—always pulling pranks, hiding my things, and generally being a nuisance. Even now, as an adult, he can't resist winding me up at every opportunity. I don't get how anyone—never mind Maisie—could fall for someone who delights in being so infuriating.

"I can see it now," Iona says. "I couldn't at first, but now I reckon they're perfect for each other. Jamie's met his match in Maisie." Iona gives her a small approving nod. "No one can keep him in line like you can."

I cock my head then admit, "That *is* true."

Maisie glances back at Jamie, a soft smile playing on her lips.

"You know," Iona says to Maisie, "we're practically family now, what with our parents being together."

Around the same time that Maisie and Jamie began to secretly see each other, so did Bryce and Elspeth. Elspeth is Iona's maw. She's also been something of a surrogate mother to me and my brothers ever since we lost our own maw.

"Aye," Maisie agrees. "Plus, when you marry Lewis, you and Cat will become sisters."

"And if you and Jamie ever get hitched," I add, "we'll *all* be sisters. One big happy but slightly weird family."

"True! It's funny how everyone is pairing off now." Realisation hits Maisie a beat too late, and she winces. "Oh! Sorry, Cat. Not you, obviously, but—"

"Ha!" I give a dismissive wave and swirl what's left of my wine, totally unfazed. "That's okay. I'm not exactly looking to settle down. *Although* . . . I *may* have my eye on someone I could have a wee bit of fun with."

Iona, immediately interested, sits forwards. "Oh? Spill!"

"Well, let's just say I have a thing for a certain . . . bad boy."

"Oh my God. Not Robbie MacDonald?" Maisie laughs so loudly that a nearby table glances our way. "Cat, please tell me you're joking. I've seen that man pick up more tourists in here than hot dinners."

"What can I say? I'm a sucker for tattoos. And piercings."

Smirking, Maisie pours us more wine, including a glass for herself. I take a sip and savour the crisp, tangy bite. I'll stop after this one. Today was just an in-service day—a chance for teachers to prepare for the new term—but tomorrow there'll be actual students at the school. I can't show up on my first proper day with a hangover.

"What would Ally think about this wee crush," Maisie wants to know, "considering the number of times he and Robbie nearly killed each other back in the day?"

Remembering those fights, I can't hold back a grimace. I was too young to understand what started it all, but the bad blood between them ran deep.

"Pah, that's ancient history." I try to sound breezy. "People change."

"Do they, though?" Maisie questions. "Because there've been all sorts of rumours going round about why he left his job at the resort."

"You said it yourself, they're *rumours*," I point out. "And as we all know, the folk in this town love nothing more than to exaggerate a story. Besides, in the classroom, I've seen how teenagers act out when they're hurting. The way Robbie was when he was younger . . . well, sometimes the worst behaviour is just a cry for help."

Maisie isn't convinced. "That might be true, but Robbie's not a teenager. He's a grown man who still has a reputation for trouble."

"He's also gorgeous," Iona adds with a dreamy sigh. When we both stare at her astounded, she flushes. "What? I'm engaged, not blind. And I do read a lot of romance novels. There's just something about the brooding bad boy with a hidden heart of gold . . ."

"Exactly!" I point at her. "See? Iona gets it."

"I still think you should be careful," Maisie warns. "Though, I'll admit, if anyone can handle Robbie MacDonald, it's probably you, Cat."

I lean in closer. "Want to know a secret? You can't tell Lewis, Iona. And Maisie, you absolutely cannot tell Jamie. But . . . I've asked Robbie to do a bit of work around my flat."

Maisie's eyes widen. "You've what?"

"Hey, none of my brothers were willing to help, and Robbie's available for work. Plus, he's good with his hands." I wiggle my eyebrows suggestively.

"And if this gives you an opportunity to flirt with him, then that's just a perk, right?" Iona says with a knowing look.

I wink at her. "Aye. Trust me, after how dull the dating scene was up north, I *need* a bit of excitement. I'm not wanting to be his girlfriend or anything. Just, you know, have some fun. I'm calling this . . ." I pause dramatically. "Project Bang a Bad Boy."

CHAPTER TEN

CAT

I give my reflection one final assessment in the hallway mirror. My black Lycra running shorts show off my legs nicely, and the pink tank top hugs my curves in all the right places. Perfect for my "I was just about to go jogging" charade.

The doorbell rings, sending a little flutter through my stomach. I take a deep breath and open the door.

"Hi!" I beam at Robbie, who fills my doorframe like a tattooed colossus.

"Evening." His expression is neutral, although his eyes briefly flick over my outfit.

I step back to let him in, and immediately my tiny hallway feels even smaller. He has his leather jacket draped casually over one arm, and he's in a plain white T-shirt that stretches across his broad shoulders. He smells freshly showered – soap and something woodsy.

"Sorry about my outfit." I gesture down at myself. "Squeezing in a run after this."

"Hmm. Right." His pierced eyebrow lifts, scepticism written all over his face.

"Anyway, let me show you around! I'll take your jacket."

I grab it then realise there's nowhere to hang it. "Er . . ." I balance it precariously on top of a stack of moving boxes. "I'll need to get some hooks. Maybe that's something you could help with. Anyway, the tour!"

I lead him into the living room, hyperaware of his presence behind me. Robbie glances around, taking in the cracked walls, peeling wallpaper, and worn carpet. He lets out a low whistle.

"So," I say brightly, "just needs a bit of TLC, right?"

"More like CPR." His gaze lingers on the stack of paperbacks piled haphazardly in one corner. "That's a lot of books."

I raise my hands in a "what can you do?" gesture. "English teacher. It comes with the territory."

He crouches to read some of the spines. "Ah, *Trainspotting*. Brutal but honest. Shows a side of Scotland tourists never see."

I put a hand on my hip. "Have you actually read it? Or just seen the film?"

"Read it. Just because I work with my hands doesn't mean I can't use my brain."

"I didn't mean—"

"Sure you did." He straightens. "Anyway, we're not here to talk books."

"*Actually* . . ." I grab my tablet. "I have a few ideas for custom bookshelves I'd love to get your opinion on."

I pull up my Pinterest board and hold the tablet between us, forcing Robbie to lean in. His proximity—his body heat—makes my pulse quicken.

"How about something like one of these for the living room? Built-in shelving with space for all my books. Is that something you could do?"

Robbie studies the images, and I take the opportunity to

study him up close. His profile is all strong lines and hard edges, softened by dark lashes that cast shadows on his cheekbones. He really is beautiful.

"Aye. If you need something made of wood, I can make it. Whatever it is."

I like that. There's something undeniably sexy about a man who knows exactly what he's capable of.

"Brilliant," I say. "Shall we look at the rest of the flat?"

I lead him through each room, watching as he taps walls here and there and takes mental notes of all the work that needs done. In the kitchen, he glances at the drawer that's *still* sitting on my floor.

"Ah. So, about that—"

"You got a screwdriver?"

"Er, aye, I think I do, actually." I fetch it for him, and within thirty seconds, the drawer that caused me *so* much grief last week is back on its runners, opening and closing smoothly.

"Easy fix," he says, then he grimaces up at the flickering fluorescent light. "That, on the other hand, needs replaced."

"To be honest, I'd love to replace the entire kitchen at some point. But that'll have to wait. For now, the priority is to get the place livable."

Once he's finished looking around, we head back to the living room, where we agree on a list of everything he's going to tackle.

"All in, should take about two weeks, give or take." He tells me his daily rate, which is not insignificant, especially for someone who's newly self-employed.

"Wow." I play with my braid. "How about we haggle that down a bit, and in return, I'll make sure everyone in town knows you're the best handyman in the Highlands?"

"Nope." He glances out of the window, completely unfazed

by my little negotiation attempt. "People already know I'm good." His blue irises meet mine once more. "They think I'm trouble, but they know I can fix anything. My rate's my rate. Take it or leave it."

Again with that confidence. It's infuriating and attractive all at once.

"Is there really nothing we can do?" I try once more, giving him my best pleading look, complete with dimples.

He doesn't even respond, just folds his arms.

"All right, fine!" Although, as soon as I say it, a thought flashes through my mind: *I can't afford this!* I quickly flip it, though, just like the self-help book I read earlier this year taught me. *I* can *afford this.*

It's all about the power of positive thoughts and manifesting abundance, baby. I used the same technique when buying this place, and look how that turned out! It's not every twenty-four-year-old who can say they're a home owner.

The universe provides for you when you put good energy out there. Or at least, that's the theory. True, my bank balance may be low, but things will sort themselves out. I'll just . . . leave it to the universe to handle the details.

"Just a reminder," Robbie says, "but my rate assumes you'll be out at your job while I'm working. If you distract me with chat and . . ." He waves a hand at my outfit. ". . . *this*, I'll have to increase my quote accordingly."

I gasp, outraged by his insinuation. Also, it turns out Project Bang a Bad Boy might be more difficult than I was expecting. Still, I can't help feeling a teensy bit smug that my choice of attire is getting under his skin.

"I'm not sure what you're implying, but I assure you, this is purely functional sportswear."

"Mm-hmm." He pulls a tape measure from his pocket. "Anyway, I need to take some measurements and jot down a few things. Won't take long."

While Robbie moves around the flat, his tape measure snapping, I pop on the kettle. I take down two mugs—one with a Shakespeare quote and the other featuring a Highland cow—and pop a teabag in each. When the kettle clicks, I fill the mugs and leave them to brew.

"Do you normally have two drinks at once?" Robbie asks, returning to the kitchen.

"One of these is for you, silly."

"No, thanks."

"I've got beer if you prefer?" I open the fridge to reveal several bottles of Golden Stag Lager. Maisie mentioned it was his usual order at the Pheasant.

"Er . . . no." He pops his notepad into the back pocket of his jeans. "That's me got everything I need. If you're happy with the quote, I can start tomorrow."

Part of me itches to come up with an excuse for him to stay longer, but no, best not to push my luck. Besides, he's going to be here every day for the next two weeks. That's plenty of time to wear down his grumpy exterior.

"Tomorrow is perfect."

CHAPTER ELEVEN

ROBBIE

The scraper makes a satisfying ripping sound as I tear away another strip of the hideous floral wallpaper. Whoever thought this pattern was a good idea should be banned from interior decorating for life. Beneath it, the wall is a patchy mess, uneven and cracked. That'll need sorted before any new paper or paint goes up.

It's my second day of working in Cat's flat, and I've been at this task for hours. It's tedious, but a bit of mindless work is exactly what I need right now, or so I keep telling myself. Each strip I peel away is another minute where I *shouldn't* be thinking about the resort, or the accusation hanging over me, or the fact my own father is willing to believe I stole from guests. But try as I might, those thoughts keep creeping back in.

The front door clicks open. "Just me!" Cat calls. A few seconds later, her voice fills the living room. "Wow! I've been dying to see the back of this wallpaper since I set foot in here. Great work, Robbie!"

I pause the rock music playing through my phone, checking the time as I do. Bang on four o'clock, just like yesterday. Don't teachers have marking or lesson planning or whatever to do? And wouldn't it make more sense for Cat to do that in her classroom than here, surrounded by dust and mess?

"Cheers." I get back to it with the scraper. "Should have it all down before I leave today."

She moves into my peripheral vision. "No rush. Honestly, I could watch you strip all night—and I don't just mean the wall-paper. Last week's shirtless wood-chopping show was quite the spectacle." She fans herself.

Christ, here we go again. I shake my head and focus on the wall. The seven-year age gap between us feels like twenty when she comes out with stuff like that. There's something distinctly immature about her approach, like a teenager who's just discovered flirting and is trying it out for size. Didn't I make it crystal clear when I accepted the job that there was to be none of this nonsense? And yet here we are. She's persistent, I'll give her that.

"Can you pass me that bucket?" My strategy for dealing with Catriona McIntyre's flirting attempts is to simply not engage.

She goes over to the corner, picks it up, then sashays back and hands it to me with a flourish. "Here you go. Need anything else? A drink? A snack?" She pauses and bats her eyelashes. "Me?"

Jesus Christ. She's barely in the door! There's no build-up whatsoever. It's straight from zero to sixty.

"Nope. Just the bucket, thanks." I take it and get back to work.

Apparently, she gets the message because she leaves me to get on with things in peace—for all of ten minutes. Then she calls, "Robbie? Could you help me with something? I'm too short."

With a sigh, I put down my tools and head into the bedroom, where she's standing by the built-in wardrobe, a box in her hands.

"Can you put this up there for me?" She indicates the top shelf. "It's winter clothing."

On the face of it, it's an innocent enough request, so I do as she asks. But then—because of course there's a "but then"—she shifts slightly as I stretch upwards, and her breast grazes against me.

Oh, for crying out loud. There's no way that wasn't on purpose. Right, that's it.

My hand finds her hip—not gentle, not rough, just . . . firm. I step into her space like the air between us belongs to me now, close enough to her that she has to tilt her head back to keep looking at me. Then, because I don't stop walking, she retreats, backing away until there's nothing but solid wall behind her and me in front of her.

I slam my hand flat against the plaster above her head, hard enough to make her flinch. Her eyes go wide as saucers, and for once—*for once*—she's quiet. I lean in close, so close I can feel the heat rolling off her skin.

"Catriona," I growl, my voice low with warning.

She's breathing fast now, her chest rising and falling with every breath.

Damn it. Don't look at her tits, Robbie. Focus!

"You think this is a game?" The words are rough-edged, practically a snarl. "Because if it is, I'm not playing. You hired me to do a job, and that's what I'm here to do. So whatever you think you're doing, it needs to stop."

She lifts her chin a wee bit higher. "I thought you'd be up for some fun." She says it steadily enough, but a faint quiver slips through. She's not as sure of herself as she's pretending. "I mean, you're Robbie MacDonald. Bannock's bad boy. Why are you being so . . . boring?"

72

I let out a slow breath, then I breathe in again and her scent wraps around me—coconut shampoo mixed with something floral, like she's just stepped out of a summer garden. Almost instinctively my hand tightens on her hip. She's warm. So warm.

"Boring?" I manage.

She holds my gaze defiantly, the tilt of her head exposing the delicate line of her throat. "Yes! Boring!" She jabs at my chest with her finger. "It's because of my brothers. Right? God, is your reputation a lie? Is there even an adventurous bone in your body?"

Bloody hell, she is incorrigible. But maybe there's something to what she's saying. Maybe I *should* just give in, fuck her, and be done with it. Maybe *then* I could get on with my work in peace, and God knows I could use the release after the week I've had.

My gaze drops to her lips, pink and slightly parted, like she's daring me to take what she keeps offering. I can't remember the last time I was this close to a woman and *didn't* take her to bed.

But no, I can't—and yet she's not listening to me! So maybe I need to teach her a lesson. The thought slips in uninvited, a mental image of me yanking down her tight work trousers, laying her facedown over my lap, and skelping her arse until she finally gets the message. My dick twitches at the thought. I'd like to do *that*. A lot. She'd fucking deserve it too.

But then, out of the corner of my eye, I spot a photo on Cat's bedside table. A family photo, showing her with her brothers and parents.

Shit. Her parents.

An altogether different image crashes into my head, a memory of a stormy winter night seven years ago. I was on my motorcycle, and the rain was lashing down hard. It was fucking miserable. But then my headlights caught something off the side of the road. A car, smashed into a tree, steam rising from its crumpled bonnet. I pulled up and killed the engine. Got off my bike. Approached the wreck, and—

Abruptly I push away from the wall, putting distance between me and Cat. "I fucking told you that nothing is going to happen between us."

She blinks, startled—but only for a moment. Then she harrumphs and folds her arms across her chest. "Well, if you *really* aren't up for a bit of fun—if you're really going to be so boring—we'll have to talk about something else. Like . . . why you left your job at the resort."

At this, I turn away from her and walk out of the bedroom. "No," I call over my shoulder. "We're not going to talk about that. I'm off—I'll be back tomorrow. And from now on, I'll only be working when you're *not* in the flat."

"Oh, come on!" She follows me. "Whatever happened, I bet there are things you need to get off your chest. You need to talk to *someone*, and who's it going to be? There's your da and Johnny, but they both work at the resort, so maybe it's not so easy to talk to them about what happened."

I grab my phone from the living room, deciding my tools can stay where they are until tomorrow. I just want to get out of here. But when I make for the front door, Cat blocks my exit.

"Who else have you got? Because, let's be honest, you're a bit of a lone wolf, Robbie. Who else around Bannock are you going to open up to, if not me?"

"Opening up isn't really my style." I drum my fingers against my thigh and eye her with impatience. "Besides, I'm fully aware this is just another ploy to get close to me. Now, could you move out of my way?"

She does, holding up both hands and taking an exaggerated sidestep. "Fine! But not everything I do has an agenda, you know.

Maybe I just think you could do with having someone in your corner. But whatever. Keep bottling it all up if that's working for you."

The annoying thing is, it *hasn't* been working. There really hasn't been anyone I can vent to, other than the punchbag in my garage. And no matter how hard I go to town on that thing, I don't feel any better.

Still, I make for the door.

"You don't have to be some stereotypical man who refuses to open up," Cat insists. "What pressing plans do you have for this evening? Can you really not spare ten minutes for a drink and a chat?"

I pause, my hand on the door handle. "I'm not one of your students that you have to counsel."

"No, but you *are* acting like a moody teenager. Lucky for you, I'm a great listener, so why not open up? What's the worst that could happen?"

I release a long, irritated sigh and pinch the bridge of my nose. "You're like a bloody terrier, you know that? Won't let go until you get what you want."

She grins, unapologetic. "Guilty as charged."

I hesitate a little longer, torn between my instinct to shut her out and the nagging voice in my head that says she might actually have a point. "Fine," I mutter eventually, dragging a hand down my face before pointing at her like this whole thing is somehow her fault. "Ten minutes. No more."

She beams then bounces through to the kitchen. "I'll crack open a couple of beers!"

"No! No beer. I'll take a tea, though."

She sticks her head out of the kitchen door, a genuine smile lighting up her face—not the flirtatious one she's been throwing me since she got home, but something warmer, more real. "One tea coming right up. How do you take it?"

"Milk, no sugar."

I follow her through and sink onto one of her kitchen chairs, suddenly exhausted. When did I last actually talk to someone about my problems? Not Johnny—I'm always trying to protect him. Not my da—that relationship has been strained for as long as I can remember. And I don't exactly have mates I pour my heart out to. There's Drew, but that relationship is based on jokey banter. We don't do personal stuff.

Cat places a steaming mug in front of me—it has a Highland cow on it—then sits opposite me with her own mug. She waits, patient for once, giving me space to find my words.

"I've been accused of stealing from guests at the resort," I say finally. "Valuable stuff. A watch, diamond earrings, a signet ring, cash."

Her eyebrows lift slightly, but that's the only sign of surprise. She nods, encouraging me to continue.

"Da found out my keycard was used to access the rooms where items went missing, but I swear I didn't go into those rooms." The words come easier now, spilling out like I've uncorked something. "Someone's set me up. I don't know who or why, but they've done a good job of it."

I take a sip of my tea, the warmth spreading through my chest. "Da suspended me, but I quit instead. Told him where he could stick his job."

"What about CCTV?" Cat questions. "Doesn't the resort have footage that could clear things up?"

I shake my head. "Not in the guest corridors. Privacy reasons. The only cameras are in public areas, like the lobby and restaurant."

I hesitate, wondering if I should tell her the rest. Something about her steady gaze encourages me to continue.

"My da made my brother escort me to my locker to collect my things. When I was taking out my jacket, a ring fell out. One of the stolen items."

Cat's brows draw together. "Wait . . . what?"

"I swear I'd never seen it before in my life, but there it was, planted in my locker."

"What did you do?"

"I asked Johnny to lie." The admission feels heavier than I expected. "I begged him to say he found it somewhere else, not in my locker. He agreed, but he wasn't happy about it. Johnny's always been the good one, you know? The rule follower."

I run a hand through my hair, frustration bubbling up again. "Anyway, my da said he and Johnny have to keep their distance from me for now. He doesn't want it looking like they're interfering with the police investigation. I do get that . . . kind of. But it's still shit."

Cat's quiet, processing everything I've told her. Finally she says, "And . . . you just walked away? You aren't trying to clear your name?"

I shrug. "How? I'm not welcome at the resort right now, so what am I supposed to do?"

"Have you at least approached a lawyer?"

"The police haven't charged me yet, so no. I'd rather not involve a lawyer unless I have to." I grimace. "Apart from anything else, they're bloody expensive, right?"

"So . . . you're doing *nothing*? I hate to point this out, Robbie, but you have a bit of a reputation around town. It'd be all too easy for people to believe you did this."

"Aye," I say glumly. "I realise that."

"So you have to *fight* this."

I stare at her for a moment, thrown by her total lack of doubt. Most folk would at least have asked if I did it.

"How?"

"Well, *someone* put that ring in your locker." She leans forwards. "If it wasn't you, who might it have been? Is there anyone who has it in for you?"

I scoff. "Where do I start? I've made a lot of enemies over the years."

She sets her mug down. "C'mon, consider the question properly. Surely the easiest way to clear your name is to come up with another name, the name of the person who actually did it. So give me some names!"

"Where did this Sherlock Holmes act come from?"

She grins. "I'm a fan of a good whodunnit. They're a great break from the more high-brow literature I had to study at university. Now, suspects. Go!"

I consider her question. "Well . . . one person who's never liked me is Ally McIntyre."

Cat rolls her eyes. "Right. My brother framed you. Sure."

"Why not?" I say, warming to the idea, if only to wind her up. "He's always around the resort these days, thanks to his adventure business. He and Aidan are constantly there to pick up customers for outdoor activities, or to drop them off. He's got the motive—he and I have never got along—and considering all the time he spends at the resort, he's had the opportunity too. Aye, I think there's a strong possibility it was him."

Cat fixes me with a flat stare. "Right. Ally, who's married to a woman he loves, who's running his dream business with his best mate, and who's just become a father to a second wee boy. Oh, and who lives with his family in a gorgeous house, where I know for a fact they're all very happy. You're saying Ally decided to risk all that, and potentially end up in prison, by nicking some items and framing you? Just to settle some ancient grudge against a guy who drove him up the wall when he was a lad? Aye, that sounds *dead* logical." Her words drip with sarcasm.

"All right, well . . . let's put him down as a maybe." I wink at her, enjoying the way her cheeks flush with indignation. Truthfully, I don't for a second think Ally's behind this, but ruffling Cat's feathers is too tempting to resist.

She sighs. "Who else?"

I give it some proper thought. "Well, there is Samantha, who works at the resort and has never particularly liked me. She's tried to report me to my da a few times in the past, and I reckon she's frustrated I've never been disciplined to the extent she'd like."

The memory of my departure from the resort flashes back to me. "Oh, and here's a funny thing. When Johnny was leading me to my bike, after I told Da I'd quit, we passed Samantha and she had this strange smile on her face, like she was pleased I was finally getting my comeuppance. She even asked me if I was having a bad day in this really smug, unpleasant way."

"Samantha . . . Drummond?" Cat says. "I don't know her well, but I know who she is. She's the head of housekeeping, right? So it'd have been easy for her to access the guests' rooms?"

"Aye," I agree. "She had the means, and the motive. Shit. It might actually have been her."

"See?" Cat sits up straighter. "We're getting somewhere already! Although . . ." She frowns and taps a finger against her mug. "Would she really risk jail just to see you properly punished? Nah, she'd need another motive too. Like needing the money."

"Well, she got divorced last year."

"Oh!" Cat bounces in her chair. "That fits! The divorce

could've hit her hard—legal fees, splitting assets, maybe even alimony payments. If the opportunity came along to pocket some valuable items from guests and frame you in the process, that might've been too tempting for her to resist."

I nod, scratching my jaw. "Maybe. And . . . I don't know if this is relevant, but for all her disapproval of me, she did try it on with me once, last year. I reckon she wanted a rebound fling or something, but I turned her down pretty firmly. Let's just say she didn't take it well."

"Ohhhh, that's *absolutely* relevant! Haven't you heard the saying *Hell hath no fury like a woman scorned*?"

I huff out a laugh despite myself. "Aye, well, it does seem like something she'd hold against me."

"So"—Cat ticks off points on her fingers—"money trouble, possibly. Bruised ego from your rejection, definitely. And access to guest rooms, yep. I reckon she fits the profile!"

I can't help but give a small smile at her enthusiasm. "All right, let's say it was her. How do I prove it and clear my name? Especially when I'm not exactly welcome at the resort."

"Hmm." Cat purses her lips thoughtfully. "Well, right now we're just guessing that Samantha might be having money problems. Truthfully, we've no idea. So how about, as a next step, I try to dig into that? Bannock being the way it is, if she's been struggling financially, *someone* around town will have heard of it. I could have a few conversations, see if anything interesting comes to light?"

"Why you?"

She blinks, then a smirk tugs at her lips. "Robbie, most folk around Bannock can't resist a good chinwag, but *you*? You aren't exactly known for your small talk or your sunny disposition. If you start chatting with people and asking questions, they'll think something dodgy is going on and clam up. Me, on the other hand? Folk won't bat an eye if I poke around."

Hmm, she's got a point there. "Well . . . if you think playing Miss Marple will help figure this out, go ahead."

She beams as though I've just handed her some kind of golden opportunity. "Great! I'll see what I can find out. This is actually kind of exciting! Maybe I should buy a cork board, so I can set up something like you always see on those detective programmes, with mugshots and Post-it Notes and red string connecting different ideas . . ."

I narrow my eyes at her. "You realise this is my life we're talking about? Not a bit of entertainment for you?"

Her smile falters, and she has the decency to look embarrassed. "Oh. Of course. Sorry, when I said it was exciting, I meant—"

"Aye, I know what you meant. It's fine." I drain the last of my tea. "It doesn't matter why you're helping, I still appreciate it. I'm not sure it'll come to anything, but what the hell, you might as well see what you can find." I stand. "Anyway, I best go."

"Already?" Disappointment is clear in her voice. "Are you sure you don't want to stay a bit longer? After everything you've been through, maybe you could do with some . . . relief?" She wiggles her eyebrows suggestively.

I grunt and shake my head. I'll give it to her, this lass is nothing if not persistent.

"That's *definitely* my cue to go," I say. "See you, Cat."

CHAPTER TWELVE

CAT

I'm connecting a piece of red string between *Samantha Drummond* and *Possible money problems?* when my phone pings. I ignore it and focus on securing the string with a tiny drawing pin.

It's Friday night, and I'm sitting cross-legged on my bed in pyjamas with a green clay mask on my face. The cork board I ordered yesterday sits propped against my pillows like some kind of investigative masterpiece. Ideally, I'd be doing this in the living room, but Robbie's turned it into a plaster-dusted war zone. My bedroom, which has yet to be plastered, offers a small sanctuary from the chaos.

When I opened the package this afternoon, Robbie shook his head and muttered "Christ" before resuming his battle with the walls.

He doesn't know it yet—emphasis on *yet*—but this cork board is going to blow the case wide open. Admittedly, it's not exactly teeming with evidence. So far, it's mainly just a few colour-coded note cards listing stolen items and Samantha Drummond's name underneath *Prime suspect*. Not quite Netflix docuseries material, but at least I'm getting organised. I'll just have to wait for Bannock's gossip mill to churn out some more clues.

When I decided to move back to Bannock, I pictured spending my weekends hanging out with friends and barhopping in Inverness. Instead, here I am, alone, in a glorified building site, playing detective. But honestly? At the end of a busy week in a new job, where I've not only had to make cheery small talk with colleagues but get to know and teach a bunch of judgemental teenagers, the last thing I want to do is go out and socialise.

Plus, staying in isn't so bad. Despite the "under construction" vibes, Robbie's making impressive progress, and I can already visualise how amazing this place will look when he's done.

Grabbing a fresh Post-it, I scribble: *Seeking vengeance following romantic rebuff?*

I attach it to the board and connect it to Samantha's name with another piece of red string, completing my triangle of suspicion. Does the red string serve any real purpose? Probably not. But does it make me feel like a badass detective? One hundred per cent yes.

Today's fieldwork, sadly, has been far less gratifying than assembling my conspiracy web. At work I casually dropped Samantha's name into conversations with a few teachers. Then, wandering through town on my way home, I paused to chat with a few folk and slyly fish for clues. But the only whiff of scandal I picked up was to do with her divorce, which raised a few eyebrows at the time.

Apparently, she and her husband had always presented themselves as the perfect couple—matching Christmas jumpers, coordinated social media posts, the works. Other than that wee blip of gossip, most people just described her as polite, though she keeps herself to herself these days. My sweep of the town yielded precisely zero useful intel. So, aye, looks like I'll need to dig a wee bit deeper if I want to crack this case.

My phone pings again. This time I check it. It's the Scottish Sirens group chat.

> **MAISIE**
>
> Guess who just walked into the Pheasant looking all broody?
>
> He's chatting up some tourist with legs up to her eyeballs

I frown at my screen, then another message comes in.

> **MAISIE**
>
> Looks like your bad boy is getting lucky tonight

My stomach drops. Robbie? At the pub? Flirting with some tourist?

> **MAISIE**
>
> He just touched her arm and she didn't pull away. Just saying . . .

"Oh, for fuck's sake." I jump to my feet and hurry to my wardrobe.

The cheek of it! Robbie left shortly after I got home. Had he stuck around, I'd have been very interested in his company. Exhausted from work or not, I'd have shown him a good time. But no, apparently he'd rather spend his Friday night getting chatted up by some *tourist*.

Well, one thing is for sure: I'm wide awake now. Funny how fast tiredness vanishes when you find out the bad boy you've been shamelessly flirting with for days might be going home with someone else.

I yank off my pyjama top and bottoms then reach for my jeans, but freeze when my mirror reflects a green-faced goblin back at me. Shit! The face mask!

A mad dash to the bathroom follows, where frantic scrubbing turns my face a blotchy pink, water splashing everywhere. Not exactly glamorous, but at least I'm no longer green.

Back in the bedroom, my phone pings again.

MAISIE

She's pretty. Tall, blonde, you know the type

Oh, hell no.

Tossing my jeans aside, I pull out my pleated tartan miniskirt instead, the one that makes my legs look fantastic. Comfy briefs are swapped for blush-coloured French knickers. No harm in a girl being prepared, eh?

Humming away to Chappell Roan's "Pink Pony Club", I pair the skirt with a black vest top and my favourite red cardigan, the one with the zip and cute wee hood.

A quick brush through my auburn hair, some mascara, cherry chapstick, and I'm good to go.

Well, almost.

After some determined rummaging at the back of the wardrobe, I pull out the pièce de résistance, a pair of black knee-high boots with heels sharp enough to do damage. I put them on, enjoying the satisfying *zrrrp* of the zip.

I check my reflection in the mirror, grin, then tap out a quick message to the group.

CAT

On my way!

No sooner do I hit send than another message pops up.

IONA

Lewis and I have plans tonight 🍷 🥗 📺

Then there are two more pings.

IONA

But I'll expect a full debrief later, okay?

You've got this, McIntyre 💪

I thumbs-up her message then pocket my phone and head into the kitchen. The makeshift drinks cabinet—a cardboard box with *Booze* scrawled across it in black marker—holds exactly what I need: Glen Garve Whisky. I twist off the cap and take a generous gulp straight from the bottle. Liquid courage in its rawest form. It burns like fire all the way down but leaves behind something bracingly warm.

I wipe my mouth, replace the cap, and stride to the front door.

Time to stake my claim.

◆ ◆ ◆

The Pheasant is buzzing, the cosy stone-walled pub having drawn its usual Friday night mix of locals and tourists. I scan the room, soaking up the warmth and chatter, the scent of wood polish and beer thick in the air.

Then I see him. At a corner table, half-drunk pint in hand, leather jacket hanging on the chair behind him. And aye, he's got company. Across from him sits a woman with honey-blonde hair that falls in perfect waves around her shoulders. Her skin has that sun-kissed glow that screams, "I live in a place with reliable sunshine." She's laughing at something he's just said, her head tilted back to reveal a slender neck.

Shit. Robbie's surly quips aren't that funny. This lassie is seriously keen.

I thread my way towards the bar, ignoring the appreciative glances from a group of male tourists clustered around a table. Any other night, I'd be flattered, but tonight I only have eyes for one man.

And damn, Robbie looks good. Dark jeans and a black henley that clings to his broad shoulders and shows off his muscled forearms, the sleeves pushed up just enough to reveal the edge of a tattoo. His onyx hair is as shiny as ever, and a single lock has fallen forwards over one eyebrow.

The blonde laughs again, her fingers grazing Robbie's hand for a fleeting moment. I narrow my eyes.

"Wow," Maisie says when I reach the bar. She's wiping it with a cloth but stops and leans over it to give my ensemble a once-over. "Those boots are lethal."

"That's the idea." I nod towards Robbie's table. "So, who the hell is she?"

The words tumble out sharp and bold, causing a few of the locals perched at the bar, including old Hamish, to eye us curiously. Nothing like a hint of small-town drama to liven up a Friday evening.

"American. Californian, I think. Been here about twenty minutes." Maisie lowers her voice. "Between you and me, this might be for the best. I wasn't sure you and Robbie was such a great idea."

I frown. "Why not?"

"Because he's *Robbie MacDonald*," she says, as if that explains everything. "And your brothers would have a collective aneurysm."

"My brothers don't dictate my love life."

"Oh, love life? Thought this was just Project Bang a Bad Boy."

"It is," I insist, watching as the blonde clinks her beer glass against Robbie's. "But still, I don't like seeing him with *her*."

Maisie sighs. "Cat, I love you, but sometimes—"

"Sometimes I know exactly what I want," I finish for her. "And right now, I want that tourist to know she can't just swan in here and steal my bad boy." I straighten my shoulders. "Time to show her what a Highland lass in killer heels can do."

Before Maisie can respond, I'm making my way across the pub. Robbie looks up as I approach, surprise flickering in his eyes before they travel the length of my body in a way that sends a thrill through me. He lingers on my legs—can't blame him, considering the amount of thigh I'm showing. Only after he's finished his visual tour does he meet my gaze again, his familiar scowl settling in.

"Sorry I'm late, babe," I announce loudly. "Got held up at work." Leaning down, I press a kiss to Robbie's stubbled cheek. He goes rigid.

"Oh!" The blonde's pretty blue eyes widen and she looks between us. "Are you guys an item? I'd no idea. Robbie, you didn't mention . . ." Her accent is definitely American, and aye, between her blonde hair and golden tan, she's bonny all right.

"No, we're n—"

I slide onto Robbie's lap before he can finish. "Och, you're such a joker, Robert!" I wrap an arm around his shoulders. "We've been together, what, three months now?"

Up this close I can see flecks of silver in Robbie's blue eyes, which right now are shooting daggers at me. I give him my most innocent smile and tighten my grip on him.

A small voice in my head whispers that this is childish, manipulative even, but I push the thought away. Too late to back out now. I'm in deeper than Nessie in Loch Ness.

Robbie's hands find my waist—his fingers brushing the sliver of bare skin just above my skirt, sending tingles blooming across my stomach—and for one blissful second I believe he might play along. But then he's lifting me off his lap and setting me firmly on my feet.

"Sorry about this," he tells the American, his voice tight with barely contained anger. "I'm doing a bit of work in Cat's flat. That's all." His eyes slide to mine, and wow, he is not happy. "We're *not* dating."

The blonde glances between us, confusion evident on her face. "You know what? I . . . think I'm going to call it a night. It was nice meeting you, Robbie." She gathers her jacket and handbag and gestures between us. "Good luck with . . . whatever this is."

She walks away and Robbie turns to me, his eyes flashing, his jaw tightening. "What the hell was that?"

"What?" I try for innocence, but it falls flat even to my own ears.

"You had no right to do that. No right at all."

I slide into the vacated seat. "I'm basically your private investigator. If you're going to flirt with anyone, it should be the lass working on your case."

Rather than responding, Robbie drains the rest of his beer then goes back to glaring at me.

"What's so wrong with me anyway?" The words burst out,

fuelled by a mixture of irritation and something that feels uncomfortably like rejection.

Robbie shakes his head. "Nothing's *wrong* with you. Well, other than the fact you clearly don't take no for an answer. And that wee performance you just pulled? Downright self-centred. You can't just waltz in and act like folk belong to you."

My cheeks warm. Suddenly I don't feel quite so bold. "I'm sorry," I say, and mean it. "That was . . . immature of me."

"Aye, it was." Robbie stands and pulls on his leather jacket. "I'm heading home." He strides for the door.

"Wait!"

Several patrons glance our way as I hurry after him, nearly tripping over my boots in my rush. By the time I burst out onto the lamplit street, Robbie is almost at his motorcycle.

"Robbie! Please, can't we talk?"

He doesn't answer. Not even a glance in my direction as he throws a leg over his bike.

I decide to change tactics. "How much did you drink in there?"

"I'm quite capable of getting myself home." He still won't look at me. He grabs his helmet from where it's secured near the rear of the bike.

I fold my arms and do my version of stern teacher. "I can't let you drive after imbibing alcohol, I'm afraid. For your own safety and that of others."

Perhaps I'm being manipulative again, clinging on when I should probably let him go. But I just can't leave things so sour.

Robbie glowers at me. "Who says 'imbibing'? Besides, yesterday you were the one offering me a beer from your fridge before I rode home."

"Aye, well. You wouldn't want to be reported to the police for drink-driving now, would you?" It's a low blow, and I know it. With everything else Robbie's dealing with, the last thing he needs is more trouble with the police. But still, I stand my ground.

Robbie gives me a hard look, then he sighs, secures his helmet back onto the lock by the rear wheel, and snaps it shut with a sharp click.

"Luckily for you," I say, trying to lighten the mood, "I have a perfectly good bed in my flat. You can crash at my place."

"No chance. If you're not allowing me to take my motorcycle, then I'll walk." He turns and heads up the street, aiming for Bannock Woods and the footpath that leads to his cottage.

"But . . . that'll take an hour!"

"I know," he calls over his shoulder. "That's why I wanted to ride home."

I stand there, watching him go. I glance down at my heeled boots then back at Robbie's retreating form.

"Wait up!" I call, breaking into a run despite the impractical footwear.

CHAPTER THIRTEEN

ROBBIE

"Robbie! Wait up!"

Cat's voice carries through the trees from somewhere behind me. Fuck's sake. Why won't she and her poor excuse for a skirt leave me alone? I'm furious with her right now. She had no right to do what she did in the pub. And now I have to walk home? Just fucking great.

I march deeper into Bannock Woods, the moonlight filtering through the canopy above, casting shadows across the forest floor. The night air is cool against my heated skin. Somewhere in the distance an owl hoots, the sound echoing through the darkness.

"Robbie, please! Slow down!"

Twigs snap as she hurries to catch up, but I don't turn around. Maybe if I ignore her, she'll take the hint and piss off.

No such luck. Within moments she's at my side, breathless from jogging to keep up with my long strides.

"Look, I'm sorry about what happened back there," she says, "but you don't have to storm off like this."

"I'm not storming off. I'm going home, and you should do the same."

"You want me to go home? Through the woods? At night? Alone? That's not very gentlemanly of you."

I stop abruptly and turn to face her. The moonlight catches in her long auburn hair, giving it a silvery sheen. Her hazel eyes are bright, her cheeks flushed. Angry though I am, I can't deny she looks especially beautiful tonight.

"Gentlemanly?" I laugh, the sound harsh even to my own ears. "We both know I'm no gentleman, and I didn't ask you to follow me. You know the way back."

"But—"

I step closer to her, towering over her. "Why don't you tell me what this is really about? Why are you so desperate to sleep with me?"

She opens her mouth to respond, but I cut her off.

"Let me guess. You're going through some delayed teenage rebellion. A bit tragic in your twenties, don't you think?" She flinches, but I don't stop. "You're an English teacher. You're into books. So maybe you want to gather a story or two of your own before you inevitably settle down with some dull, boring man in a dull, boring house with two well-behaved but dull and boring children, a boy and a girl. Am I right?"

Her eyes narrow. "That's not—"

"I bet you only want this so when you're old and grey, you've got at least one interesting tale to tell. 'Oh, did I ever mention the time I slept with Bannock's bad boy?'" I mimic her voice, making it high and breathy. Then I shoot her a steely look. "I know your type, Catriona McIntyre."

"You don't know anything about me!" she snaps. "And that's not fair. I've been trying to help you clear your name!"

"Aye, and I appreciate that, but it doesn't mean I'm going to sleep with you."

"I never said it did!" Her fists clench at her sides. "And I'm not some daft wee girl playing at being adventurous. I'm experienced! I know what I want."

I scoff. "Oh, really? Don't tell me. When you were at university, did you have missionary sex with a few polite, well-educated uni boys?" I gasp mockingly. "How very daring of you!"

Her cheeks flush darker. I've hit a nerve. Good. Maybe now she'll leave me alone.

I turn and walk off. The path to my cottage is familiar—I've walked it countless times—but in the darkness, with the trees looming overhead and shadows playing tricks on my eyes, it feels different. Wilder. Less safe.

Footsteps behind me. Christ, she's persistent.

"Come on, Robbie!" Cat's voice carries through the stillness like a thread tugging at my resolve. "One night—that's all I'm asking for, and I bet you want it as much as I do. So what's the harm in a bit of fun?"

Something inside me snaps. The frustration, the desire I've been fighting, the sheer bloody-mindedness of this woman—it's too much. I spin around and close the distance between us in two quick strides, then I plant my hands on her shoulders and press her back against the nearest tree.

Her breath hitches, her eyes widening, but it isn't fear staring back at me. It's something far more dangerous. Anticipation.

"I went to the Pheasant tonight for one reason only." My face is inches from hers, and my frustration bleeds into every word. "Not to make small talk with locals over a pint. God no. No, I went to pick up a woman to help me forget about the shit week I've had. And I found one—until you scared her off with your wee act. Because you just couldn't resist sticking your nose into something that didn't concern you."

"Oh, Robbie," she says, completely unfazed by my words. She slips a finger under the waistband of my jeans—not tugging, not teasing, just resting there. "You were looking for a woman, and here I am. And I'm not going anywhere until you stop pretending you don't want me."

Fuck. All the reasons I've been telling myself to steer clear of Catriona McIntyre are dissolving under the buzz of alcohol and that scent of hers—a heady mix of something floral and sweet that makes my head spin. Plus, her finger is *right there* . . .

My cock twitches to life, betraying me just when I need it to stay the hell in line. I grit my teeth hard enough to crack enamel, determined not to give her the satisfaction of seeing just how much she's getting to me.

"Cat," I say slowly, deliberately, "I guarantee you can't handle me." I lean closer to her, pinning her further against the rough bark of the tree. "Sex with me isn't soft or sweet, lass. It's raw, and it'd leave a good girl like you in tears. This is your chance to get out of here, and I suggest you take it. Because if you stay any longer, I may not be able to go on resisting you."

She doesn't flinch. If anything, fire sparks in her eyes. "So you *do* want me?"

A sneer tugs at my lips, and I press closer still to her. She doesn't try to get away from me. If anything, she pushes right back, and that's when I know she feels it—my cock stiffening, pressing ever more insistently against her.

Leaning close to her ear, I whisper, "Of course I want you. Can't you feel how much I fucking want you?" Then I yank myself sharply back from her, creating space between us before I lose all sense entirely.

Her eyes drift down—shamelessly—to where I'm hard against my jeans. Her tongue darts out, wetting her bottom lip.

Christ.

"This is your chance to go," I warn again. "I suggest you scram."

"No." That's all she says before stepping forwards until there isn't even a breath of space between us. Her fingers find me through the denim, curling around me, squeezing just enough to drive me insane.

"I want this," she insists.

Fuck. I can't go on resisting. Without a word, I reach down and unbuckle my belt, the metal clinking loudly in the quiet of the forest.

"Here?" Her earlier boldness wavers.

"It's now or never, princess."

I unzip my jeans and shove both them and my boxers down, revealing my cock to the cool night air. It stands tall, hard as steel, the moonlight catching on the silver barbell pierced through the head. Cat's eyes immediately lock onto it, and her sharp intake of breath is loud enough to make me smirk. For once she doesn't have some smartarse comment ready. In fact, she looks completely out of her depth. I knew she was too much of a good girl for this.

"Thought so," I say, reaching for my jeans. "You can't handle me."

But before I can pull them up, her hand shoots out to stop me. Tentatively—almost shyly—her fingers brush the piercing, and the contact sends a jolt straight through me. Her bottom lip caught between her teeth, and her eyes wide with what I think might be awe, she explores it some more. Her touch is cautious but curious, like it's something dangerous but too damn fascinating for her to resist.

"Holy shit, Robbie," she says eventually. "That's . . . unbelievably sexy."

She presses at it a little harder now, testing the metal as if she can't quite believe it's real. The barbell shifts slightly under my skin, sending a shiver all the way up my spine. And when she twists it experimentally between her thumb and forefinger . . . oh, man. Pleasure zips through me like an electric current, sharp enough to make me hiss softly through my teeth.

"I didn't know about this piercing," she murmurs, her eyes never leaving it. "Your eyebrow, your nipple—I've seen those. But *this* . . . this is a surprise. A very nice surprise."

Her deliberate wee touches drive me crazy. They're maddeningly perfect and perfectly maddening all at once. Already my breathing is wrecked, shallow and uneven.

Finally she stops toying with my piercing and wraps her hand around my thick shaft instead. Heat shoots through me like a flame licking over my skin. My breath catches, only for a second, but that's enough for her to notice and for her lips to curl into a sly little smirk.

But then she blinks, and suddenly her eyes are all wide and full of mock innocence. It's like she heard every word I said earlier about her being a good girl, and now she's decided to weaponise it against me.

"Tell me what to do," she murmurs, pleading and breathy like some bashful virgin. "Please!"

Fuck, the act is pretty convincing. I could almost believe this really is her first time.

"On your knees," I bite out.

She doesn't even hesitate, just sinks onto the forest floor, bare knees and all. Her eyes briefly flick up to mine before dropping again and focusing on my hard length.

"Open your mouth," I order.

Her soft lips part without a single word of argument, and she moves closer to me, her warm breath ghosting over my skin. My cock twitches in response.

"This is your last chance," I grind out, even though every nerve in my body is screaming at me to shut up and let her do this. "You're too good for this. Too good for me."

Instead of answering, she tilts her head, and her tongue flicks across my piercing.

Christ!

A moment later her tongue slips out again, only this time it lingers, prodding at the metal, exploring it, swirling round and round it. Bloody hell. If she doesn't stop teasing and take me into her mouth soon, I'm going to lose my mind.

My hands move almost of their own accord, finding their way to Cat's hair—soft, silky, and begging to be tangled between my fingers. I fist a handful at the back of her head, not *too* rough, but enough to make sure she knows exactly who's in charge here.

"Enough games. Take it, lass. All of it."

There's no pause, no hesitation. She dives straight in, and the wet heat of her mouth engulfs me.

An involuntary groan escapes my throat. It feels incredible. Still, I grit out, "More!"

Cat obliges, sinking further down onto me. I forget everything—the resort, the accusations, all of it. I'm lost in the sensations of her mouth around me.

She starts to move, her lips sliding up and down my shaft in slow, deliberate strokes. But I'm not in the mood for slow tonight. I'm wound too tight, too frustrated, too desperate for release.

"Faster!" I order, the command biting through the air.

She glances up at me, her eyes flashing with a hint of defiance, like she wants to test me just for the fun of it. But then she does pick up the pace, her tongue swirling around the head of my cock with every upward motion. I groan again, my fingers tightening in her hair as I guide her movements.

"That's it," I mutter, my voice strained. "Good girl."

The praise seems to spur her on. She grips my thighs and takes me deeper, her throat relaxing as she swallows more of me—more than I expected she could handle. My head falls back, and I drag in a shaky breath. The night sky stretches above me, its vastness framed by dark branches, but all I can focus on is the wet heat of her mouth, the pressure of her tongue, the softness of her lips as they tighten around me, creating a suction that's driving me to the brink.

"Fuck. You're better at this than I thought."

Cat hums in response, the vibration buzzing through my entire body. Her movements quicken, her lips gliding over me with a slick, intense rhythm. Each pass pulls me deeper into her mouth until I'm hitting the back of her throat with every descent.

Tension coils in my gut. I'm close—too close.

"Look at me," I command.

Her eyes snap up to mine.

"I'm going to come. Don't swallow it."

My release crashes into me like a storm tearing through the woods—wild and unstoppable. A guttural sound escapes my throat, and my hips buck hard, but she doesn't move away. She stays with me through every shudder until I'm left trembling and raw.

When I'm done, I ease away from her, every nerve in my body still thrumming. "Open," I rasp.

Cat parts her lips immediately, her tongue glistening with what I just gave her. The sight sends a fresh jolt of heat through me, stirring something primal deep in my gut.

"*Now* swallow."

She obeys, her throat bobbing, then shows me her mouth to prove it's gone.

I smirk and run a thumb over her swollen lips. "Good girl."

All the tension drains from my body, replaced by a pleasant, satisfied heaviness. I tuck myself back into my jeans while Cat gets to her feet and brushes herself down.

"I bet," I murmur, "that if I slipped my hand under your skirt, I'd find you soaked."

Her cheeks flush, but not from embarrassment. She nods.

"Take your underwear off and give it to me."

Cat arches a brow but does as she's told, shimmying her knickers down her legs then stepping out of them and bending to retrieve them. I take them from her, letting my fingers brush hers as I do. Then I lift the lace to my nose for a slow inhale. Her scent is intoxicating: sweet with an edge of musk that floods my veins like whisky straight from the bottle.

"These are mine now," I say simply, slipping the knickers into my back pocket. "Goodnight, Cat."

Without another word, I turn and stride off through the woods towards my cottage. I don't need to look back to know she's still standing there in that indecent little skirt with nothing underneath now to shield her from the chill. She'll be wondering what the hell just happened—and no doubt cursing me under her breath—but that's fine by me.

Let her wonder. Let her curse my name with every step back to Bannock. As for me, I'll be grinning to myself the whole walk home.

CHAPTER FOURTEEN

ROBBIE

I pull up outside Cat's flat, kill the engine on my bike, and sit there for a moment, gathering myself. The morning air is crisp, carrying the scent of dew and pine from the nearby woods. I probably should've just texted to say I wasn't coming today. Last night was . . . complicated. But I need the money, and the sooner I finish this job, the sooner I can move on to the next one.

It's just work, I think to myself as I swing my leg off the bike. *Same as yesterday. Same as the day before. Best not to overthink it.*

I make my way up to her door and knock. At first there's no response, so I have to rap again. Finally there's shuffling from inside, then the door swings open to reveal Cat in a baggy T-shirt and tartan pyjama bottoms, her hair a tousled mess. She takes me in then blinks, suddenly wide awake.

"Oh. I . . . wasn't expecting you today."

She looks different this morning. Her usual sparkle is missing. She's pale and washed out.

"Oh?" I raise an eyebrow. "We agreed I'd work on Saturday to get the job done quicker. Don't you remember?"

"Aye, I do." She hugs herself awkwardly, looking everywhere but at me. "But I thought . . ."

I know exactly what she thought—that last night changed things. That I wouldn't show up today because of what happened in the woods. But this is a job. This is how I pay my bills now.

"Well, I'm here." I step past her into the flat. "Might as well crack on."

"Actually, could we maybe not do this today? I'm not feeling great."

I turn back and hold her gaze, observing the regret swimming behind her eyes. "Look, I know this is about last night. It's like I've been telling you all along: I'm here to work. If we cancel today, it'll just be awkward on Monday, so why don't we get the awkwardness over with now, eh?"

She nods slowly, then her face crumples and she bursts into tears.

Shite. This is . . . new. I've had women get clingy after a hook-up. I've had them get angry when I made it clear it was just a one-time thing. But tears? Full-on sobbing? This is uncharted territory.

"Cat . . ." I rub the back of my neck, completely out of my depth here. "Come on now. You don't have to cry."

She tries to swipe the tears away with the back of her hand, but they keep coming—fat drops rolling down her cheeks no matter how she tries to hold them back.

"I'm s-sorry," she chokes out.

God, what the hell do I do now? I don't know the first thing about comforting someone who's upset. It's not like it's a skill I learnt from my maw—she was hardly the epitome of maternal warmth. I can't remember the last time I even heard from the woman. Hasn't so much as sent a birthday card in years.

My first instinct is to leave. I've got enough on my plate without adding emotional support to the list. The police could show up at my door any day now with a warrant for my arrest. I don't need this.

But something stops me from walking right out. Maybe it's because Cat listened to me the other day when I needed someone to talk to. Or maybe I'm just not as much of a heartless bastard as I pretend. After all, I suppose there *were* times, when Johnny and I were lads, that I'd comfort him if he was upset. But . . . that was years ago. And anyway, this? A grown woman in tears? That's an entirely diffcrent beast. Right?

"Come on." Awkwardly I place a hand on her back and guide her through to the kitchen. "Sit down. I'll, er, make tea, okay?"

She doesn't protest, which I take as a yes. Good. I can manage tea. It's just hot water and a bag. But the kettle's hum doesn't entirely cover her sniffling. Christ, what the hell have I got myself into?

Once the tea is ready, I hand Cat a mug then lower myself into the chair across from her. A bit late, I say, "Er, is it okay if I sit?"

Part of me hopes she'll give me an out and say she'd rather be alone. But she nods and wraps both hands around the mug like she's trying to draw every bit of warmth from it.

All right, now what? I've no idea what to say next. The silence stretches, broken only by the occasional hiccup or sniff from Cat.

"Honestly," I say eventually, largely just to break the tension, "your family and breakdowns recently."

Cat looks up, her eyes red-rimmed and puffy. "What does that mean?"

I take a sip of my tea. "Well, about a month and a half ago, I ran into Jamie on the old stone bridge. It was pissing down, and he was just standing there in the rain, getting soaked through. He looked like the weight of the world was on his shoulders."

"Jamie?" Cat's nose crinkles as if I've just short-circuited her brain. "As in, my brother Jamie?"

"Aye. Things weren't going well between him and Maisie at the time. He and I had a bit of a heart-to-heart, if you can believe it."

"Wow." Cat wipes at her eyes. "I . . . had no idea. Jamie's always acted the clown. Hell, even when he finished that hill race without his kilt, and with his arse—and everything else—out for the whole of Bannock to see, it was all jokes and laughs. It's stupid, but I suppose I forget he has hidden depths under all that daftness." She gives a watery smile. "As families go, we're close. We really are. But I suppose everyone's got bits of themselves they keep tucked away."

I take another sip of tea then say, "So, you going to tell me what this is about?"

Cat draws a shaky breath. "Last night I had this really vivid dream. It was me, my brothers, and my parents at Loch Bannock. We used to have picnics there in the summer." Her voice wavers. "It felt so real, you know? When I woke up, I missed them so much it physically hurt. Then *you* showed up at the door, and it all just became a bit much. Because you were the one who . . ."

She trails off, but she doesn't need to finish. I know exactly what she means. I was the one who came across the crash. Who saw her parents dead in their car. Who called the ambulance for Jamie.

"I'm so embarrassed," Cat says quickly. "And . . . I want you to know this has nothing to do with last night." Her cheeks flush.

"The dreams . . . they come when they come, and when they do, they knock me for six every time."

It hits me then that she's not just the flirty, cheeky lass who's been throwing herself at me and trying to get into my pants. She's someone who lost her parents when she was, what, seventeen? Someone who's been carrying around a whole lot of pain and sadness beneath that bubbly exterior.

I reach for her hand across the table, intending to give it a squeeze, but chicken out halfway through and tap my fingers against the tabletop instead. *Nice, Robbie. Moral support through Morse code. Real smooth.*

To my surprise, Cat snorts out a laugh through her tears. "God! Comforting someone doesn't come easily to you, does it?"

I grimace. "Sorry."

"I'm sorry too." She sniffs again. "About the tears, but also about last night. I've been silly around you. I'll be more sensible from now on, I promise. I'll let you get on with your work without bothering you. And I'm still going to help you clear your name."

"You don't have to—"

"I want to," she insists, wiping away another tear. She gives me an embarrassed grin. "God, what must you think of me? It's funny: you think you have it all together, but then every so often, *boom*! It hits you again, out of nowhere. Grief, I mean."

She's quiet for a moment, then: "Did I ever even thank you? I'm not sure I did."

"Thank me for what?"

"For calling the ambulance and saving Jamie's life." Her eyes, still wet with tears, are earnest. "He can be a real pain with his constant teasing—I don't think anyone in town would disagree with that—but I don't know what I'd have done if I'd lost him too."

I wave away her gratitude, uncomfortable with the praise. "I was just the first on the scene. Anyone else would have done the same."

"Well, thank you anyway."

Something about her sincerity, about the raw vulnerability she's showing, makes me want to offer her something in return. I'm not used to opening up, but I did it the other day about the resort, and somehow it feels right to do it again now.

"That night changed me too, you know," I say, staring down at my mug.

I can feel Cat's gaze on me, waiting for more.

The memory surfaces again: the lashing rain as I approached the car wreck. Jamie slumped in the backseat, blood pouring down his face. And in the front, Mairi and Angus McIntyre . . . they were already gone.

"I got into a lot of trouble growing up. More than my fair share, as you've probably heard." My mouth curls into a humourless half-smile. "For a while, as a young man, I was into underground fighting. It gave me an outlet for all my anger."

I remember the rush of it—the roar of the crowd, the sharp crack of knuckles against flesh, the taste of blood and victory.

"It was brutal, but it made me feel alive. And the money didn't hurt either."

I glance up at Cat, whose eyes are wide, and who's looking at me like I've just confessed to being Batman or something. "You were an underground fighter? I had no idea."

"Not something I advertise." I shrug. "Anyway, the night of your parents' accident, I was riding back from a fight in Inverness." My jaw tightens at the memory of it. "I knocked a bloke

106

out cold in that fight, and for a moment, I didn't think he was going to get up again." I can still see Big Cal lying there, motionless on the concrete floor.

"He did, though. He was all right. But then on the ride home, I came across the crash. Coming face to face with . . . well, death . . . it made me realise how bloody fragile life is. After that, fighting didn't feel like freedom anymore. It felt like . . . tempting fate."

I let out a slow breath, the admission leaving me feeling oddly exposed. "That was it for me. Never fought again—not properly anyway. It's just me and my punchbag these days."

Cat reaches over and gives my hand a gentle squeeze. There's nothing flirty about it. It's just a simple, heartfelt gesture. And unlike my attempt to do the same to her, it's natural. I can't remember a woman ever having comforted me like this before. When women touch me, it's with intent, with desire. This is . . . different. Nice.

"I believed you when you said you weren't responsible for the thefts," Cat says, "but hearing all this? Now I'm doubly sure. I trust you, Robbie. And I'm sorry I haven't found out anything concrete about Samantha yet. Maybe I could try to do a bit more digging today while you get on with some tasks around the flat?"

I look at her, still puffy-eyed from crying, and before I know what I'm doing, the words slip out. "Or . . . we could go for a ride on my bike?"

Cat blinks at me in surprise.

"Well, someone made me leave it here last night," I point out, a hint of teasing in my voice. "And as I was on the prowl, the pillion seat is on, and there's a spare helmet in the saddlebag."

"A . . . ride?"

"Aye. As you've already pointed out, I'm hopeless at

comforting people. All I know is that, when I'm feeling down, going out on my bike always makes me feel better."

She studies me—eyes still red but brightening slightly—then says, "What about your work here? You said—"

"I can miss a day. I wouldn't mind a ride anyway."

"And the investigation?"

I can't help but smirk at this. "With all due respect, I doubt going around Bannock and bursting into tears in front of people is likely to help me *too* much."

She rolls her eyes at this, and just like that, some of her spark is back.

"You ever been on a bike?"

"Nope."

"Well, once you've experienced a motorcycle, I doubt you'll ever bother with a horse again."

Cat snorts then pats under her eyes. "So, this is how you win women, is it? Take them out on your motorcycle and show them a good time? Well, newsflash: despite how I acted last night, the last thing on my mind is getting frisky with you. At least, not today."

I huff out a dry laugh. "Understood and agreed, but this is just about getting out of Bannock for a while and clearing our heads. I think we could both do with that. What do you say?"

She considers, then nods. "Well, I'd better get dressed then." At the doorway to her bedroom, she pauses and shoots me a glance over her shoulder. "What should a girl wear for her first dose of biker therapy?"

CHAPTER FIFTEEN

CAT

"Safety first, McIntyre." Robbie hands me a helmet with a no-nonsense look, his eyes briefly taking in my outfit—fitted jeans, comfy checked shirt buttoned over a simple tank top, and the denim jacket I grabbed at the last minute.

"What? Not biker chick enough for you?"

"It'll do. Just glad you didn't come out in that tartan miniskirt you were wearing last night."

Despite myself, I grin. It's hard to believe this is actually happening. Just minutes ago, I cried in front of Robbie MacDonald. Broke down and sobbed like a wean. And instead of turning on his heel and leaving, which would have been the easy option, he stayed. Made me tea. Listened. And now . . .

I slip the helmet on, watching as Robbie does the same then swings a leg over his motorcycle in one smooth, practised motion. His powerful thighs grip the machine like he and it were made for each other—man and metal in perfect harmony.

When I climb on, I'm surprised by how intimate it feels. The so-called passenger seat is no more than a small shelf that leaves me balanced just behind him, my thighs bracketing his hips. As I settle in, I'm wrapped in his scent, a heady mix of leather, soap, and something raw and masculine.

Robbie snaps down his visor and I follow suit. The engine growls to life beneath us, sending vibrations through my entire body that are both terrifying and exhilarating.

"Arms round me," he shouts over the rumble.

I hesitate, my hands hovering near his waist. "I thought we agreed there would be no funny business?"

"This isn't funny business. It's basic safety. You need to hold on properly or you'll end up on your arse when I accelerate."

"Fine." Tentatively I place my hands at his waist.

The motorcycle lurches forwards, and just like that, I abandon any pretence of casual contact and instead wrap my arms tightly around him and press my chest against his back, my pride forgotten in the name of self-preservation.

We roar down Main Street, then the motorcycle picks up speed as the houses give way to open countryside. We take a bend in the road, and Robbie leans the bike into it, the ground seemingly inches from my knee. I squeal, my heart hammering in my chest, a cocktail of fear and exhilaration flooding my system. The speed, the closeness, the danger . . . it's intoxicating.

Fields and forests blur past us in streaks of gold and green. Every curve in the road brings a fresh surge of adrenaline, chasing away the last of my gloom until I'm grinning so hard my cheeks ache.

With every mile we cover, I grow more attuned to Robbie: the solid wall of his back, the way his muscles shift subtly as he steers the bike, the sensation of my jean-clad legs against his. My mind flashes to last night in the woods. His commanding tone, the cool metal of that tantalising piercing against my tongue, his wickedly addictive taste. My entire body had burned with want when he walked away with my knickers stashed in his pocket.

Not the time, McIntyre. Not the time. I shake the memory away, focusing instead on the landscape rushing past us.

All too soon, Robbie slows the bike and pulls off onto a small dirt track that leads to a viewpoint overlooking Glen Garve. He kills the engine, and my ears ring in the hush that follows.

I slide off the bike, trying not to look like a newborn foal finding its legs, but my thighs are wobbly. Turns out gripping onto Robbie for dear life uses different muscles than galloping across a field on horseback.

Robbie takes off his helmet and glances over his shoulder at me, a few strands of dark hair falling across his eyes. He flicks them back with one swift movement, like he's part motorcyclist, part shampoo advert. "So? What did you think of your first ride? Bit of an adrenaline high, eh?"

I tug off my helmet and shake out my hair. "It was fine," I say with a nonchalant shrug, even as my heart still pounds from the thrill.

Smirking, Robbie climbs off the motorcycle. "Fine? You nearly squeezed the life out of me back there. You were glued to me tighter than a limpet on a rock."

My cheeks warm, but I refuse to give him the satisfaction. "Seeing as I went on your bike," I say instead, "I'll have to get you on a horse at some point."

"Me on a horse? Nah, not happening."

Robbie secures his helmet onto the lock by the rear wheel, tucks mine in the saddlebag, then we set off along a narrow path that leads into the woods bordering the viewpoint. The trees provide welcome shade from the August sun, and I reach out to brush my fingers against leaves as we make our way along.

For a moment, I think about my parents and how as a family we'd take walks like this when I was wee. I'd sit atop my da's shoulders, feeling like I could almost touch the highest branch, or maybe even the sky. I'd give anything for just one more of those carefree afternoons.

To distract myself, I clear my throat. "So, about clearing your name—"

"Let's not talk about that right now. We came out here to take a break, remember?"

"Aye, okay."

The path narrows, forcing us to walk closer together. Even with the leafy branches overhead sheltering us, the day is warming up, and I remove my jacket and tie it around my waist. Robbie follows suit, shrugging off his leather one and tossing it casually over one shoulder. In his white T-shirt and jeans, he looks like he's stepped straight out of a 1950s film, all brooding intensity and barely contained rebellion.

"What should we talk about, then?" I ask after a moment of side ogling. Inspiration strikes, and I click my fingers. "Oh, I know! Did it hurt like hell to get a bit of metal put through your penis?"

Robbie lets out a laugh so sudden and deep it startles a pair of birds from the branches above, sending them flapping into the sky. It makes me want to keep tossing out ridiculous questions just to coax another sinful rumble from him.

"You know what, let's not talk about that either."

I grin cheekily. "We have to talk about *something*, and you're shutting down every topic I'm suggesting. If you won't let me grill you about your piercings, what *do* you want to chat about, then?"

"How about nothing below the waist?"

I roll my eyes then nudge his shoulder playfully. "Fine. But since we're not talking about *that*"—I gesture vaguely towards his crotch—"how about we talk about your driving? Maybe it just felt fast because I'm not used to motorcycles, or maybe it was because you were going way over the speed limit."

"Jesus, what is this? An interrogation? I'm a good rider. And a safe one."

"Er, you do remember I was holding on to you like my life depended on it, right?"

"You were enjoying yourself."

"Maybe, but that doesn't mean you weren't speeding. And given the whole"—I wave my hand—"police investigation thingy you've got going on, maybe it's not the best time to be racking up tickets."

"Fair point. Actually, a week or so ago I was going pretty fast when I passed one of those mobile speed vans. Didn't see it until too late. Wouldn't be surprised if I get a fine through the post."

I groan. "And that's going to help your case how, exactly? 'Sorry, officer, I didn't steal anything, but aye, I might have done ninety in a sixty.' Brilliant."

"Just because I was going a bit over the speed limit doesn't mean I steal things from people."

"No, but it doesn't paint you as Mr Law-Abiding Citizen either. And in case you've forgotten, I'm upset today because I've been thinking about my parents, who I lost in a traffic accident. I'd rather the same thing didn't happen to you."

Robbie's expression softens. "Shit, you're right. Sorry." He runs a hand through his dark hair.

"Besides, I'd hate for you to get a driving ban now I've discovered I don't completely hate clinging to your back and pretending I'm some badass biker chick."

Robbie raises one eyebrow, his piercing glinting in the dappled sunlight. "Sounds like you think this'll become a regular thing."

I shoot him a shameless wink. "Maybe it will."

He shakes his head, but I spy a faint twitch at the corner of his mouth.

A comfortable silence falls between us as we continue through the woods. I'm surprised by how natural this feels. Lately, most of my time with Robbie has been me flirting and him expertly dodging every advance. But with Project Bang a Bad Boy officially on hiatus, at least for today, I'm discovering he's actually decent company. He might not be much of a talker, but being around him is surprisingly easy.

The path soon opens up to reveal a small clearing, where sunlight glints off a pool of water, still and glassy. The branches of the trees around it are adorned with strips of cloth in every colour imaginable, fluttering and twisting in the gentle breeze. A clootie well.

"Ever made a wish here?" I ask.

Robbie crouches, picks up a smooth stone, and rolls it between his fingers like it's suddenly fascinating. "Aye. As a kid. Tied a scrap of cloth to one of those branches and wished my maw would treat me the same way she treated Johnny."

My eyebrows lift in surprise, but I don't interrupt. I give him the space to continue, if he wants to.

He lets out a short, humourless laugh. "Obviously, it didn't work. That's when I knew it was all a load of nonsense."

I let his words sink in. It's hard for me to imagine someone as big and tough as Robbie standing here as a young lad, desperate enough for his maw's love that he tied a clootie to a branch and wished for something most folk never have to ask for.

"She . . . had this way of looking at me." Robbie stands but doesn't meet my eye. "Like I was a problem she couldn't solve. Johnny? He could do no wrong. But me? I was just . . . more bother than I was worth." He pauses then shakes his head as if to dismiss the memory. "Doesn't matter now."

I reach out and lightly touch his arm. "It does matter. She should have made you feel safe and wanted, not like that."

My maw never treated me that way, not even when I went through my moody teenager phase. She'd just sigh, call me her "wee hurricane", then pull me into a hug so fierce I'd forget why I was storming about in the first place. My heart aches at the thought of Robbie growing up without that warmth.

He glances at me, just for a moment, then looks away again. "Aye, well. She left Scotland years back. Lives somewhere sunny now, I think. I've not spoken to her in . . . honestly, I don't know how long it's been."

I want to ask more, like whether his maw has ever tried to reach out, or if he's ever confronted her about the way she treated him. But before I can form a question, Robbie blows out a long breath.

"Didn't mean to spill all that. Let's leave it there, aye?"

I hesitate, my natural curiosity urging me to push for more. But I catch the tightness in his jaw, the way he's still avoiding my gaze, and I know better than to press him further. So I nod.

There's more to Robbie MacDonald than the "bad boy" label that's been slapped on him, that's for sure. He's complex, with his own struggles and vulnerabilities, just like everyone else. I'm starting to realise how shallow my previous impressions of him were, never mind my recent campaign to get into bed with him. A twinge of guilt twists in my gut.

I take a step closer to the well. "I think I'd like to make a wish."

"You actually buy into this nonsense?"

"Maybe . . . maybe not." I shrug. "But they say folk have been tying wishes to these branches for hundreds of years. Maybe there's something in it, eh?" I look down at myself, considering, then grab the hem of my shirt and tear off a small strip of fabric.

Robbie doesn't say anything, but he watches me as I approach one of the trees. I *could* wish for something for myself, but instead I make a silent plea for Robbie. *Let him be cleared of these accusations. Let the truth come out.*

I tie the clootie to a low-hanging branch then step back and brush my hands together decisively. "There. Now we wait and see if it works."

Robbie scoffs softly but doesn't say anything more.

We wander back through the woods, sunlight flitting between the trees and striping the path at our feet. The mood has changed—not quite awkward, but not exactly easy either. Heavier, if that makes sense.

When I spot a flash of chrome through the trees, I decide enough is enough. Time to lighten things up.

"Race you back to the bike! First one there gets to ask the other a personal question, so be prepared to give me a *very* detailed answer about what it was like to get *that*"—I point at his crotch—"pierced."

Before Robbie can respond, I'm off, sprinting along the last stretch of path with a whoop. Behind me, there's a muttered curse, followed by heavy boots pounding on the ground.

I'm fast—years of running alongside horses when helping out at lessons have given me speed—but Robbie's legs are much longer than mine. Just as we near the motorcycle, his strong arms wrap around my waist, lift me clean off my feet, and spin me away from it.

"Cheater!" I squeal, but I laugh when he sets me down. He does too.

I turn to face him. We're standing close now—too close, maybe. His hands linger at my waist, and I'm very aware of the warmth of them through my clothes. Our eyes lock, and everything else fades away. The flecks of silver in his gaze steal the breath right out of my lungs.

But then, as if suddenly remembering himself, Robbie steps back, breaking the spell. He reaches out and taps his motorcycle before I can gather my wits.

"I win."

"Bollocks! That wasn't fair!"

"Aye, well, you never specified the rules." Robbie scoops up his leather jacket—he must have flung it aside earlier when he swept me off my feet. "Now I get to ask you a question. Hmm . . . all right, how about this? What is it you want, Cat? And I don't just mean from me. I mean from life."

That's a big question, I think. But I smirk and lean against the bike. "What do I want? Hmm . . . my own horse. That would be nice. And maybe a flat that doesn't look like a construction site."

My bravado falters when Robbie just stands there, looking at me like he sees right through all my nonsense.

"Okay, okay! But seriously, beyond that, I'm not entirely sure. I mean, it's not like life comes with a manual. But . . ." I chew my lip, considering. "Maybe I want to stop being the girl who parties too much or flirts with every guy she meets just because she can."

I don't think I've ever been this candid with someone before, but there's no judgement in Robbie's eyes. He doesn't flinch or frown or make me feel daft. So I continue. "I've done that for a while already, and it was fun. Don't get me wrong, I had a blast down in Glasgow, but . . . maybe it's time to move on."

Robbie is quiet, his gaze thoughtful, then he nods. "Wise words, McIntyre."

I untie my denim jacket from my waist and shrug it on, not quite ready to admit to myself how much his approval pleases me. "Anyway, for now, I want to go back to Bannock, and maybe then we can have a serious chat about clearing your name. Because it's going to be all too easy for folk to accept you did it. We'll have to put up a proper fight to make them see you're innocent."

Robbie sighs. "Aye, no kidding. Story of my life." He hands me the spare helmet. "Let's head back, then."

I slide it on then swing onto the bike behind him. The engine growls awake beneath us. This time, when I wrap my arms around Robbie, it feels less like clinging on for dear life and more like holding tight to something I'm not sure I want to let go of.

CHAPTER SIXTEEN

ROBBIE

I kill the ignition outside the Otter's Holt gift shop, and the rumble of the bike gives way to the cheerful bustle of Main Street. It's busier than usual this afternoon—locals chatting, tourists wandering into shops, everyone soaking up the sunny weather. Heads, of course, turn our way. Cat McIntyre on Robbie MacDonald's motorcycle? In Bannock that's enough to set tongues wagging for weeks.

Cat swings her leg off the bike and pops off her helmet, freeing a tumble of flattened auburn hair, which she fluffs with her fingers. There's a lightness to her movements that wasn't there this morning, when she was in tears in her flat. The ride did its job, clearing both our heads. I'm still not sure what possessed me to tell her about my maw at the well, but somehow the words found their way out.

"Thanks for that." She hands me back the helmet. "I needed it."

I'm about to respond when Cat's eyes focus on something behind me. She raises her hand in a wave.

"Ally! Emily!" she calls out.

Shite.

I turn to see Ally McIntyre walking towards us, pushing a pram with one hand and guiding a toddler with the other. His wife, Emily, walks alongside them, wearing a friendly smile, though there's no mistaking the glint of curiosity beneath it. Still, her expression contrasts sharply with the thundercloud on her husband's face.

"I'm going to head off," I mutter to Cat, already kicking up the stand.

"Don't be daft." She grabs my arm, her fingers surprisingly strong for such a wee lass. "You have to meet Ciaran! He's only a few days old, and he's *so* cute."

"I really don't think—"

"Come on!" She tugs at my arm impatiently. "It'll be fine."

But it won't be fine. It's never been fine between me and Alasdair McIntyre.

As a lad, I went out of my way to make his life difficult. Every chance I got, I'd goad him into a fight or stir up trouble just to see him lose his temper. I told myself it was about loyalty—my da ran the Glen Garve Resort, the McIntyres ran the Bannock Hotel. Natural enemies, right?

But now, at thirty-one, I've got enough self-awareness to recognise the truth. It wasn't about business rivalry. It was about envy.

The McIntyres were everything my family wasn't. A proper unit. A maw who actually gave a damn about her children. A da who wasn't constantly stressed about work. Four siblings who squabbled but clearly loved each other.

Meanwhile, I had a mother who looked at me like I was a mistake she couldn't undo, a father who buried himself in work, and a wee brother I was forever looking out for—making sure

Johnny never saw the worst bits, even if that meant taking the brunt myself.

And now, surprising absolutely nobody, Ally's gone and created his own perfect family. Beautiful wife. Two sons. A lovely home. The whole fucking package.

Cat's grip tightens on my arm, her fingers digging in like she thinks I'll make a run for it—well, more like a ride for it—if she lets go. "Robbie, get off the bike. And take your helmet off. You'll give wee Ru nightmares otherwise."

"Honestly, Cat, I'm going to—"

"You owe me."

I pause and raise an eyebrow. "Owe you?"

"For last night," she murmurs with a sly grin. "Consider this payback."

Jesus. The cheeky wee minx! Wielding last night against me like some sort of weapon. Mind you, it *was* a fantastic moment of relief in what's been a shite week or so. If it makes her happy, maybe I can stomach Ally's glares for a minute or two.

With a sigh, I climb off the bike and pull off my helmet, then reluctantly I let Cat drag me over to Ally and his clan.

Ally's eyes flick from his sister to me, his jaw visibly tightening. "Cat," he says, his voice carefully controlled. "What are you doing?"

"I've just been for a ride on Robbie's motorcycle," she says cheerfully, either oblivious to or, more likely, deliberately ignoring the tension. "It was amazing!"

Ally just grunts, like he doesn't trust himself to say what he's really thinking. But I notice his knuckles whitening on the pram handle.

"Nice to see you, Robbie," Emily interjects smoothly.

I nod at her, grateful for the rescue.

"I don't think you've met our boys yet." Emily gestures to the toddler, who's regarding me with open curiosity. "This is Ru."

"Hello, wee man," I say awkwardly. I've never been particularly good with children.

Cat crouches down to Ru's level. "Hiya, pal!" She opens her arms, and the boy eagerly toddles into them for a hug.

"And this," Emily continues, reaching into the pram, "is Ciaran."

She lifts out a tiny bundle wrapped in a blue blanket. Ciaran's face is scrunched and red, like he's still annoyed at having been evicted from his comfortable home inside Emily.

Cat wastes no time before cooing and fussing over him. "Isn't he gorgeous, Robbie? Look at his tiny wee fingers!"

Emily offers her a hold, and Cat accepts without hesitation, rocking the wee guy and murmuring nonsense words to him. After a bit, she looks up at me, a sparkle in her eye. "Here, Robbie, you should have a go too."

"What? No, I—" But it's too late. Cat deposits the infant into my arms.

Bloody hell, what am I supposed to do with a baby? I've never held one before in my life. He feels impossibly small and fragile against my chest. I adjust my grip awkwardly, one hand cradling his head while the other supports his tiny body.

I glance at Emily, who gives me a reassuring nod. "You're holding him just fine. No need to look like you're defusing a bomb."

"Aww," Cat says with a grin that's far too wide to be wholly innocent. "You look good with a baby, Robbie."

Ally makes a strangled sound that might be a suppressed growl. His face is a picture of barely contained fury. It can't be easy for him, seeing his newborn son in the arms of his oldest enemy.

"Cat," he says through gritted teeth, "what exactly have you been up to with Robbie?"

There's an accusation in his tone that makes my hackles rise, but I bite my tongue.

"Nothing!" Cat protests. "He's been helping me with my flat, that's all. Hasn't laid a finger on me—at least not in the scandalous sense your face is implying."

Technically, she's not lying. I haven't laid a finger on her. She, on the other hand . . .

"Helping you with your flat?" Ally repeats sceptically. "The same Robbie MacDonald who was just fired from the Glen Garve Resort for stealing from guests?"

Ah, shit. It seems the word is out. Da could only keep it under wraps for so long.

"He wasn't fired," Cat says defensively. "He was suspended, then he quit. And he's innocent."

"Oh, grow up, Cat," Ally says. "Don't believe everything people tell you. From what I've heard, even his own father thinks he's guilty."

My jaw clenches so hard I'm surprised my teeth don't crack. Typical Ally, judging me from his high horse. I want to snap back, to tell him to mind his own fucking business, but the warm weight of the baby—*his* baby—in my arms keeps me in check.

"Ally," Emily says quietly, laying a hand on her husband's arm. "Not now."

"I'm just concerned about my wee sister," Ally says. "I've told you, Emily, what Robbie was like growing up."

"People change," Emily says pointedly.

"And even if they don't," Cat adds, "it's my business who I spend time with."

Ally sighs heavily. I can see the struggle on his face: the desire to reclaim his baby warring with the knowledge that snatching him from my arms would cause a scene.

"Besides," Cat continues, "Robbie's doing a great job with my flat. For starters, that awful wallpaper in the living room is gone. And he's fixed the leaky tap in the bathroom."

Ally's brow furrows. "And how are you paying for all this work, Cat? You said your bank account was more or less empty."

Cat gives Ally a tight-lipped smile that doesn't quite reach her eyes. "Oh, let's not get into boring money stuff now."

But wait—what? Her bank account is empty? She hired me to do a job. She'd better be able to pay for it.

Emily, clearly sensing the rising tension, steps forwards and gently takes Ciaran from my arms. "We should probably get going. Ru's due his nap, and this little one will be wanting a feed soon."

"Of course," Cat says. She crouches down to say goodbye to Ru, but I'm barely paying attention now.

She *will* be able to pay me, right? Because I've worked my arse off the last few days. After everything—losing my job, being accused of theft, finding that ring in my locker—I can't cope with another betrayal right now. I really can't.

◆ ◆ ◆

As soon as Cat shuts the front door of her flat behind us, I can't hold it in any longer.

"So, am I grafting away for free then?" I lean against the wall and fix her with a look.

She freezes, one arm half-out of her jacket. "Och, don't mind Ally. He's always fussing about something."

"He said your bank account is empty."

"Well . . . it's not *completely* empty."

"But empty enough that I should be concerned about getting paid for all this?" I push open the living room door and gesture at the work I've done—stripped walls, repaired skirting boards, surfaces prepped for painting. And that's not everything. Besides, I'm supposed to be here for a couple of weeks. I've booked out the time for Cat.

She sighs dramatically. "You worry way too much. Just relax, would you? I'll find a way to pay you."

"Find a way?" My voice rises. "Cat, we had an agreement. I've been busting a gut."

"And I was never *not* going to pay you," she protests. "I'll get paid from school soon, and anyway, my brothers always help out if I'm in a bind."

I stare at her, incredulous. That's her plan? Big brothers to the rescue? The same brothers who were too busy to help her with the flat? Does she really believe Ally will whip out his wallet for me when he looks ready to throttle me every time we cross paths?

"And if they don't help?"

"Then I'll take out a loan or something." She shrugs and moves through to the kitchen. I follow.

"Look, Robbie, I can't go on living in the flat in the state it's in." She fills the kettle like this is no big deal. "The work needs done, and I need your help to do it. I'll sort out the money. Promise."

"Sort it out how, exactly?" I fold my arms across my chest. "And you should have really figured this out *before* hiring me."

"God, you can be so negative, you know that? I put the idea out into the universe." She makes a sweeping gesture with both hands, like she's releasing something into the air. "I visualised having enough money, and now I just need to wait for the universe to manifest a solution."

I stare at her, trying to decide if she's joking. "You're having me on, right?"

"It's called manifestation," she says, as if that explains everything. "You focus on what you want—the money, or whatever—and then opportunities show up."

I rake a hand through my hair and let out a sharp laugh. "Jesus. Your brother's right: you do need to grow up. You really thought the *universe* was going to pay me?"

Her cheeks flare rosy pink. "I'm serious!" she claims, though there's a slight wobble in her voice now. "It works for loads of people. I read this book—"

"I don't give a shit what book you read!" My words bounce off the walls, louder than I intended. But it's all pouring out now: the stress, the humiliation of losing my job, the way everyone always assumes the worst of me. "This is my livelihood. I'm trying to set myself up as a self-employed tradesman. I need actual money, not your fucking universe magic!"

She steps back as if I've slapped her, but I press on before guilt can soften me.

"How am I supposed to keep working for you when I don't even know if you'll pay me? You said you wanted to help me clear my name, but it turns out you're not helping at all. You're just . . . using me."

"That's not true!" The tremor in her voice almost breaks me, but not quite. "You're getting this all wrong. I really do want to help you."

126

"Right," I scoff. "Just like you 'helped' me last night by chasing off the woman I was chatting to."

Cat's chin juts out stubbornly. "That was different. I was—"

"You know what? I don't want to hear it."

I move back into the hallway and head for the door, feeling like a right idiot. I actually opened up to her today—told her about my maw, about wishing at the clootie well as a bairn. I never tell people that stuff. *Never.* And this is why. People can't be trusted.

"Robbie, please!" Cat follows me, her voice softening. "I'm sorry. I should have been upfront about the money. But I promise I'll sort it out."

I open the door then pause. For a second, I'm tempted to believe her. But no, I've been let down too many times before.

"Save it. I'll swing by tomorrow for my tools. After that, you're on your own."

I pull the door shut behind me, cutting off whatever she was going to say next.

CHAPTER SEVENTEEN

ROBBIE

Age eight

The rain hammers against the window like it's trying to get in. I press my nose to the cold glass, watching puddles grow in the garden where me and Johnny were meant to be playing today.

"Get away from there, Robbie! You'll leave smudges all over the glass." Maw's voice makes me jump. She's sprawled across the sofa, painting her nails bright red, a glossy magazine balanced on her knees.

I shuffle away from the window. "But I'm bored."

"Find something quiet to do then. And keep your brother out of trouble." She doesn't even look up.

Johnny is sitting cross-legged on the carpet, his wee face scrunched up as he tries to fit puzzle pieces together. He's only four—four years younger than me—which means I'm supposed to be the "responsible one". That's what Maw always says.

"Want to play a game, Johnny?" I crouch beside him.

His face lights up. "Yes! Ball game?"

I glance at Maw, who's still focused on her nails. "Let's go in the hallway. More space there."

Johnny follows me, giggling with excitement, and I fetch the soft indoor ball from under the stairs. The hallway isn't big, but it's long enough that we can stand at opposite ends.

"Ready?" I ask, and Johnny nods, bouncing on his toes.

I squat down and roll the ball along the floor to him. He stops it then rolls it back.

After some more passing backwards and forwards—and only losing it under the shoe rack once—we move on to gentle throws. Johnny's idea of "catching" is to grab the ball and hug it to his chest like he's trying to keep hold of a wriggly puppy. Still, he manages not to drop it most of the time.

"Look, Robbie!" Johnny tosses the ball up and catches it himself. "I did it all on my own!"

"Nice one, wee man!" I say, imitating the kind of voice I imagine Da would use if he ever bothered to play with us.

We get braver as we go, me throwing just a wee bit higher each turn because Johnny keeps squealing with laughter when he manages to hold on. It's actually a pretty fun game.

Then Johnny decides he wants to show off, and he flings the ball way too hard. It sails past my hands and straight towards Maw's prized photograph on the wall—the one of her and Da on their wedding day, back before she had us.

Time slows down just enough for me to think *Oh no*, then the photo frame hits the floor with a crash, glass shattering everywhere, the sound like thunder in our quiet house.

I freeze. Maw's smiling face peeks up at me from under jagged shards. And then she appears in the doorway, only in real life she's not smiling. Nope, her cheeks are red with anger.

She looks from the broken frame to me, barely even glancing at Johnny. "ROBBIE! What have you done now?"

"I didn't—"

"It was me, Mummy," Johnny pipes up, his voice small. "I throwed the ball too hard."

Maw ignores him completely, her eyes fixed on me. "Why can't you ever be responsible? I leave you alone for five minutes and you break something. Just look at this mess!"

"But Maw, Johnny was the one who—"

"Don't you *dare* blame your brother!" Her voice drops to that scary quiet tone that's even worse than shouting. "He's just a wee boy. You're supposed to know better!"

She kneels next to Johnny and brushes his hair from his forehead, her face softening. "It's not your fault, sweetheart. Your brother should have known not to play ball in the house."

Then she turns back to me, and her face hardens again. "Stay right there. Don't touch anything." She stomps off towards the kitchen, muttering under her breath.

Johnny's bottom lip trembles. "I'm sorry, Robbie."

"It's okay. Don't worry about it."

I spot a large piece of glass near my foot and bend to pick it up, thinking I should at least try to help clean up. But the edge is sharper than it looks. I hiss as it slices into my finger.

"Robbie's bleeding!" Johnny calls out, just as Maw returns with a dustpan and brush.

She gives my finger the briefest look before rolling her eyes. "For God's sake, Robbie! I told you not to touch anything." She grabs my wrist roughly. "You can't stay still for a moment, can you? No, you never do as you're told."

She drags me to the kitchen, Johnny trailing behind us with

worried eyes. Maw runs my finger under cold water, her movements quick and impatient.

"Always making more work for me," she mutters, fetching a plaster and wrapping it around my finger with none of the gentleness she shows Johnny when he's hurt. "Always causing problems. Why do you have to be so difficult?"

Back in the hallway, she points at the stairs. "Both of you, out of my sight. I'll clean this up myself. You'll only make it worse."

Johnny looks like he might cry, so I take his hand. "Come on, let's go to my room."

We sit on my bed, listening to Maw banging around downstairs. Johnny leans against my shoulder, and I let him play with my toy cars, even the wee motorbike I usually keep on my shelf.

The front door opens around six o'clock, and Da's heavy footsteps echo in the hallway. Johnny and I creep to the top of the stairs to listen.

"How was your day?" Da asks, his voice tired but kind.

"Terrible," Maw replies. "Your eldest has been a nightmare. Smashed our wedding photo, after I *specifically* told him not to play ball in the house."

Da sighs, and I can picture him rubbing his forehead the way he always does. "Robbie! Come down here, please."

I trudge down the stairs, Johnny following close behind.

"Just for once, could I please come home and hear that you *didn't* get up to mischief? Apologise to your mother."

"But Da, *I* didn't—"

"I don't want to hear it! Just apologise to your mother. Is that really too much to ask?"

I curl my hands into fists, my fingernails digging into my palms. My chest feels tight, like something is squeezing it.

"Young man, apologise to your mother right now!" Da's voice gets that stern edge that means I'm in real trouble.

I look at Johnny, who stares back at me with sad eyes. I look at Maw, who's waiting with that smug face she gets when things go her way. I look at Da, who's too tired to even listen to my side.

Without a word, I turn and race up the stairs, slamming my bedroom door behind me. I kick my schoolbag across the room, scattering books and pencils everywhere.

It's not fair. It's *never* fair.

I throw myself onto my bed and punch my pillow, pretending it's something else. Someone else.

It doesn't help, but at least up here, no one can see the hot tears that spill down my cheeks.

◆ ◆ ◆

The punchbag swings wildly as I slam my fist into it again and again. Each hit sends a jolt of pain up my arm, but I welcome it. Physical pain is simple. Straightforward. Nothing like the mess churning inside my head.

Sweat drips down my bare back. The garage is stuffy despite the door being wide open, but I don't care. I need this. Need to hit something until my muscles scream and my lungs burn and my mind goes blissfully blank.

But it's not working today.

I land another punch, harder this time, but it's still no good. I step back, chest heaving, and grab a towel to wipe my face. The memory of Cat standing in her kitchen, talking about the fucking *universe* paying me, sends a fresh wave of anger through me. Gritting my teeth, I slam my fist into the bag again.

What kind of person hires someone when they've got no

money to pay them? What kind of person talks about *manifestation* like it's an actual strategy for paying bills?

A spoilt one, that's who. A princess who's never had to worry because there's always been a big brother to fix her problems for her.

I've spent days working my arse off in that flat, thinking I was earning money I desperately need to keep afloat while this theft accusation hangs over me. And all the while, she was relying on the *universe* to sort things out.

Jesus Christ!

My fist connects with the bag so hard it nearly comes off its hook.

The worst part is, I actually opened up to her. Told her about my maw, about the night I found her parents' car, about how I gave up fighting. I never tell people that stuff. There's only Johnny, and even then, I prefer not to burden him with my mess.

And shit, even if I wanted to, I couldn't talk to Johnny right now. Da's made sure of that. My own brother—the one person who's always had my back—is off-limits because of this investigation.

I pause, breathing hard, and lean against the workbench. My gaze falls on something crumpled in the corner of the garage. A small scrap of blush-coloured lace.

Cat's knickers.

I stare at them for a long moment, remembering how I took them from her last night. How I walked away with them in my pocket.

Before I can think better of it, I cross the garage, pick them up, lift them to my face, and inhale deeply. Her scent hits me like a physical blow—sweet and musky and unmistakably *her*. In an instant, I'm back in those woods, with her on her knees, her mouth on me, her hands gripping my thighs. The memory sends heat surging through my body, pooling low in my gut.

"Fuck," I mutter, tossing the knickers aside like they've burned me.

I stride back to the punchbag and hit it again, harder than before. What is wrong with me? I should be furious with her. I *am* furious with her. But even now, part of me wants to get on my motorcycle, ride to her flat, and finish what we started in those woods.

And that's exactly why I need to stay the hell away from Catriona McIntyre.

I keep punching, trying to drive her from my thoughts. Left jab. Right hook. Repeat. My knuckles are raw despite the wraps, but I don't stop.

This is why I keep to myself. Every time I let someone in, they let me down.

My maw was the worst for it, blaming me for anything that went wrong, looking at me like she wished she'd had a different kid altogether.

I pause, breathing heavily. Even now, I don't understand what I did to make her hate me so much. Aren't mothers supposed to have some primal urge to protect their kids? Survival of the species and all that. Well, apparently I was *so* fucking unlovable my mother was able to override that maternal instinct.

When she left, when I was eleven, she said to me, "I can't do this anymore. Not with you always making everything so bloody difficult." Like I was personally responsible for driving her out of our house. Not Johnny. Not Da. Me.

Now, as an adult, I know that's bullshit. I know she was unhappy in her marriage, unhappy with small-town life, unhappy with being a mother. It wasn't my fault.

But as an eleven-year-old? I believed her. And that belief shaped everything that came after—the scrapping, the vandalism, the stupid choices. If I was going to be blamed for everything anyway, why not actually do something to deserve it?

I slam my fist into the bag one last time then rest my forehead against the cool vinyl. What I really want is a proper fight, the kind I used to have in those warehouses in Inverness. The adrenaline, the danger, the clarity that comes when it's just you and your opponent and nothing else matters.

But I gave that up. I made a promise to myself: no more fighting. No more risking lives, mine or anyone else's.

I step back from the bag and unwrap my hands, flexing my fingers. They're going to be stiff tomorrow, but that's the least of my worries.

Cat's knickers catch my eye again, sitting on the garage floor. Common sense says I should lob them into the rubbish and be done with them, with *her*. I actually reach for them to do just that, then I hesitate. Can't bring myself to do it. Bloody pathetic.

Ugh. *Get a grip, Robbie.* What I need right now is a plan. I need to figure out who framed me, and I need to do it without Cat's help. I can't rely on her, or anyone else for that matter.

I'm about to head inside for a shower when there's the rumble of a car working its way along the dirt track to the cottage. I tense. Is it the police, coming to arrest me? Maybe they've concluded their investigation and decided I'm guilty. Or perhaps it's Cat, come to apologise—or to stir up more trouble.

Either way, I'm not in the mood for visitors.

I step out of the garage, squinting in the late afternoon sunlight. A red car parks beside my motorcycle, then the driver's door opens and a familiar figure steps out.

David Adefope. Johnny's boyfriend.

He's dressed in what can only be described as an assault on the senses: a yellow shirt so bright it practically glows in the sunlight, electric blue trousers, and thick-rimmed turquoise glasses that ride low on his nose until he nudges them back into place.

"Oh my!" His eyes widen as they take in my bare, sweat-slicked upper half, and for a second his jaw actually drops. Then he throws a dramatic hand over his face and peeks at me through his fingers. "I resist temptation! I'm taken—and it's your brother I'm with!"

Despite everything, I can't help but chuckle. His embarrassment is pure theatre—I know he's loving every second. "Relax, David. It's just a chest."

"Easy for you to say," he replies, still covering his eyes, his fingers spread wide enough for him to ogle me shamelessly. "Some of us aren't used to Greek gods strutting around half-naked on a Saturday afternoon."

Smirking, I grab my T-shirt from the workbench and tug it over my head. Just moments ago, I'd have bitten someone's head off for disturbing me, but actually, David being here? I'm strangely glad for the company.

When Johnny first introduced me to David, I was a wee bit surprised. My brother, quiet and reserved, with this loud Londoner who dresses . . . well, like he's on his way to a pantomime rehearsal? But then I saw how Johnny lit up around him, how David could make my brother laugh like nobody else could, and that was enough to win me over.

David and I are about as different as two men can be, but I've always looked out for Johnny, have done my entire life. Anyone who loves him gets my respect too.

He walks over to the garage, his eyes flicking around, taking in my tools and the punchbag still swinging on its chain, then they land on Cat's knickers on the floor. He raises an eyebrow but, to his credit, doesn't comment on them (thank Christ).

"Well?" I say. "Don't get me wrong, it's nice to see you, David. But why are you here?"

"So, the thing is . . ." David leans against the garage door-frame. "Johnny's been having a tough time this last week."

I frown. "*Johnny's* been having a tough time?"

"Okay, so maybe he's not the only one," David concedes with a small smile. "But he's been out of sorts. At first I just thought it was because he was worried about you. I mean, he's always worrying about you, but more so recently, of course."

This catches me off-guard. I'd have said it was the other way around—that I'm the one always worrying about Johnny. But before I can question this, David continues.

"Plus, obviously he's frustrated he's been told to keep his distance from you while the police are investigating. But then today, when I was talking to him, I realised something else was eating him up, and I finally got it out of him." David crosses his arms and fixes me with a piercing stare. "He confessed to me what you made him do, not tell anyone where he found that signet ring. More than that, *lie* to your da and the police about it."

I pause a moment before answering, then point out with half-hearted grouchiness, "Seems like he didn't do a very good job of not telling *anyone*."

David waves away this comment. "I don't count. The point is, we both know what Johnny's like. He's not one to step out of line or do things he's not supposed to. So, not only has he been worrying himself sick about you, but the thought that he did something wrong by lying has been gnawing away at him."

Guilt tugs at my conscience. I've always tried to protect

137

Johnny, shield him from the worst parts of life. It bothers me that he's suffering on my account.

"So, here's what I need to know," David says, straight-faced now. "Did you do it?"

"Are you being serious?" I step towards him. Old instincts—get bigger, get mean—kick in before I can think better of it. "You come here to my own home and ask me that?"

"I need to hear you say it." David doesn't back down even though I tower over him. "Did you do it?"

"No. Of course I bloody didn't."

David watches me for a few moments more, then he nods. "Yeah, I know you didn't. I just needed to hear you say it." His shoulders relax. "Anyway, Johnny isn't supposed to talk to you about the investigation, but . . . I'm not Johnny!" He grins, our charged moment of just a few seconds ago apparently already forgotten. "And when I suggested that maybe *I* could come here and talk to you, the biggest smile lit up Johnny's face. Honestly, you should have seen it. It was adorable."

A reluctant smile twitches at my lips. I can imagine the look on my brother's face.

"I don't have much of an update," David continues, "but Johnny *has* mentioned that nothing else has been stolen since you left, which is a pain."

I groan. That just makes me look guiltier, as if my absence has magically solved everything and I was the problem all along.

"*However*," David says, "Johnny *was* able to get me some things that may prove useful. Let me fetch them from the car. Drumroll, please!"

He's as bad as Cat.

"This isn't a game show, David," I growl, although there's no real heat behind it.

"Fine, fine. No appreciation of drama, you Highlanders." He lets out an exaggerated sigh. "But trust me, you're going to want to see this."

He heads back to his car, whistling as he goes, and despite myself, the tiniest spark of hope flickers in my chest.

CHAPTER EIGHTEEN

CAT

I open the front door to the Bannock Hotel—my childhood home—and peek inside. Reception is empty. Result. Still, I'll need to be quiet. Lewis is probably through in the restaurant, setting up for dinner service.

I make a beeline for the supply cupboard, ease it open, and cast a quick glance over the shelves. Spotting what I need, I nab two bottles of shampoo and a conditioner then tuck them into my tote bag. Next target: the ever-essential toilet roll.

Guilt nips at me. Here I am, a grown woman with a teaching job, pinching toiletries from my brother. But is it *really* stealing when technically a portion of this hotel belongs to me? Besides, there are a ton of products here. Surely one or two going missing won't make a difference? Plus, I need to save every penny to pay Robbie back.

My stomach twists at the memory of how we left things earlier. The look on his face when he realised I might not be able to cough up what I owe. God, I've made a mess of things. I should never have trusted that stupid manifestation book.

I'm reaching for another roll of posh toilet paper when there's a soft whine behind me. I freeze then slowly turn around.

Bruce, the hotel's black Labrador, stands in the doorway, his tail wagging furiously. He lets out a delighted wee whimper.

"Shh, Bruce," I whisper, giving his head a quick pat. "Not now, boy. Shoo!"

But Bruce has no intention of leaving. If anything, he gets more excited, his tail thumping rhythmically against the doorframe, the noise echoing through the quiet hallway.

"What are you up to there, Bruce?" a familiar voice calls.

Oh, shit.

A moment later, Lewis appears in the doorway. "Cat! What are you doing skulking about?" He spots my tote bag, which is now twice its normal size and bulging suspiciously at the seams, and lets out a heavy sigh. "Really, Cat? Nicking from your own family? Classy."

I flash him my signature mischievous grin, the one that's got me out of trouble more times than I care to admit. "Come on, it's hardly a daring heist. Just a few bits and bobs."

"That's not the point." Lewis crosses his arms and gives me a stern big-brother stare. "You can't just help yourself every time you fancy something."

Ouch. The sting of truth isn't lost on me. I wonder if this is how all my brothers see me—the sibling who takes rather than contributing.

Bruce gives my hand a slobbery lick of consolation then trots off down the corridor in pursuit of peace and quiet. Wise dog.

"Fine, fine. I hear you loud and clear," I mutter, trying for my most repentant expression.

"Aye, I've heard that before, though, haven't I?" Lewis

doesn't budge. "Like all those times you'd ring Ally for a wee 'loan' after overspending. You promised him every single time it'd be the last." He shakes his head. "Honestly, I used to think he was daft for caving as often as he did. And now I hear you've hired MacDonald to work on your flat without having the cash to pay him?"

Jesus, word really *does* travel fast in this town.

"Aye, all right, I get it!" I throw my hands up, my embarrassment morphing into defensiveness. "Maybe I didn't think things through with the money, but—"

"No, you didn't," Lewis interrupts. "Do you ever think maybe it's past time you were a bit more responsible and grew up, Cat?"

He's the second brother today to tell me to grow up, and something inside me snaps. "Enjoying life up there on Mount Judgement, are you? You've seen my flat, yet here you are in this lovely place, which belonged to our parents and is just as much mine as yours. So I think you can excuse me for nabbing a few mini bottles of shampoo. You've done pretty well out of this arrangement, Lewis."

The moment the words leave my mouth, I regret them. They hang in the air between us, sharp and ugly.

Lewis stares back at me, stunned. A flicker of hurt crosses his face before he composes himself.

"If you'd wanted to stay in your old room," he says quietly, "you'd have been very welcome to. You're the one who didn't want to. No one asked you to buy an old rundown flat without warning anyone what you were up to."

His measured response only makes me feel worse.

"Aye," I admit, heat creeping up my cheeks, "but let's be

honest, I'd have ended up leaving eventually. The hotel . . . it's your and Iona's home now. Not mine."

Lewis scrubs a hand over his face. "Shit, Cat. I . . . don't know what you want me to say to that."

Guilt gnaws at my insides. Lewis pours his heart and soul into this place, giving it everything he's got. His hard graft turned the business around, kept our parents' legacy alive, and here I am accusing him of hoarding it all for himself, when that's not exactly how things happened.

"I'm sorry, Lewis." My throat is tight. "That was bang out of order. I didn't mean it. You, Ally, and Jamie have always been there for me, and I just—" I choke on a sob. "Oh Lewis, I've messed up. I . . . I wanted the flat to feel like *mine*—a proper home—but I've gone about everything all wrong." A hot tear slides down my cheek, and then another. "Now I don't know how to fix this. I feel like such an idiot."

Lewis's face softens and he steps forwards and folds me into a big bear hug. "Hey now, it's all right," he soothes, holding me tight.

I hug him back, grateful for his steady, familiar comfort. Honestly, what a roller coaster of a day—blubbering this morning, shrieking with glee on the back of Robbie's motorbike, getting all introspective at the clootie well, and now crying again. Talk about emotional whiplash.

"You know what?" Lewis says. "You're right about the hotel."

I pull back from him and swipe at my tears. "What?"

He gives a half-smile. "I'd never want you, or Jamie or Ally for that matter, to feel like I've pinched something that belongs to all of us. But . . . it's complicated, you know? The hotel isn't something we can easily divide up between us. Unless we sold it, of course, but—"

"God no! I don't want you to sell this place. The Bannock Hotel belongs in McIntyre hands. *Your* hands. Lewis, this is your home, your dream. You're the one who's kept everything that Maw and Da built going, and that's amazing. You and Iona will raise your own family here, I bet, just like our parents did with us. And that's exactly how it should be." I squeeze his arm so he knows I mean it.

Lewis visibly relaxes, his shoulders loosening. "Thanks, but still . . ." He looks thoughtful for a moment, as if piecing something together in his mind. "I think we *do* need to sort something out financially between the four of us, especially now you've got your own place, Ally's got his, and Jamie's practically living with Maisie." He nods, growing more certain of the idea. "Aye, it's what Maw and Da would want. They'd also want their youngest living in a clean and pleasant home, so . . . let me have a look at my finances and see if I can't work out something that'll allow you to finish your flat renovations."

I blink at him, not quite believing my ears. "Are you sure? Don't you want to wait until we figure everything out properly with Ally and Jamie?"

He laughs softly. "To be clear, Cat, anything I send over now will come out of your share once the four of us finalise an agreement. Think of this as an advance."

I fling my arms around him and hug him again, fiercely this time. "Thank you, Lewis!"

"You're welcome. But in the future, maybe think a bit more carefully before making any big financial commitments. I'm always happy to talk things over and give you advice, but it's generally better to do that beforehand."

I release him and nod solemnly. "Right. No more impulse spending or casual pilfering from the supply cupboard. That's a

Cat McIntyre promise. Operation Responsible Adult starts now."

I dig into my tote and return the shampoo and conditioner bottles to him, a little sheepishly. "Sorry again."

Lewis chuckles. "Don't worry about it. And you can keep the loo roll, Cat. That's on the house."

CHAPTER NINETEEN

CAT

I knock on Robbie's door with my knuckles, three determined raps. There's movement inside, then the door swings open, and—oh, sweet Jesus. Robbie stands before me, freshly showered, his dark hair still damp. He's wearing a plain black T-shirt that clings to that ridiculous chest of his, faded jeans that hang just right on his hips, and he's not even bothered with socks. He's so bloody attractive my brain temporarily short-circuits, and I forget why I'm here.

"What do you want, McIntyre?"

His growl snaps me out of it.

"Can I come in for a sec?" I try not to flinch under his steely glare. "I've got news. Something you'll actually want to hear."

Robbie folds his arms, looking like a bouncer about to turn me away. His mouth opens—probably to tell me to get lost—but I jump in first.

"Please, Robbie. I promise it won't take long." I give him my most hopeful look.

His eyes narrow, and for a second I think he's going to slam the door in my face. But then he steps aside with a resigned sigh. "Fine."

I follow Robbie into the living room. The place is rustic and cosy, somewhere that'd be perfect to hole up on a rainy day with a mug of hot chocolate. A thick burgundy rug sprawls in front of the log burner, its deep red echoed by the big squashy sofa and armchair. But this is no granny's sitting room. Shelves made from rough wood are fixed to one wall, their black iron brackets giving off industrial vibes. On them sit empty vintage whisky bottles, a lamp with an exposed filament bulb, and—because of course—a miniature model motorbike. To top it off, on the wall opposite there's a framed quote about raising hell, most likely from some heavy metal band.

My eyes flick to the coffee table, where there's an open file of paperwork. Robbie reaches over and snaps it shut, but not before I spot the Glen Garve Resort letterhead.

I'm dying to ask about it but bite my tongue. Instead I say, "Did you make those shelves?"

He gives a tight nod.

"Very cool." I sink into the sofa, which envelops me like a hug.

Robbie drops into the armchair and drums his fingers on his thigh impatiently. "So, what do you want, Cat? Make it quick."

Charming. But after what I did, I can't really blame him for being frosty.

"Good news! I've got the money to pay you now. So it'd mean a lot if you could come back and see the job through."

Robbie's expression remains dubious. "Is that right?"

"It is." I pull out my phone, open my banking app, and hold it out to him. "See for yourself."

He leans forwards to look at the screen then sits back again, giving nothing away. "Let me guess. You ran to your big brothers for help?"

A flush creeps up my neck. "I did speak to Lewis, and we sorted some things out."

Robbie rolls his eyes.

"But it's not what you're thinking! The money is my inheritance, not some handout."

Robbie's features shift. Less thunderstorm, more overcast drizzle.

"That said, Lewis did have a few choice words about my recent decisions. I realise it was reckless and selfish of me to hire you before I had the funds."

"It was," Robbie says gruffly, but with less bite than before.

"I'm sorry. Really." I take a breath. "But now that I have the money, will you come back and finish the work?"

He drums his fingers once more, slower this time, thinking it over. "On one condition," he says eventually. "You pay me for what I've already done. Right now."

"Of course." I make the transfer and show him the confirmation. Some of the tension bleeds out of his shoulders.

"See?" I flash him a relieved smile, glad the crisis is over. "You can trust me, Robbie. I'm in your corner."

He raises a brow. "Paying me what I'm owed isn't exactly some grand gesture of loyalty."

"True, but I sorted things, didn't I? Besides"—I grin coyly—"I've been loyal in other ways. For starters, I haven't spilled any of your secrets, such as the one about you having metal, you know . . . *down there*."

"Robert MacDonald!" a voice exclaims from the doorway. "Have you got a willy piercing? We're practically brothers, and yet you've never mentioned it!"

I whip around to see David Adefope standing there, dressed in an eye-wateringly bright outfit, carrying a tray with mugs, a cafetiere, and a plate of biscuits. He's looking at Robbie with a mixture of shock and delight.

"Er . . . we're not brothers, David," Robbie mutters, actual spots of colour blooming on his cheeks. It's absurdly endearing.

"Not *yet*," David agrees, setting the tray down on the coffee table. "But let's be honest, it's only a matter of time before your brother pops the question. I mean, who wouldn't want to lock *this* down?" He gestures to himself.

"David? What are you doing here?" I rise and give him a hug.

David moved to Bannock a few years ago. Although I've been away for most of that time, we always hit it off whenever we cross paths. Outgoing personalities just gravitate to each other, I suppose.

"I could ask you the same." He squeezes me then looks between me and Robbie with undisguised interest. "And more importantly, how do you know about Robbie's . . . embellishment? Is there something going on between you two?"

"Nope," Robbie says.

David smirks. "Then why have your cheeks gone all pink?"

Robbie shoots him a murderous look.

"I once dated a guy—before Johnny, of course—who had an intimate piercing," David says, totally nonchalant, as if dick piercings are just part of everyday chat. "What type is yours? Is it a Prince Albert? An ampallang? A frenum ladder? Or—"

"We're not discussing this," Robbie says.

David pouts for a moment, but then he brightens and turns to me. "Fancy a coffee?"

"I'd love one!"

"She's not staying."

149

David just winks. "I'll grab you a mug, Cat." He vanishes into the kitchen.

No sooner has he left than my gaze zeroes in on the plate. "Oh! Tunnock's wafers. My favourite." I snatch up one of the shiny red and gold parcels, peel back the wrapper, then sink my teeth into the glorious chocolate, biscuit, and caramel goodness.

"Help yourself," Robbie grumbles.

David reappears with another mug and pours coffee for us all. "So, Cat . . . I noticed some knickers in Robbie's garage. Were they yours by any chance?"

"Er . . . blush-coloured and lacy?"

Robbie, who's grabbed a wafer of his own, nearly chokes. David nods.

"Aye, they're mine," I say, entirely unbothered. I take another bite of the Tunnock's.

Robbie takes a swig of his coffee, looking anywhere but at me. David's got a glint in his eye and is clearly ready to dig for more juicy details, but—feeling a sudden pang of sympathy for Robbie—I jump in before he can strike.

"So, are those papers about the case?" I nod at the file on the coffee table.

The atmosphere in the room shifts. David looks to Robbie, but neither speaks.

"I'll take that as a yes, then." Connecting the dots, I ask, "David, did Johnny give you those papers to bring over?"

"He did," David admits. "Said they might be helpful."

My curiosity flares, and I lean forwards. "So, what's in here, then?"

"Doesn't involve you, Cat," Robbie says.

That stings a bit, but I don't back down. "I believed you were innocent from the start," I remind him. "And I've been doing my own digging, trying to help." I glance at David. "I even set up a cork board at home, to track suspects and motives."

He nods approvingly. "That's what I call commitment."

Robbie snorts, and David fixes him with an unamused look then folds his arms. "Stop trying to scare her off, Robbie. You need to let people help you. I know you're not half as scary as you pretend to be, and I reckon Cat knows that too."

"I do."

Robbie stares at me—a bit suspicious at first—but then his face softens, only for half a second. Blink and you'd miss it.

"Okay. I'll let you lot help."

David puts down his coffee and claps his hands together with delight. "Brilliant! Let's get stuck in." He opens the file, and we all scoot closer, studying its contents. It's a collection of records— keycard data, rotas, maintenance logs, that kind of thing. Bits and pieces that Johnny must have thought might help us figure out what really happened.

"This is great!" I exclaim. "If I'd known we were going to be working on this, I'd have taken the cork board with me. Probably makes more sense for you to have it anyway, Robbie."

He doesn't bother to respond to that. Instead he jabs a finger at the keycard records. "According to these, I accessed the rooms in question when the items went missing, even though I didn't." His lips form a grim line. "But how am I supposed to argue with what's written down in black and white?"

"Whoever framed you must have messed up somewhere," David says. "We just need to keep looking."

We examine the maintenance logs and the staff rotas, sipping our coffees. Occasionally David or I ask Robbie to decipher some abbreviation or other.

"Well, according to these, Samantha was working on all three days," Robbie says after a while. "Then again, a lot of people were, so that doesn't mean much."

"It means we've got reason to keep her as a suspect," I say. "That's something."

Robbie and I give David a quick summary of why Samantha is at the top of our list. When we're done, he nods. "Definite motives there."

"Aye, but still a complete lack of proof." Robbie flips to the next page, and as he does, a folded note slips out and flutters to the floor.

I grab it and scan it.

Robbie,

I hate that I can't be there for you right now, but I hope something here helps. Know that I'm on your side. Be careful and stay strong.

Johnny

P.S. Destroy this note after reading it. It's safer that way.

I hand the note to Robbie, who reads it then slips it into his pocket.

"Johnny asked you to destroy that."

"Aye, I'll get rid of it soon."

I wonder if he's in no hurry to let go of the only scrap of contact he's had from his brother lately.

We top up our coffees and pore over the paperwork some more, but there's no dramatic breakthrough. No dazzling clues. Just more frustration.

Eventually Robbie snaps the file shut and rubs a hand over his jaw. "Nothing. It was a great idea Johnny had, sending us this stuff, but we're no further forward and I don't know where we go from here."

He practically deflates in the armchair, his usual scowl replaced by something almost vulnerable.

"Any bright ideas?" I ask David, willing him to come up with something—anything—that might lift Robbie's mood.

"Funny you should ask. As it happens, I do have an idea."

I sit up a little straighter. "Well, go on, then."

"You and I, Cat, are going to go on a spa day."

I blink at him. "A . . . spa day?"

"Yep, at the resort. And while we're there, we're going to do a bit of . . . investigating."

The penny drops, and a grin tugs at my mouth. The look on Robbie's face, though, suggests he thinks we've both lost the plot.

"No offence, but neither of you is exactly MI5 material. If you get caught poking around for my sake—"

"None taken," David cuts in breezily. "And Robbie, some-times in life you have to take risks for people who matter. Right, Cat?"

"Right," I say firmly.

Robbie glances between us, and for just a second, I see it—the surprise that we'd bother sticking our necks out for him. And that's what gets me most, the fact Robbie MacDonald doesn't even realise he's worth fighting for.

Well. We'll just have to show him he is.

CHAPTER TWENTY

CAT

The Glen Garve Resort swimming pool is everything you'd expect from a luxury establishment: crystal-clear water, elegant blue tiles, and not a hint of the heavy chlorine smell I remember from the public pools down in Glasgow. Sunlight streams through floor-to-ceiling windows, casting dancing patterns across the water's surface as David and I wade in.

"This is the life," he sighs, sinking up to his shoulders. He's rocking pink swimming shorts that are as loud and cheerful as he is. "Considering Johnny works at the resort, it's criminal he and I don't relax here more often. Mind you, if we did, we'd probably just end up in the bubble pool, making out like teenagers."

I splash water at him. "Too much information, thank you very much."

"Oh, please." David rolls his eyes. "As if you're some innocent wee lamb."

I laugh then turn and tip backwards so I'm floating on my back. The ceiling above is painted with clouds that seem to drift lazily across an azure sky. It's peaceful here, the kind of place where you can forget all your troubles and just . . . exist.

But today isn't about relaxation. We're here on a mission.

I straighten and plant my feet on the tiles beneath me. "I know we've been through this," I say, keeping my voice low, even though there's only one other couple in the pool and they're way too busy chilling to pay us any attention. "But . . . Operation Undercover Spy kicks off at one, right?"

David nods then ducks under the water. When he resurfaces, droplets cascade down his face. "Yep. That's when Samantha takes her lunch break, and Johnny said she'll be out of her office for at least twenty minutes, probably more. More than enough time for us to have a snoop around her things and see if we can't find anything incriminating."

I glance at the ornate clock mounted on the wall. Half past eleven. No rush.

"I still can't believe we're actually doing this," I say, half-excited, half-terrified. "If we get caught . . ."

"We won't." David's tone is breezy, though I can't tell if he's genuinely confident or just putting on a brave face. "*Anyway*, let's talk about something else, like . . . oh, I don't know, you and Robbie. I couldn't help but notice some interesting tension between you two yesterday."

"Oh?" I aim for nonchalance but miss by a mile.

"C'mon, Cat, your underwear was on his floor. Care to explain how it got there?"

I open my mouth then shut it again, and suddenly I'm *fascinated* by the ripples in the water. But who am I kidding? There's no way I'm keeping this to myself. So, a smile creeping onto my lips, I meet David's gaze again. "Let's just say I got acquainted with his below-the-belt piercing in a rather intimate way. In the middle of the woods, no less. But he didn't even return the favour! Just asked for my knickers then walked off with them like they were some kind of trophy."

David lets out a low whistle. "Okay, I need more details. Wait—no, I don't. That's my boyfriend's brother! I shouldn't want to know about Robbie's . . . hardware. I may have teased him yesterday about it to his face, but I really shouldn't gossip behind his back." David taps his chin. "And *yet* . . ."

I snort. "How about I leave it at this: it wasn't exactly a romantic stroll in the moonlight. It was . . . intense."

David grins wickedly. "Oh, I bet it was."

"But that was Friday," I say, shifting gears. "Yesterday, the way I view Robbie changed a bit."

David cocks his head. "How so?"

I hesitate, thinking back to the clootie well, to Robbie's quiet confession. "Robbie mentioned something about his maw, about how he wished she'd treated him more like how she treated Johnny. It made me realise there's so much more to him than I thought."

David's playful demeanour slips away, replaced by something gentler. "Ah. Fiona."

"Has Johnny spoken about her? I know she left when Robbie and Johnny were young, but I was even younger, so I barely remember her."

David paddles over to the pool's edge and props his elbows up on the tiles, water beading on his arms. I follow suit.

"Johnny's told me bits here and there. She . . . struggled. She was quite a bit younger than Craig—had Robbie when she was barely out of her teens."

"That is young," I agree.

"Some people do just fine becoming parents at that age. Others, though, aren't ready for the responsibility, and Fiona fell into the second category. From what I understand, she felt trapped. Craig was working all hours here at the resort, and there she was, stuck at home with a baby, and then another one a few years later. Small town, no career, just nappies and housework day after day."

I think about my own maw, how she managed to balance running the hotel with raising four children. But she had my da, and they were a team. Plus, she chose that life—she wasn't thrust into motherhood before she was ready.

"And Fiona . . . took things out on Robbie?" I ask carefully.

David nods. "Johnny says she'd compare them constantly. 'Why can't you be more like your little brother?' That sort of thing. Johnny was the 'easy' child—quiet, obedient. Robbie was . . . well, Robbie. And he got the blame for everything, whether it was his fault or not."

I think about the man I've come to know the past week and a half. Guarded. Defensive. Quick to assume the worst in people. It makes a painful sort of sense now.

"Johnny only hears from her every now and then," David goes on. "A text on his birthday, maybe a call at Christmas. She travels a lot. Has flings. Lives this wild, free life—the complete opposite of what she had here."

I fiddle with the strap of my bikini top, letting David's words sink in. "So she just . . . left them? To go live her best life?"

"Pretty much," David says with a small shrug. "Left them both behind for adventures and hot men in hotter climates."

Something uncomfortable shifts in my stomach. I think about my own life—the wild nights out in Glasgow, the string of casual hook-ups, the constant chase for the next thrill. My Project Bang a Bad Boy plan suddenly seems not just mortifying but cruel.

"God, I feel awful," I mumble.

David lifts an eyebrow. "About what?"

"When I first saw Robbie again, I literally made a plan called Project Bang a Bad Boy. I even told Maisie and Iona about it." I cringe at the memory. "I treated the whole thing like it was a challenge, something to spice up my return home to Bannock. Didn't even think of him as a real person."

David's expression softens. "Cat—"

"Chasing excitement, not caring about who gets hurt along the way . . . not so different from Robbie's maw, right?"

"Cat," David says firmly, "there's a world of difference between being young and wanting a bit of fun, and abandoning your children because you resent the life you've built. Don't be so hard on yourself."

I sigh. "Maybe, but it still feels wrong now. What if what Robbie really wants isn't some wild fling, but someone stable? Someone who won't leave him, the way his mother did?"

David doesn't answer right away, and I can tell he's genuinely considering my words.

"I've been thinking," I continue, "if I keep pursuing Robbie, it can't be because I want a bit of fun with the town bad boy. It has to be because I genuinely care about him." I pause, struck by the truth of what I'm saying. "And I think I *do* care about him. I've seen beyond his reputation, and . . . I like what I see."

"Well," David says with a small smile, "that sounds like growth to me. Johnny would be thrilled to hear you talking like this about his brother, by the way. He worries about Robbie— says he's too isolated, too stuck in his own head."

I think about Robbie in his secluded cottage, with his motorcycle and his punchbag and his walls built so high that hardly anyone gets to see the man behind them. The man who stopped fighting after witnessing death. The man who saved my brother's life.

"Robbie deserves better than being someone's rebellious phase," I say.

"He does," David agrees. "And for what it's worth, I think you two might actually be good for each other. Yesterday, when he was looking at you . . . I don't know. There was something there I haven't seen before."

My chest flutters for reasons entirely unrelated to our impending spy mission. "Really?"

"Really. But let's not get ahead of ourselves. First, we need to clear his name." David glances at the clock. "Speaking of which, we should probably hit the steam room and sauna before our little . . . investigation. Make it look like we're actually here for the facilities."

I nod, pushing away from the edge. "Race you to the steam room?"

"You're on, McIntyre."

We splash towards the steps, our laughter echoing off the high ceiling.

◆ ◆ ◆

After the steam room and sauna, David and I meet up in the resort's plush lobby. My hair is still damp, and water occasionally drips onto my collar, but I barely notice. My stomach is too busy tying itself in knots.

David glances around and then lowers his voice so only I can hear him. "Ready for phase two?" He's wearing a navy-blue polo shirt with tiny embroidered flamingos on the collar, his idea of understated spy attire.

I nod then take out my phone and open the staff corridor layout Robbie sent me earlier. "Just to confirm what we're doing . . ." I tilt the screen so David can see it. "Samantha's office is here, just past the locker rooms. And we access the staff area from here."

Despite the knots in my stomach, excitement builds inside me. I'm reminded of chasing thrills down in Glasgow—snogging strangers in dark corners, getting up to no good on sticky dance floors, dancing on tables when I'd had one too many. But this time, the stakes are higher than being chucked out of a nightclub.

"Let's go," I say, tucking my phone away.

We casually make our way through the resort's grand hallways, past guests lounging in armchairs and staff carrying trays of drinks. I saunter along like I'm heading for a hot stone massage and not about to channel my inner cat burglar.

As planned, we find Johnny near the entrance to the staff corridor. When he spots us, his eyes light up with perfectly feigned surprise.

"David! What are you doing here?" He pulls his boyfriend into a hug before turning to me. "And Cat! What a lovely surprise."

I bite back a smile at his acting. For someone who's supposed to be a rule follower, Johnny's quite good at this subterfuge business. Only . . . there's no one else around in this part of the resort, so it seems a little unnecessary.

"We've just been enjoying the spa facilities," David says, playing along. "The steam room was divine."

Johnny leans in, ostensibly to give David another hug, and whispers, "I've checked. Samantha's not in her office, and the locker rooms are empty. Most of the staff are helping with a wedding, so the corridor should be quiet."

He glances around to confirm we're alone then taps his keycard against the reader. The door unlocks with a soft click.

"There's CCTV in the corridor, but it's not actively monitored. They only check the footage if something goes wrong." Johnny holds the door open for us. "So don't let anything go wrong."

I nod, my mouth suddenly dry.

"And if you do get caught," he adds, his expression serious, "please leave me out of it. The last thing Robbie needs is for the police to think I'm interfering with their investigation."

"We'll be careful," I promise.

He nods, but I can't help but notice the tension tightening his shoulders. "Good luck." He ushers us through then walks off, allowing the door to click shut again behind us.

"Right," David says, his usual cheerful demeanour replaced with steely resolve. "Let's do this."

We move quickly down the corridor, our shoes squeaking on the polished linoleum, a far cry from the soft hush of the guest hallways. My heart is thumping like mad. If anybody clocks us back here, there'll be questions I absolutely cannot answer. But luck is on our side: the corridor remains deserted all the way to Samantha's office. David opens her door and we slip inside.

The office is small but neat, with a large desk dominating the space. There's a window behind it that looks out onto the resort's gardens, and a cupboard against one wall. A few framed certificates hang on display: management qualifications and employee of the month awards.

I eye the window. If someone wanders past, we'll be busted faster than you can say "criminal mastermind". I dare a quick peek through it, but it's clear outside. For now.

"I'll keep watch," David says, positioning himself by the door. "You search."

I nod and approach the desk, my fingers tingling with nervous energy. This is it, our chance to find something that proves Robbie didn't commit the thefts.

I start with the drawers, carefully sliding each one open. The first contains standard office supplies—pens, paper clips, sticky notes. The second is filled with resort paperwork—schedules, inventory lists, nothing interesting.

When I open the third drawer, though, I hit the jackpot. There's a leather-bound planner, and when I flip it open, several folded papers fall out. Bills, by the look of them. I scan through them quickly: credit card statements with eye-watering balances, utility bills marked FINAL NOTICE, a letter from a debt collection agency.

"Oh my God," I whisper, flipping through more pages. "David, I was actually right. She's in serious financial trouble."

Mixed in with the bills are receipts for luxury purchases: a nine-hundred-pound handbag, the latest phone, a weekend "wellness retreat" down south. There's also a receipt for shoes that cost more than I spend on food in a month. Samantha's living well beyond her means, trying to maintain a lifestyle she clearly can't afford.

"This is it," I say, excitement bubbling up. "This is the motive. She needed money, and this proves it."

I pull out my phone and take photos of the evidence, flipping through pages as quickly as I can while still making sure the images are clear.

"Cat!" David hisses suddenly. "Footsteps. Someone's coming. Hide, quick!"

I fumble with the planner, trying to shove it back into the

drawer, but unhelpfully, my fingers have gone clumsy with panic. The footsteps are getting louder. Two sets of them, moving quickly.

David darts across the room and squeezes into the cupboard, pulling the door almost closed. I try to follow, but one glance tells me there's no way we'll both fit. It's barely big enough for David alone.

The footsteps are right outside the door now. In a moment of desperation, I dive under the desk and tuck myself into the cramped gap where your legs are meant to go, yanking the chair in after me. I realise I've left the drawer slightly open, and the planner might not be exactly where I found it, but there's no time to fix it.

The door opens with a soft creak, and I hold my breath, praying I won't be seen. As long as no one walks around this side of the desk—or decides they fancy sitting down—I should be fine. At least, that's what I keep telling myself.

Both sets of footsteps enter the office, the sharp click-clack of high heels closely followed by a heavier, more deliberate tread.

"We have to be quick," a woman says. Samantha, I assume. "I've got to inspect the bridal suite in fifteen minutes, and if it's not perfect, today's bridezilla will have my head."

"Quick is my speciality," a man jokes, and they both snigger like teenagers.

There's a soft thump above my head, followed by a jangle of keys. A handbag dropped onto the desk, perhaps. Then, to my horror, I catch a flash of black tights and heels through the gap between chair and desk. Samantha moves to the window and fiddles with the blinds, then shadows swallow the room.

Now another set of legs appears, these ones masculine and in practical navy work trousers. The pair giggle again, then comes a soft thud—someone being lifted or pushed against the desktop.

"In your office again?" the man murmurs, his voice low and teasing. "You really do like living dangerously."

Samantha lets out a breathy laugh. "Don't pretend it wasn't your idea in the first place. Besides, the risk of getting caught makes it all the more exciting."

"True. Plus, there's something about you in your natural habitat, where you're always telling people what to do . . . it drives me mad, you know?"

Oh God. This is not happening. I'm not hiding under a desk while our prime suspect gets it on with some bloke right above me. Except . . . I am, and it absolutely is happening. So I can add voyeurism to today's list of misdemeanours. Brilliant.

There's a rustle of fabric—a skirt being hiked up?—then the sharp whisper of a zip being undone. Shoes scuff dangerously close to my hiding spot. The air fills with soft moans and stifled laughter, the sort that definitely wouldn't pass muster at a staff meeting.

I squeeze my eyes shut, except that only seems to make my other senses sharper. The smell of lilies from Samantha's perfume. Their voices getting breathier and less coherent.

Oh God. This has to be the most mortifying moment of my life, and that's saying something, considering some of the situations I found myself in during my uni days.

The desk jolts suddenly, and I bite my lip to keep from yelping. Then an urgent rhythm builds: creaking wood, scraping shoes, Samantha's increasingly theatrical sighs ("God yes!", "More!", "Harder!"). My only comfort is all this noise probably means they won't hear me quietly dying under here.

Suddenly there's a loud clatter. I crack open an eye to see a handbag has toppled off the desk, spilling its contents across the floor: lipsticks, receipts, coins, a compact mirror, among other things.

"Oops," Samantha laughs breathlessly, but neither of them stops what they're doing.

My gaze snags on a piece of paper that must have fallen out the handbag—not because I'm particularly interested in Samantha's shopping lists, but because looking at it is infinitely preferable to looking up. But, even from my awkward angle, certain details leap out at me. There are initials scrawled across it. "RM" appears more than once.

RM . . . Robbie MacDonald?

My heart rate spikes. I squint harder, trying to make out more of the note without moving from my hiding spot. There seems to be some kind of timeline or schedule on it, and then—my breath catches—I spot the name "Ashford". That's the guest whose watch was the first item to go missing. This could be the evidence I've been looking for!

My fingers itch to reach out and grab the note. Too risky? But they're distracted, right? Just as I'm considering making a desperate lunge for it, Samantha and her companion shift positions again, and I hurriedly withdraw my hand.

The desk shudders violently, as though they're determined to win a prize for Most Inappropriate Use of Office Furniture. Samantha gasps loudly, followed by a responding grunt from her mystery man as he . . . well . . . finishes what he set out to do.

Silence falls, except for their ragged breathing and my internal wailing for mercy.

"That was . . ." Samantha trails off, still catching her breath.

"Aye," the man agrees eloquently.

Then comes the moment I've been dreading. Samantha

crouches to scoop up her scattered possessions. I freeze completely, not even daring to blink. The chair may be mostly shielding me, but if I so much as twitch, I'm toast.

Thankfully, she seems distracted, adjusting her skirt as she hurriedly crams spilled items back into her bag. When she reaches for the note, though, her hand hovers over it for a second, like she's surprised to see it. Then she snatches it up too.

"Bugger, look at the time! I need to run." She stands, and I hear the soft snap of a mirror opening, then the slick click of a lipstick cap. A faint powdery scent drifts down as she dabs at her face with something, then comes the *spritz-spritz* of perfume. The blinds are whisked open again, flooding the room with light and spilling across my contorted shape beneath the desk.

Please don't look down, please don't look down, please don't—

Miraculously, neither does. Footsteps retreat towards the door, and with a click, it closes behind them.

I remain utterly still, not moving or breathing or existing at all. It's like time itself has stopped out of respect for my dignity's passing.

At last, David stumbles out from his cupboard sanctuary. He pulls back the chair, crouches, then mouths at me, "What. Just. Happened?"

I groan, scrubbing both hands over my face before wriggling out from under the desk. My whisper comes out fierce and ragged: "I thought we were searching for evidence of theft, not playing accidental extras in an office-based porno!"

He grins then quickly sobers when he realises I'm actually shaking.

"I saw a note," I murmur, frustration knotting my insides. "It fell out of her bag. I saw Ashford's name on it, and RM."

"Robbie MacDonald?" David asks.

"My thoughts exactly. It definitely looked dodgy, but she scooped it up before I could grab it."

"Shit. Actually, do you think she put it back in there?" He points and—small miracle!—what's sitting on the desk but Samantha's handbag? She left it behind.

I pounce on it and rifle through it, searching for that crucial note, but . . . it's not here.

No, it has to be. I search again. For a head of housekeeping who supposedly has a reputation for orderliness, she sure keeps a lot of junk in her handbag, but the note is definitely not among its contents.

"She must have pocketed it," I say at last, defeated. "It's probably halfway through a shredder now, or being burned as we speak." A hot flush of failure prickles up my neck. We were so close! Close enough to smell her perfume and hear every mortifying noise.

"Absolute disaster," David whispers. "But we need to go. We've been here too long."

He's right, so we slip out into the corridor and make our escape, my legs still trembling from both the cramped position and the sheer mortification of what I just endured.

I really hope Robbie appreciates what we've gone through for him. Because some things, once seen—or heard—can't be forgotten.

Ever.

CHAPTER TWENTY-ONE

ROBBIE

Cat's phone sits on the kitchen table, its screen lit up with photos of Samantha's financial mess. David and Cat are recounting their adventure at the resort while I pace. I can't seem to shake this jittery energy, like I've necked five espressos.

"So, let me get this straight." I force myself to stop and lean back against the counter. "You actually hid under the desk while Samantha and some bloke . . ." I trail off, unable to keep a smirk from my lips.

Cat groans and buries her face in her hands. "Don't remind me. I'm going to need therapy."

"It wasn't great for me either," David says. "I had to listen to the whole thing while crammed in a cupboard, being prodded in the ribs by an overly amorous mop."

I snort and grab one of the cakes I bought while they were risking arrest on my behalf. The sugar rush is probably the last thing I need right now, but fuck it. For the first time since I found that ring in my locker, I feel like I might actually have a shot at clearing my name.

David picks one up too. "Decided to treat us, did you?"

"Well, while you two were playing James Bond, I was stuck here climbing the walls. Figured the least I could do was provide post-mission sustenance."

Cat reaches for a chocolate cupcake and peels the wrapper back. When she takes a bite, a smudge of frosting gets on the tip of her nose. My fingers twitch with the urge to wipe it away, but I resist. Barely.

"So, these bills," I say instead, tapping one of the photos on Cat's phone. "They definitely show she's in financial trouble?"

Cat nods, still chewing. "Serious trouble. Credit card debt, final notices, even a letter from a debt collection agency. And yet she's still buying designer handbags and booking spa weekends."

"Living beyond her means," David adds, reaching out and wiping the frosting from Cat's dainty wee nose. "Classic motive for theft."

I lean closer to examine the photos more carefully, and my shoulder brushes against Cat's. The contact sends a jolt through me that I pretend not to notice.

"And you're sure the note you saw had Ashford's name on it?" I ask. "The guest who lost the watch?"

"Positive," Cat says. "And your initials too. RM, several times."

My stomach tightens. "Can't be a coincidence."

"But without the actual note . . ." David doesn't bother finishing the thought. Doesn't need to. We're all thinking the same thing.

"I know." Cat's shoulders slump. "I should have grabbed it when I had the chance."

"Hey." I catch her gaze. "You did brilliant. Both of you. Most folk would've bottled it, but you went through with it, and you got these photos."

"They establish motive," David says. "But we still need to prove she actually took the items."

I run a hand through my hair. "And that she framed me. Cat, can you tell me more about the man? Anything you can remember might help."

Cat wrinkles her nose, thinking. "I didn't see much. Just his legs, really. Navy work trousers. Plain, nothing fancy."

Something clicks in my head. Navy trousers? Not the tartan ones most of the staff wear? The maintenance team wear navy trousers. They're more practical.

The conversation I had with Drew just before everything went to shit floods back to me. He asked if I'd ever considered hooking up with another staff member. Even mentioned Samantha. What was it he said?

"She's always giving you the stink eye. Maybe she's just mad because she wants you."

Christ. Was he fishing? Trying to find out if I was interested in Samantha because *he* was already involved with her?

And if he and Samantha *are* screwing, then . . . might Drew also have been involved with the thefts?

No way. Drew and I get on well. He was one of the few people at the resort I actually liked. He wouldn't betray me. Would he?

Then again, I haven't heard from him since I was suspended. I assumed he'd been warned off, like Johnny, but what if he's been avoiding me because he feels guilty?

"Robbie?" Cat's voice pulls me from my thoughts. "You've gone quiet."

"Aye. Just thinking. Navy trousers narrows it down."

"To who?" David asks.

"Well . . . maintenance staff, mostly. But there are a few of us.

Big resort, you know." I decide to keep my suspicions about Drew to myself, at least for now. No point throwing accusations around until I've considered it a bit more.

Cat polishes off her cupcake and reaches for another. "Stress eating," she explains when she catches me watching her. "Being an accidental voyeur really works up an appetite."

David lets out a snort just as his phone chimes. He checks it then stands up. "That's Johnny. He's home now—finished his shift at the resort. I should probably head back." He glances at Cat. "You heading out too or sticking around?"

Cat hesitates, her eyes flicking to mine. "I might stay a bit longer, if that's okay?"

I shrug, aiming for casual. "Fine by me."

David gives me an amused look that I choose to ignore. "Well, then. I'll leave you two to . . . discuss the case."

He winks at Cat, who rolls her eyes but smiles. After thanking him again for his help, we see him to the door.

Once his car disappears down the dirt track, Cat and I are left alone. The cottage suddenly feels smaller, more intimate.

"Cup of tea?" I offer, keen for something to do with my hands.

"Sure." Cat follows me back to the kitchen and drops back into her seat while I fill the kettle. I can feel her watching me as I move around, pulling out mugs and teabags. "So," she says after a bit. "Your maw."

I pause, my back to her. "What about her?"

"When we were at the clootie well, you mentioned she treated you differently from Johnny. David filled in some gaps today, about how she was young when she had you, how she felt trapped."

171

I turn slowly and lean back against the counter. "Did he now?"

"I'm just trying to understand you better." Cat's voice is soft, lacking the flirtatious edge of our earlier interactions. "After everything today, don't you think I've earned a little trust?"

The kettle clicks off. I pour water into the mugs, buying myself some time. "What do you want to know?" I ask finally.

"Did she really blame you for everything?"

I hand her a mug and take a seat across from her at the table. "Pretty much. If Johnny broke something, it was my fault for not watching him properly. If the house was a mess, it was because I was too destructive. If she was unhappy . . ." I trail off and take a sip of tea.

"And your da?"

"Never took my side. Not once." The bitterness in my voice surprises even me. "Still doesn't."

Cat studies me over the rim of her mug. "And that's why this accusation hits you so hard? Because it's happening all over again—being blamed for something you didn't do?"

I stare at her, surprised by her insight. "Aye. Something like that."

She reaches across the table and places her hand over mine. The touch is gentle, undemanding. "We're going to fix this, Robbie. I promise."

"I know." And I do. Somehow, this woman who bounced into my life with her dimples and her ridiculous flirting has become one of the few people I actually trust.

Cat withdraws her hand, but her eyes stay on mine. "About the knickers David spotted in your garage . . ."

The abrupt change of subject catches me off-guard. "What about them?"

"When David mentioned them yesterday, I thought you were going to combust from embarrassment." A smile plays at the corners of her mouth. "What exactly have you been doing with them, Robbie MacDonald?"

Images flash through my mind—her on her knees in the woods, the silky fabric pressed to my face, my hand wrapped around myself in the darkness of my bedroom. I clear my throat. "I thought we'd moved past this."

"Past what?"

"This." I gesture vaguely between us. "The flirting. The games."

"Who says I'm playing games?" Cat's voice drops lower, and she leans forwards slightly. "Maybe I just like you."

I snort. "You don't even know me."

"I know more than you think," she counters. "I know you saved my brother's life. I know you gave up fighting after you saw death up close. I know you're talented at repairing things that seem broken beyond saving." She pauses, her eyes meeting mine with unexpected intensity. "And I know you're not the bad boy everyone thinks you are."

I look away, uncomfortable with how accurately she's seeing me. "You don't give up, do you?"

"Not when I see something worth sticking around for."

There's a weight to her words that wasn't there before. When I meet her gaze again, the playfulness has been replaced by something more serious, more genuine.

For a moment, I consider closing the distance between us. Taking her face in my hands and kissing her until neither of us can breathe. But I hold back.

Because the truth is, I don't know if I could handle something casual with Cat. Once I've had a proper taste of her, I'm not sure I'll be able to share. And a woman like Cat—young, vibrant, with her whole life ahead of her—isn't looking to settle down with Bannock's resident fuck-up.

"It's getting late," I say instead. "And you've had a busy day. Don't want you driving home knackered."

Disappointment flashes across her face. She studies me, then she nods, taking the hint. "Didn't even have a chance to finish this." She has a final swig of tea. "But you're right, I am tired." She stands. "Will you be at my flat tomorrow? To continue the work?"

"Aye. I'll be there." I walk her to the door.

She pauses on the threshold, looking up at me with those hazel eyes that see too much. "See you tomorrow, then."

"See you tomorrow."

I watch her walk to her car, fighting the urge to call her back. She drives off, but the energy between us lingers in the air, crackling and restless.

CHAPTER TWENTY-TWO

CAT

As I unlock my front door, the distinctive thump of heavy bass greets me, along with the sharp tang of fresh paint. I dump my bag of marking in the hall then open the living room door, only to stop short.

Wow, what a transformation! The walls are covered in fresh white emulsion, making the space feel bigger and brighter.

Robbie has his back to me, his old jeans and vest dotted with flecks of white. Apparently, he's not heard me over his music yet, so I take the opportunity to admire him. There's something mesmerising about the way he moves, each stroke of the roller in sync with the pounding heavy metal blaring from his little speaker. And honestly, if there's a more perfect sight than Robbie MacDonald's arse in worn jeans, I've yet to see it.

He must sense my presence because he turns. His eyes flick over my work outfit—fitted pinstripe trousers and a grey blouse—before meeting mine. "Afternoon, Cat."

And there it is, that energy crackling between us, the same electricity I felt yesterday in his kitchen when I basically told him I was developing feelings.

Just as I'm getting lost in that electric pull, Robbie leans over, turns down the speaker, then nods at the freshly painted walls. "What do you think?"

I walk further in and give him what I hope is a casual smile, even though my pulse is anything but calm. "I love it! You've done a brilliant job. It looks amazing in here."

"Amazing might be pushing it, but it's getting there." With the toe of an old trainer, he nudges the worn and threadbare carpet. "Wait till I rip this thing up and buff the original floors. Then you'll really think it looks good."

I give the room another once-over, this time taking an even closer look at Robbie's handiwork. The walls, now smooth from his plastering and gleaming with fresh paint, are barely recognisable.

Robbie grabs the hem of his vest and uses it to wipe a smear of emulsion from his forearm, unwittingly flashing me a tantalising glimpse of his abs. "I'd like to finish this room before I call it a day, but there's still a fair bit left of the second coat to do. Do you mind if I stay on a while? Shouldn't be more than an hour or two."

"Of course," I say, perhaps a little too eagerly. "Can I help? Four hands are better than two, right?"

Robbie arches an eyebrow but then gives an easy shrug. "Suit yourself, but . . ." His eyes flick down to my blouse, lingering just a heartbeat too long before he glances away. "You might want to throw on something you don't mind ruining."

"Give me two minutes."

In my bedroom I change quickly into a pair of old grey joggers and a faded T-shirt that's seen better days, then twist my hair up into a messy bun. When I return to the living room, Robbie has a second paint tray filled, with a spare roller beside it.

"You ever painted a room before?"

"Honestly? No," I admit, a tad embarrassed. Any time something needed done at the hotel, Da or one of my brothers handled it. If I so much as picked up a paintbrush, they'd shoo me away like an annoying wee fly.

"Right. Well, there's a bit of a technique to it," Robbie says, without judgement. He takes the roller, dips it into the tray, then rolls it back and forth on the ridged part until the paint is evenly coated. "Don't overload it. You want it covered, not dripping."

He steps up to the wall. "Start in the middle and work out like this." He makes a large W shape with smooth, practised strokes. "Then go back over it to fill in the gaps and even it out. It stops streaks and gives you good coverage."

He hands me the roller, his expression encouraging. "Your turn."

I copy him as best I can, but after half a minute, he shakes his head. "Not quite." He steps in behind me, placing his big hand over mine, and suddenly I'm cocooned in his heat, that spicy, masculine Robbie smell curling around me.

"Like this," he says, guiding the motion, firm but gentle. The roller glides across the wall like magic.

"Got it?" His breath tickles my ear.

"I think so," I manage, even though my mind is *far* more focused on the feel of his body than painting techniques.

He steps back and I immediately miss his warmth. "Good. You keep working on this bit, and I'll finish up over here." He moves over to another wall.

I'd much rather work side by side, but maybe this is safer. Less chance of getting distracted by those tattooed arms of his flexing with every paint stroke.

For a few minutes, we work in companionable quiet, the

steady thrum of rock music and the swoosh of our rollers filling the space. But after a while, I decide this is the perfect opportunity to learn a bit more about Robbie.

"So, did you always know you wanted to do this sort of hands-on stuff?"

"Suppose I just kind of fell into it. Wasn't much of an academic at school, but I liked the practical classes, especially woodwork."

"Right, but how'd you go from *that* to being good at, like, everything?"

"I wouldn't say I can do *everything*."

"Says the man who completely renovated his own home."

Robbie rubs the back of his neck with his free hand, and for a second, he seems almost bashful. He's clearly not used to compliments.

"Aye, well, I did a few apprenticeships after school—never really stuck with one long enough to call it a proper trade, mind." He shrugs. "But I probably picked up most of my skills at the resort. There's always something breaking there. Leaky taps, temperamental heating systems, fancy light fixtures going on the blink . . . in maintenance, you learn quick or drown in work orders."

I'm tempted to ask if there's any part of him that misses his role at the resort, but I don't want to drag him into heavy chat. Instead I say, "Your love of woodwork obviously stayed with you after school. Those shelves you built for your living room are gorgeous."

"Och, that's just me fiddling about in my free time." Once again, he's playing things down.

"Well, if society ever breaks down and we're flung into a post-apocalyptic world, you'll be sorted with your survival skills.

Meanwhile, my contribution will be—what? Reciting sonnets by the campfire?"

He snorts. "I suppose someone will need to educate the roaming hordes. You could give them lessons in literature, spread civilisation one Shakespearean reference at a time." He points his roller at me, mock serious. "Never forget, McIntyre. The pen is mightier than the sword."

I grin at him. "Was that Robbie MacDonald giving me an actual compliment?"

"Don't get used to it."

AC/DC takes over the conversation, filling the room with "Thunderstruck". Robbie moves closer to me and tops up both trays. We load up our rollers with fresh paint and push on.

It strikes me how different our interactions have been recently. Days ago, all I saw was Bannock's bad boy—a thrill to chase, a conquest to make. Now I see a man who's been misjudged his whole life. Someone more thoughtful, talented, and vulnerable than his reputation suggests.

And I care about that man.

"You're quiet," Robbie observes, breaking into my thoughts. "For a change."

"Just thinking."

"Care to share?"

I'm thinking about how yesterday I told Robbie I liked him, and instead of kissing me, he said it was late and time for me to go. And I'm thinking that, thanks to the way I acted around him at first, I may have blown any chance of something romantic happening between us.

But instead of saying what's in my head, I go with, "Oh, I was just thinking about the case. About Samantha and her mystery man. Any guesses who it could be?"

Robbie pauses. "Aye, I have an idea. But if it's who I think it is, that's a real kick in the balls."

"Oh?" I pause too. "Who do you think it is?"

"Not now," Robbie says, tension growing in his jaw. "I've been trying to treat the painting like therapy. Trying *not* to think about it."

Respecting his wishes, I let the matter drop.

We move onto the last wall, Muse's "Super Massive Black Hole" filling the silence. We start at opposite ends and gradually work our way towards each other until we're painting shoulder to shoulder, so close I can feel the heat radiating off him.

Every so often, our arms and shoulders brush, sending tingles blooming across my skin. There's something about having Robbie next to me—his size, the way he fills the space—that makes me feel both utterly safe and completely on edge at the same time.

I don't want this to end, but all too soon Robbie steps back and surveys the walls with a critical eye. He nods. "That's us done for today."

He sets his roller down and wipes his hands on an old rag, taking the opportunity to put a bit of polite space between us. And just like that, the bubble we were in bursts. Suddenly it's just me, him, and four damp walls.

I stand there clutching my roller, wishing I could think of some excuse to keep him here. Anything to stretch these moments out. But nothing comes.

"Is it all right if I nip to the bathroom first to wash up?" Robbie asks, already edging towards the door. "Then I'll get out of your hair."

"Aye, of course." I try not to sound as deflated as I feel.

He disappears, and I busy myself fiddling with paint trays and pretending to tidy up, but really I'm just listening out for his footsteps and desperately hoping he won't leave the moment he's rinsed off the worst of the paint.

Time drags. Rationally, I know he's only washing his hands, but it feels like ages. Finally he appears again in the doorway, just long enough to give me a nod before stepping aside for me to take my turn. Again, he's careful to keep a bit of distance between us.

I duck into the bathroom and attack my hands with soap like they've personally offended me. A sinking feeling settles below my ribs, the kind you get when you reach the end of a good party and everyone else goes home but you're not ready for it to be over.

Through the open bathroom door—did I leave it like that as an invitation?—I hear the music being turned off and the sounds of Robbie gathering his things. He's getting ready to leave. Just as I'm reaching for the towel, his footsteps enter the hall.

"Well, I'll be off, then," he calls. "See you tomorrow?"

"Aye . . . see you tomorrow."

I'm expecting to hear the clunk of the front door, but instead there's a soft tread outside the bathroom, and I glimpse movement in the mirror. Robbie fills the doorway behind me, one hand braced against the frame.

"I just wanted to say . . . oh, hang on. You missed some." He steps closer and wets his thumb under the tap, then wipes it gently across my cheek, sending a jolt straight through me. "That's better."

I meet his eyes in the glass—so blue they look almost unreal—and my heart gives an unhelpful flutter.

"Do I have any more on me?" My voice comes out softer than I mean it to.

"Don't think so . . ." He bends slightly to get a closer look, and his gaze lingers on my lips for half a second too long. I swear he's about to close the gap, but he doesn't.

God. If I have to go on waiting for him to make a move, I'm going to explode. So I do what I do best: I throw caution out the window. Rising onto my tiptoes, I press my lips to his.

For the briefest second, it feels awkward—a fumble of noses, a rush of want—then heat blooms under my skin. But just as I'm starting to melt into him, Robbie jerks back, his jaw clenched, his eyes dark with something that looks like hunger.

"Cat." His voice is rough. "If this goes any further, I won't be able to hold back. As soon as I've got you in my hands, I'm going to want to taste you . . . fuck you. And it won't be gentle."

A delicious shiver dances down my spine at the crassness of his words. "I can handle you," I say, trying like hell to sound cool and not as desperate as I feel.

Robbie's pupils dilate, nearly swallowing the icy blue. But still he hesitates. "Your big brothers won't be happy."

"I don't care. This is between us. Just . . . kiss me already."

Robbie growls, then he pulls me towards him, his mouth crashing against mine.

The smell of him—paint, sweat, and that dark, masculine note—fills my senses as he kisses me deeply, his tongue ploughing into my mouth, demanding and dominant. His large hands slide down my back to grip my backside, and I press closer to him, feeling him thickening against me. My body responds instantly— hot, wet, aching for him—and the sound that escapes me is half-moan, half-surrender as I lose myself in the sheer power of him.

When he breaks the kiss, his eyes are molten. "Take off your top."

I've never removed an item of clothing so fast in all my life.

He runs a hand over his mouth, his eyes lingering on the

freckles across my chest, my heaving cleavage, and my hardened nipples beneath my bra.

"Last chance to back out."

"I don't want to."

"Then let your hair down."

I do, auburn waves tumbling around my shoulders. I feel a flash of vulnerability, standing here half-naked, my cheeks flushed. But Robbie reaches out and brushes a loose strand from my cheek, gentle as anything.

"You're beautiful, Cat." He says it like it's the most obvious thing in the world, and for once I'm speechless.

His voice turns rougher. "Take off the bra."

I do, letting it drop to the floor.

He looks at me—really looks. His eyes roam over my bare skin, lingering on my chest in a way that makes my nipples tighten even more. The heat in his gaze is almost as tangible as a touch. Only when I'm squirming under the weight of it does he finally reach out and cup me in both hands, his thumbs grazing over my nipples. I gasp and arch into him.

"Quite the handful you've got here, McIntyre," he murmurs, making even my surname sound sexy.

He sits on the edge of the bath and pulls me close, and suddenly his hot mouth is on my breasts, his stubble brushing exquisitely against my bare skin. He licks, nips, and sucks at my nipples until I'm trembling all over.

I bury my fingers into his black hair, surprised by how silky and smooth it feels. He lets my right nipple go with a pop then sits back to examine the results of his handiwork—my breasts now pink, the nipples redder from his attention. It's like he's marking me in some way. It's the sexiest thing I've ever experienced.

He stands and pushes me firmly against the bathroom wall, the cool surface a stark contrast to his heated body. Then he steps back and eyes me with a commanding look that has me ready to do anything he wants. I'm basically putty in his hands. It's like that night in the woods, when he took control so decisively and left me aching for more.

He pulls his vest over his head in one swift motion, revealing his broad chest. His nipple ring glints in the bathroom light, and those mesmerising tattoos snake across his skin like secret stories. I drink in the sight of him, not knowing where to focus first.

My eyes trace the raven on his left biceps, wings raised as if about to take flight from a branch. A chain with a broken link wraps around his upper chest, its detailed metalwork appearing almost three-dimensional against his skin. On the side of his neck, a belladonna flower blooms. Beautiful but dangerous, just like the man himself.

I reach out to touch the chain, but Robbie growls and grabs my wrists—first one, then the other—and pins them over my head with one big hand. His eyes lock on mine—hungry and intense—and I go utterly still, savouring every delicious moment of surrender.

Robbie's mouth claims mine again, fierce and hungry, his erection pressing insistently against my lower abdomen, the tension between us almost unbearable. But when I writhe closer, he pulls away, leaving me aching. I whimper in protest.

And then . . . his hand slips inside my joggers. "Christ, Cat, you're soaked," he groans in my ear. His thumb circles my clit, his fingers sinking into me. "So tight. You're going to squeeze my cock like a vice once it's inside you."

The combination of his words and touch sends me over the

edge. I clench around his fingers, my body shuddering with release.

Robbie looks down where his hand disappears between my legs. "Wait, Cat . . . are you . . . ?"

Rather than respond with words—couldn't if I wanted to—I cry out. Robbie watches my face, mesmerised.

"I-I didn't mean to," I gasp, the aftershocks rippling through me. Honestly, I didn't even know it was possible to come that quickly with someone. Guess there's a first time for everything.

Robbie releases my wrists and slips his fingers from inside me. "Never apologise for coming, Cat." He kisses me softly, then drops to his knees.

My breath catches. "What are you doing?"

He yanks my joggers and knickers down. "Going to eat you out, obviously."

"But . . . I've just come!" I protest, half laughing, half shocked.

"And you're going to do so again," Robbie says matter-of-factly, more to my pussy than me. He hooks a leg over his shoulder then buries his face between my thighs.

His tongue is hot and hungry on me, flicking over my already sensitised clit with a skill that turns my legs to jelly. I gasp, one hand fisting his hair, the other gripping the sink for balance.

"Oh, Robbie . . . yes!" The sounds tumbling out of me are unfiltered: breathless whimpers, desperate pleas.

"Christ, you taste good," he mutters before diving back in. His hands keep my hips pinned against the wall exactly where he wants me while his mouth works me relentlessly.

Clearly, he's been craving me far more than I realised.

His tongue and lips don't let up for another half minute, until I'm shamelessly writhing against him.

"Are you close again, Catriona?" The way he says my full name sends another wave of heat through me. All I can do is nod frantically.

"Next time you come," he rasps, standing, "I'm going to be inside you."

God above. If it's possible to combust just from anticipation, I'm about to go up in smoke.

Robbie unbuttons his jeans and pushes them down, revealing black boxer briefs stretched tight over muscular thighs—and even tighter over the impressive bulge straining at the front. Then his boxers join the jeans on the floor, leaving him gloriously naked. My eyes settle on his massive erection with that glinting piercing.

"Please," I whisper, "let me touch you."

His eyes hood with lust. "Aye. Touch me, lass."

But instead of going straight for what's standing proud between his legs, my fingers trace the chain tattoo across his chest. He shivers under my touch, a reaction I hadn't expected from someone so commanding. I let my fingertips drift over to his nipple piercing, then down the ridges of his abdomen, following the grooves and dips of his muscles before finally reaching his cock.

The piercing glints at me, wicked and tempting, and I can't resist running a thumb around it, just to see how he reacts this time. Robbie's hips jerk forwards—almost involuntarily—his breath coming out in a ragged growl. Emboldened, I wrap my hand around him properly, revelling in the weight and heat of him, the way he pulses faintly in my grip. And his skin—so soft over all that hard steel beneath.

Robbie hisses and captures my wrist. "Enough," he says firmly.

In one powerful movement, he lifts me up and presses my

back against the wall. I wrap my legs around his waist, and the tip of his cock nudges my entrance, the cool metal of his piercing making me shiver.

"Now, McIntyre," Robbie says, his voice strained, "please tell me you're on birth control. I never normally do this without protection, but I'm clean and want to feel all of you."

I nod eagerly, trying my best to squirm against him. "Clean too, and on the pill."

I've barely finished speaking when he pushes inside me in one swift motion. I gasp at the stretch. He's big enough that it takes a moment for my body to adjust. His piercing touches the deepest place at my core, sending shock waves of pleasure through me. It's an alien feeling, but so fucking good.

Robbie slides out then in again, setting a relentless pace from the start. The musky scent of our sex fills the small bathroom, and I moan loudly with each thrust.

"So tight," Robbie growls against my neck, his breath ragged.

He pounds me so hard it blots out everything else. All I can do is hold on while he slams into me again and again, tension building inside me. Our bodies are slick with sweat now, every muscle straining towards something wild and inevitable.

I'm right there on the edge when Robbie suddenly squeezes my hips hard. His jaw clenches, our eyes meet—a flash of heat and vulnerability—and then I tumble headlong into oblivion. The orgasm rips through me, sharp and sweet, and I shatter around him, crying out louder than I knew I could. Robbie's right there with me, jerking deep inside me, hot and desperate.

For a while afterwards, all I can do is cling to him, our bodies trembling in the aftermath, Robbie's heart thundering against my chest. He presses his forehead to mine, eyes closed, breathing deeply. When he opens them, they're raw and unguarded.

"You okay?" he asks.

I nod, not quite trusting my voice yet. I feel . . . claimed. Marked. Thoroughly and completely satisfied in a way I've never experienced before.

He pulls out and sets me down. My knees wobble treacherously, but before I can fall, he scoops me up, one arm under my knees and the other supporting my back. He carries me through to my bed and lays me down, then he leans over me and brushes a strand of hair behind my ear.

"I should . . ." he begins, then trails off, as if unsure what comes next.

I press a soft kiss to his lips. "Stay," I whisper. "At least for a bit."

At first I think he might refuse. But then he nods and lies down beside me, pulling me close as if he's not quite ready to let go of the moment either.

CHAPTER TWENTY-THREE

CAT

It's funny how a man who radiates a certain kind of danger can make you feel so safe.

I lie across Robbie's chest, my fingers tracing the intricate Celtic knotwork spiralling up his right arm. His heartbeat thuds beneath my cheek, calm and steady—a rhythm I could happily get used to.

I wander my fingertips across his warm skin, now skimming the rugged silhouette of a Highland landscape along his ribs. "What was it you wanted to tell me earlier?" I ask, tracing the peaks and valleys.

"Earlier?" There's a sleepy heat to his voice.

"You came back to the bathroom when I was washing up. Looked like you had something important to say."

"Oh." He yawns, his chest rumbling softly beneath my cheek. "I was just going to ask if I could rip up the carpets tomorrow."

"Didn't we already agree on that?"

"Aye. Oh, all right, I just wanted an excuse to keep talking to you."

Something fizzy and ridiculous bubbles up inside me, and I

lift my head to look at him. "I never thought I'd say this, but I'm kind of grateful for those fusty old carpets."

He flashes me a roguish grin then gives a wee shiver when my wandering finger grazes over his nipple ring. "You're trouble, you know that?"

"Aye, I know. So, tell me, which piercing came first?" I circle the cool little hoop with my fingertip, deliberately brushing his nipple at the same time.

"Eyebrow. Got it when I was sixteen. Nipple at nineteen. The other one at twenty-two."

I glance down at "the other one", still a bit in awe of what I experienced. "Did it hurt? Getting that one done, I mean."

"Did it hurt getting your nose done?"

He taps the little stud at my left nostril. So, naturally, I reach down and give *that* piercing a gentle tap back. He jolts, just the tiniest bit, like I've sent a current through him.

"That isn't the same," I say. "A nose and a cock? There's just no comparison. I didn't flinch when you prodded my nose. If I had a clit piercing, though . . . well, we could compare notes then."

Robbie's eyes darken. "The mouth on you, McIntyre. You ever stop to think what it does to a man, hearing you talk like that?"

"Oh, I know exactly what it does." I wink.

There's a gruff sort of scoff from deep in his chest. "To answer your earlier question, aye, it hurt. Quite a bit, actually." He shrugs, all casual, as if getting a hole punched through your bits is no big deal. "But once it healed . . ." His lips curl into something wicked. "Let's just say sex, which was incredible before, became something else entirely."

The thought of him using this . . . personal upgrade on other women has a flare of possessiveness sizzling through me.

"So?" His gaze sharpens with interest, and my jealousy quickly dissipates. "What did *you* think?"

"I liked it," I admit. "As in, *really* liked it. It heightened everything."

Something primal flashes across Robbie's face—male satisfaction that he's given me a first experience. And he has. I'm deliciously sore in the best way, my body still humming with memories of him everywhere.

I nestle my head back against his chest, breathing in the warm, salty-spicy scent of his skin. For some long, blissful moments, neither of us says a word. There's only our steady breathing and the gentle thump of his heart beneath my ear. Robbie's fingers slide through my hair in slow, lazy strokes that make me melt even further into him. I want to stay like this all night, tangled up with him, safe and warm and far away from anything or anyone else.

But after a few more minutes of perfect, contented silence, Robbie shifts. With an almost apologetic half-smile, he gently extracts himself from under me.

"It's getting on," he says, sitting up and swinging his long legs over the side of the bed. He stands, and with his back to me, I get a good glimpse of the majestic stag tattoo spanning his shoulder blades. The antlers stretch wide, and the detail is exquisite. "I should go."

I reach for his arm. "Stay for dinner. I owe you a meal for staying late to work on my flat."

Robbie hesitates, looking over his shoulder at me then towards the door.

"Come on, it's just pizza. Frozen, but it'll save you cooking."

He relents with a small nod. "All right."

I wrap myself in a dressing gown, and Robbie asks if he can use my shower. Says he's got some paint-free clothes he can change into afterwards. I fetch him a towel, briefly entertaining the idea of asking to join him, but I dismiss it. Whatever that was between us just now, it was . . . a lot. We probably both need a breather—ten minutes or so to regroup.

So, instead, I go in after he's finished, and when I emerge, I feel almost like myself again. Or at least, as much as a woman can after being thoroughly ruined by Robbie MacDonald.

I find him sitting at my tiny kitchen table, in a clean white T-shirt, his hair still damp. He looks hot—ridiculously so—but I preferred him sprawled out naked on my sheets. Actually, scrap that. I preferred him sweaty, paint-smudged, and enthusiastically pounding into me. But this is fine too.

He's taken out the chicken pizza I put on, cut it up, and served it onto plates. Even raided my fridge and found that sad little bag of rocket and some cherry tomatoes, tossed them in olive oil and balsamic vinegar, and made a simple side salad. Got us each a glass of water too.

"Wow, this is great!" I say enthusiastically.

"Hmm. Don't take this the wrong way, but your fridge is tragic. This was the best I could do. Anyway, tuck in."

We both do.

"You know," I say after a few bites, "if we bump into Ally again, I can no longer claim you haven't laid a finger on me."

Robbie rolls his eyes but doesn't reply, just tears into another slice of pizza.

"Speaking of Ally—well, all my brothers, really—can I ask you something? Do you think there's an expiry date for being seen as the irresponsible wee sister? Or will they still view me that way that even when I'm ninety-two and zipping about on my mobility scooter?"

Robbie's lips twitch, but there's something thoughtful in his eyes. He swallows. "I'm probably not the best person to ask. People still see the version of me they remember from years ago, not who I am now. But your brothers' nagging and fussing? Well . . . it shows they care, right?"

I'm not quite sure what to say to that. The irony isn't lost on me—Robbie defending my brothers' interference when he and Ally spent half their teenage years scrapping like terriers. But he's got a point. They do care.

We eat some more, then Robbie takes a swig of water, his throat bobbing as he gulps it down. I'm momentarily distracted—not by the muscles working in his neck (although that's hardly an eyesore)—but by the belladonna tattoo peeking out just above his collarbone. I want to know more about his tattoos.

Leaving my last slice of pizza untouched, I stand, pad around the table, and swing a leg over his lap, settling myself astride him like it's the most natural thing in the world. He leans back, eyebrows rising like he's not sure whether to laugh or brace himself for impact.

"Take your top off."

He lets out a low chuckle but obliges, baring all that beautiful artwork for me to admire again. Earlier, I was too blissed out to ask questions, but not now.

"Good lad," I murmur, staring like the lech I am. "Talk me through each of these." I trace the raven on his biceps with one finger, following the sweep of its wings and the elegant curve of its beak.

"Well, that's a raven."

I swat at him playfully. "I know that. But why did you get it?"

He shrugs. "Thought it suited me. Dark and brooding."

Well, I can't argue with that.

"But also, ravens are adaptable. They survive when others don't."

"All right. And the broken chain?" My finger follows the tattoo that wraps around his upper chest, lingering on the link that's broken.

"That one's about my da."

I wait, giving him space to elaborate.

"Despite living in the same town and working at the same place, we've never . . . connected. I got that tattoo after a bad argument a few years back."

"What happened?"

"An issue with a guest, this entitled arsehole who kept making inappropriate comments to the female staff. I told him to back off, and he complained to management. My da called me into his office and tore into me without even asking me for my side of the story."

Robbie glances down at the chain. "Of course, I wouldn't have got inked just for that one incident, but . . . it was the straw that broke the camel's back."

My fingers itch to squeeze his hand, to offer him some kind of comfort, but before I get the chance, his phone buzzes on the table, slicing through the moment.

"Sorry." He reaches around me to grab it then scans the message that's come in. His brow furrows. "It's David." He turns the phone to show me.

Johnny overheard something earlier, and it's not good news. The police are nearly done with their investigation, and they still think it was you. If you've got a trick up your sleeve to clear your name, now is the time to play it!

"We need to do something," I say, still perched on Robbie's thighs, though the mood has shifted in a flash from intimate to mission-planning mode. "We need to sort this."

"Aye, but how?"

I think for a moment. "Earlier, when we were painting, I asked you who you thought Samantha is sleeping with, and you said you had an idea. Who do you suspect?"

"I was thinking it might be Drew Miller. Do you know him?"

"Hmm . . . I know the name."

"He stays a wee way outside Bannock, but he works at the resort. You've probably seen him around town before."

Robbie takes a few minutes to fill me in on why he suspects Drew, and afterwards, we agree Robbie should go straight to Drew's place and speak to him. If Drew *is* sleeping with Samantha, he might know something about the thefts. He might even have been involved in them, though Robbie hopes not. He claims Drew's "one of the good guys".

I offer to go with Robbie, but Robbie reckons Drew will be more likely to talk if it's just him.

"All right, well . . ." I give his nipple ring a cheeky tap. "You'd best put your top back on before you go. And come back here afterwards, please. I want to know how things go. Also, I know you're *so* much older than me, but if you've got the stamina for it, we could always go another round."

In one swift motion—far too practised, if you ask me—he

flips me over so I'm sprawled across his lap, like some saucy damsel on the cover of a historical romance novel. My leggings and knickers are tugged down before I can even pretend to protest.

He delivers a sharp (but not too sharp) skelp to my bare arse. I yelp—more surprised than pained—but laughter is already threatening to burst out of me.

"I've warned you several times to watch that mouth of yours, McIntyre." He slaps my arse again, this time a wee bit harder.

"Ooft!" I wiggle on his lap, trying—and failing—to sound affronted as warmth spreads, well . . . everywhere. He spanks me once more, the sting blooming across my skin. I bite down on a giggle, loving the way every nerve ending fires at his touch. God, who knew this would be such a turn-on? And if this is my punishment for winding him up, I might just have to misbehave more often.

"I've been wanting to do that for days." His voice is rough with desire. "Still think I'm past it?" He gives one cheek a possessive squeeze.

"Prove you're not later," I challenge.

"Oh, I will."

His fingers sneak between my legs, and I moan.

"I'll be back soon, and I expect you to be wet and ready for me. Understood?"

I nod, biting my lip because words have deserted me.

He withdraws his fingers, cracks off another spank, and I damn near purr.

CHAPTER TWENTY-FOUR

ROBBIE

The countryside blurs past as my motorcycle thunders down the narrow road, each bend bringing me closer to answers, or so I hope. I push thoughts of Cat—her laugh, her touch, her taste—to the back of my mind. I need a clear head for this.

Drew lives in a small hamlet about fifteen minutes outside Bannock, just a handful of stone cottages clustered around a crossroads, with sheep dotting the surrounding hills. The sun hangs low in the sky as I approach, casting long shadows across the landscape.

His car sits in the small gravel drive, confirming he's home. I come to a stop and cut the engine, swing my leg over, remove my helmet, and take a moment to gather my thoughts. This conversation could go several ways, and I need to play it right.

Three sharp knocks on his door. Footsteps approach from inside, then the door swings open.

"Robbie?" Drew's eyebrows shoot up. "What brings you out here?" He's in jeans and a faded T-shirt, his hair a little unruly.

"Just thought I'd check in," I say with a casual shrug. "Been a while."

"Aye . . . of course." Drew hesitates just long enough to make me wonder if he'd rather I weren't here. "Come in, mate."

I follow him into his small living room. It's neater than I remember. When I was last here—helping him lug in a new washing machine—empty beer cans littered the coffee table and his gaming stuff was sprawled across the floor. Now everything has been tidied away, the surfaces wiped clean. There's even a vase of fresh flowers.

"Place is looking good. I didn't take you for the floral type."

Drew follows my gaze and laughs, though it sounds a touch forced. "Ah, well. Trying to make an effort to appear civilised these days. Beer?"

"On the bike," I say, settling into an armchair.

"Right, aye. Tea? Water?"

"I'm good."

Drew perches on the edge of the sofa opposite, his posture oddly stiff for someone in his own living room. "So . . . how've you been? This whole situation is crazy."

"Been better," I say flatly. "You?"

"Can't complain. Listen, mate, I'm sorry I haven't been in touch. Your da made it pretty clear we weren't supposed to contact you." He drums his fingers against his knee. "Also, this is awkward, but I've got to say it. I've . . . been promoted. To your old position."

I keep my expression neutral, though something twists in my gut. "Makes sense. You know the ropes."

"Aye, well, the circumstances are shite. Nobody believes you actually did it, you know."

"Nobody?"

"Okay, maybe not *nobody*. But I don't, and Johnny doesn't. Anyway . . ." He attempts a grin, though it doesn't quite reach his eyes. "You just here for a social call? If you fancy a game night, I'd be more than happy to hand your arse to you in FIFA."

His attempt at our usual banter almost makes me smile. Almost.

"Actually," I say, leaning forwards, "I was hoping to pick your brain about something."

"Oh?"

"Samantha."

The change is subtle—a shift in his posture, a twitch in his jaw—but it's there.

"What about her?"

"She still riding your arse about maintenance requests?"

Drew laughs, and this time it sounds genuine. "When isn't she? Woman's a bloody nightmare. Always finding something that needs fixed five minutes before my shift ends."

"Do you remember what you and I were talking about the day I quit?"

"Hmm. Remind me?"

"You asked if I'd ever hook up with another staff member."

"Did I? Just making conversation, I guess."

"And specifically, you mentioned Samantha." I pause. "I should really have asked you the same question, shouldn't I?"

"Christ, Robbie." He swallows. "What are you suggesting? That I'm sleeping with Samantha? That's mad."

I glance pointedly at the flowers, then back at him. "Is it?"

"Those are just—" He stops himself, and for a moment, the friendly mask slips. I see calculation behind his eyes. Then he sighs, his shoulders slumping. "Fuck's sake. How did you know?"

"I didn't. Not for sure anyway, at least not until just now."

He huffs out a laugh and shakes his head. "Remind me never to play poker with you."

I shrug, not bothering to hide my satisfaction. "So. You and Samantha."

Drew scrubs a palm over his jaw. "It just . . . happened. We were both working late, and . . . well, it's not like we planned it."

"How long?"

"Couple of months. We've been keeping it quiet. Your da has that whole thing about workplace relationships."

I nod, processing this. "And the thefts? What do you know about those?"

His brows knit together in confusion. "Nothing. Wait, why would—" His jaw drops a little. "What are you suggesting?"

"Honestly, Drew? I think Samantha framed me, and I'm trying to figure out if you were in on it or not."

"What the fuck?" He springs up like he's been stung. "Christ, Robbie, that's a serious accusation. You know I wouldn't do that. And Samantha? She wouldn't either."

"Wouldn't she? She's never liked me. And as for you . . . well, that was a nice wee promotion you got. Quite convenient I'm out of the picture, right?"

His face flushes. "Piss off! It's not like that. I didn't steal anything, and Samantha's been at the resort for years! Why would she risk it all now?"

"Money troubles after the divorce? Revenge because I turned her down when she made a pass at me?"

He gapes, momentarily lost for words. "She *what*?"

"Happened last year. I wasn't interested, and she didn't take it well."

He sinks back onto the sofa. "She never said anything about that."

"I bet there's a lot she hasn't told you. But you're right, she's been at the resort a long time. Which means she knows how everything works. And *that* puts her in the perfect position to pull off something like this. Have a think. Has she been acting strange lately? Nervous? Jumpy?"

He hesitates, and I can see him mentally replaying recent interactions. "She *has* been a bit . . . fidgety. Snapping at folk more than usual. Barely saying a word otherwise."

"When did that start?"

"I don't know, a few weeks ago? That's around the time of the first theft, I suppose, but that could just be coincidence."

"Anything else you can think of that's out of the ordinary for her?"

Drew frowns. "She went into Inverness last Monday. Wouldn't tell me why—said it was personal. I didn't push it."

Hmm. Could a trip to Inverness be relevant somehow?

"What time did she go?"

"Afternoon. Took a half day." Drew studies me. "You really think she's behind this, don't you?"

"I know *I* didn't steal those items. Someone set me up, and Samantha had motive, means, and opportunity."

Drew presses his lips together, staring at a spot on the carpet like it might offer up answers. "I don't know, Robbie. It's hard to believe."

"Harder to believe than me becoming a thief after years of honest work?"

He winces. "Fair point."

"Look, I'm not asking you to spy on your girlfriend or whatever she is. But keep your eyes open, aye? If you notice anything suspicious—anything at all—let me know."

He nods slowly. "I can do that. But what if you're wrong about her?"

"Then no harm done. But what if I'm right?"

This gives him pause. "All right. If I notice anything weird, I'll message you."

"Thanks, mate. Anyway, I'll be off." I stand and he walks me to the door, where I clap him on the shoulder. "Well, be careful. Because if she did frame me, who knows what else she's capable of?"

Outside, the evening air has cooled. I settle myself on my motorcycle, my mind racing. Drew seemed genuinely surprised by my accusation against Samantha, so I'm inclined to believe he wasn't involved. But his revelation about her being on edge? That only makes me even more certain she's behind this.

I fire up the engine.

Now I just need to figure out how to prove Samantha's guilt before the police decide they have enough evidence to charge me.

CHAPTER TWENTY-FIVE

CAT

My flat feels unnaturally quiet as I pace around and check my phone for the hundredth time. The newly painted walls of the living room gleam pristine white in the evening light.

Where is he? It's been well over an hour since he left to confront Drew.

I've tried distracting myself with lesson planning, but my mind keeps circling back to Robbie. To the way he told me about the stories etched into his skin, a rare flash of vulnerability beneath his tough exterior. To how it felt when he was inside me, his body moving against mine . . . and then afterwards, when we lay together, my head resting on his chest . . .

Christ, I've got it bad.

The growl of a motorcycle cuts through my thoughts. I rush to the window in time to see Robbie pulling up on the street below. My heart does a wee flip at the sight of him climbing off his bike.

My front door is wide open before I even hear his boots on the stairs. "Well?" I demand when he comes into view, not bothering with hello.

He smiles—not a full grin, but a definite upward tilt of his lips that transforms his usually stern face. "We were right," he says, stepping in and shrugging off his leather jacket. He hangs it on a hook by the door, one of a few he recently installed for me. "Drew is sleeping with Samantha."

I bounce on my toes, my fingers itching to grab his collar and pull him in for a kiss, but I resist. "What else did he say? Do you think he was involved in the thefts?"

"I doubt it. He seemed genuinely shocked when I asked him about them. But he did say Samantha's been acting strange lately—fidgety and on edge. And she made a mysterious trip to Inverness she wouldn't explain."

"That's suspicious as hell. C'mon, let's go through to my bedroom." My eyes widen when I realise how that sounds. "I mean, so we can talk more! The living room still smells of paint, and my bed is more comfortable than the kitchen chairs. I wasn't meaning we have to . . . you know . . ."

Robbie's lips twitch. "Shame. Thought I told you to be wet and ready for me?"

My cheeks flush, which is ridiculous considering what we were doing against the bathroom wall just hours ago. For once, I don't have a comeback. Instead I lead him through and perch on the edge of my bed. Robbie joins me, the mattress dipping under his weight, which slides me a little closer to him.

"So, what now?" I ask, trying to sound casual despite our thighs nearly touching.

"Now we focus on Samantha. Drew's going to keep an eye on her and let me know if he notices anything else unusual."

"Sounds like a plan. You sure you can trust him?"

"I think so, aye."

I nod. "Good. We're getting closer. I can feel it."

He turns to look at me properly, those blue eyes of his intense. "Thanks to you."

"Me? I just broke into an office and hid under a desk while two people shagged on top of it. Hardly Sherlock Holmes material."

"You and David stuck your necks out for me when no one else would. That counts for something."

My chest tightens at the sincerity in his voice. "Well, I'd say this calls for a celebration, wouldn't you?"

"What did you have in mind, McIntyre?"

I lean closer to him, giving him plenty of time to pull away if he wants to. He doesn't. Instead, he meets me halfway, his lips capturing mine in a kiss that starts gentle but quickly turns hungry.

I shift closer, swinging one leg over his lap and straddling him. His hands grip my hips, his fingers digging in possessively. The kiss deepens, his tongue tangling with mine, drawing a needy sound from my throat. When we break apart, we're both breathing hard.

"You do things to me," Robbie murmurs, dipping his head and nuzzling my neck, his stubble scraping deliciously against my skin. "Things no other woman has."

"Like what?" I can't help asking, even as I tilt my head to give him better access.

His hands slide under my top, rough palms skimming over my ribs. "Like . . . you make me lose control." He nips at my earlobe, sending shivers down my spine. "But also . . . you make me want more than just to fuck you."

Coming from Robbie MacDonald, that's practically a declaration of love.

I rock against him, loving the feel of the hard bulge in his

205

jeans against the thin material of my leggings. "But . . . you *do* want to fuck me. I can feel it. So fuck me."

In one fluid motion, Robbie shifts our positions, laying me on the bed and covering my body with his. I wrap my legs around him, and he kisses me deeply, his weight pressing me into the mattress. His hands are everywhere—threading through my hair, tracing the curve of my hip, squeezing just hard enough to make me gasp into his mouth.

I slide my hands under his T-shirt and explore the hot skin stretched tight over muscle. Then I tug his top up, and he lifts away from me so I can pull it over his head.

I drink in the sight of him, all tattoos and coiled power. My fingers reach for his belt buckle, but he catches my wrist.

"Not so fast. I want to savour you this time."

He tugs my top off then makes quick work of my bra. His eyes roam over me with an intensity that has me wriggling beneath him.

"You're gorgeous," he says roughly.

Before I can respond, his mouth is on my left breast, hot and demanding. I arch into him, one hand splaying across the nape of his neck to hold him closer. Every swipe of his tongue sends sparks of pleasure straight to my core.

Robbie works his way down my body, kissing and nipping as he goes, his tongue dipping into my belly button. By the time he drags down my leggings, along with my underwear, I'm practically vibrating with need.

"Please," I whisper, not caring how desperate I sound.

He stands to remove his jeans, and I take a moment to appreciate the magnificent sight of him, all hard lines and raw masculinity. Then he leans over me again, positions himself at my entrance, and pushes in, just the pierced tip, tormenting me with these shallow thrusts that have me digging my nails into his shoulders in frustration.

"Robbie," I moan, "stop teasing!"

With a wicked grin, he finally pushes all the way in, filling me completely. I cry out, loud enough that Mrs Innes next door will definitely be giving me knowing looks tomorrow.

He sets a punishing rhythm, the headboard thudding against the wall in time with his thrusts. But then, through the noise, another thumping joins in, insistent and coming from elsewhere.

"Fuck," Robbie grunts, slowing his movements. "Is that—"

The thumping gets even louder. Someone's knocking on my front door.

"Ignore it," I pant, trying to pull him back to me.

But Robbie is already withdrawing. "I don't know, Cat. Whoever that is, they *really* want to—"

"Police! Open up!"

For a heartbeat, we stare at each other in horror. Then we're scrambling for our clothes.

"Shit, shit, shit," I mutter as I yank on my knickers, top, and leggings.

I'm ready first, and I hurry to the door while Robbie tugs up his fly. I take a deep breath, try to smooth my sex-tousled hair into something resembling normalcy, then open the door to find two police officers standing on the other side. One is DS Gordon Sinclair, a stocky, greying man with the weathered face of someone who's seen it all. The other I don't know. She's a tall woman, a few years older than me, with sharp green eyes and a no-nonsense expression.

"Evening, Cat," Sinclair says with a curt nod. "It's been a while. I don't know if you've met PC Ailsa Muir?" He gestures to the younger officer beside him. "We're looking for Robert MacDonald. Is he here?"

"He hasn't done anything wrong!" The words just burst out of me.

Sinclair doesn't even blink. "We have evidence linking him to thefts at the Glen Garve Resort."

I shake my head. "No, he's innocent."

Robbie appears behind me. "I didn't steal anything," he says firmly. "You've got the wrong person."

"It's Samantha Drummond you want," I add, desperation creeping into my voice. "She's the one who framed him."

Sinclair sighs, looking almost regretful. "Robbie, you'll have the opportunity to tell your side of the story at the station. For now, I need you to come with us."

"You can't be serious," I protest.

But Sinclair nods to Muir, who steps forwards with handcuffs.

"Robert MacDonald," she says formally, "I am arresting you on suspicion of theft. You do not have to say anything, but it may harm your defence if you do not mention when questioned something which you later rely on in court. Anything you do say may be given in evidence."

She cuffs Robbie's wrists behind his back. His jaw tightens, the only sign this is affecting him.

"Never thought I'd have to bring you in again, Robbie," Sinclair says. "Thought you'd turned a corner."

Robbie meets his gaze steadily. "I did. I didn't do what you're accusing me of."

There's history between the pair. Sinclair has been in the police for as long as I can remember, and although Robbie is innocent of this, his reputation wasn't built on nothing. There was a time when Robbie kept Sinclair rather busy.

"Let's go." Sinclair gestures towards the stairs.

I trail after them, numb, my mind whirring uselessly. They're actually taking him away, and there's nothing I can do but watch.

When we step out onto Main Street, my heart drops even further. Typical Bannock—news here travels faster than rain clouds over Ben Nevis. Someone must've clocked the police car, and now a wee knot of people has gathered outside the Pheasant, necks craning for a better view.

"He's innocent!" I shout, loud and unashamed. "He's been set up!"

But my words fall on deaf ears. I catch snippets of conversation as people whisper away to each other.

"Always knew he'd land himself in bother again."

"Once a troublemaker, always a troublemaker."

"Remember when he smashed up that bus shelter?"

"I heard he used to take part in illegal fights in Inverness. Nearly killed a man once."

Robbie keeps his head high and his gaze fixed straight ahead as Sinclair guides him towards the waiting car. But I can see the tension in his shoulders, the way his hands clench into fists behind his back.

"You've got the wrong person!" I try again, my voice cracking with desperation. "He didn't do this!"

This outburst earns me some withering looks and a chorus of tuts. Mrs Fraser, whose son is in my S2 English class, approaches and lays her hand on my arm, all pity and pursed lips.

"Catriona, as a teacher at the high school, you may want to think twice about associating yourself with someone like Robbie MacDonald. It doesn't send the right message."

I jerk away from her touch. "You don't know him. None of you do!"

But it's too late. The car door slams shut on Robbie, then Sinclair slides into the driver's seat and the car pulls away. I'm left behind, feeling completely powerless. Was all our detective work for nothing?

The crowd begins to disperse, their entertainment over for the evening. A few people cast sympathetic glances my way, but most just shake their heads, like I'm nothing more than some daft girl who's been taken in by Bannock's notorious bad boy.

"Ach well, leopards never change their spots," someone says.

I'm about to round on them when a familiar voice calls my name. Turning, I see Maisie and Jamie coming over. Without a word, Maisie wraps me in a hug, and that's when something inside me snaps and tears finally break free.

"They've taken him," I sob into her shoulder. "They think he stole those things, but he didn't. No one believes us."

Jamie clears his throat awkwardly. "Well . . . I believe you." When I look up at him, surprised, he shrugs. "Robbie saved my life. The least I can do is give him the benefit of the doubt, right? Besides, if you believe he's innocent . . . well, that's good enough for me."

His unexpected support means more than I can say. I wipe at my tears.

"Come on," Maisie says. "Let's get you inside and figure out what to do next."

As they lead me back towards my flat, I cast one last look in the direction the police car disappeared. I won't give up on Robbie. I just won't.

CHAPTER TWENTY-SIX

ROBBIE

The interview room at Bannock police station hasn't changed in the years since I was last here. Same grey walls. Same scratched metal table. Same fluorescent light that buzzes like an angry wasp, flickering just enough to grate on your nerves. It's surreal to think that thirty minutes ago I was with Cat—*in* Cat—and now I'm here in this cold box.

I slump into the chair opposite Sinclair and Muir and cross my arms over my chest. The handcuffs are off now, though my wrists still feel the phantom pressure of the metal.

"Interview commencing at twenty-one thirty-seven," Sinclair says, pressing a button on the recorder that sits between us. "Present are Detective Sergeant Gordon Sinclair, Police Constable Ailsa Muir, and Robert MacDonald.

"Robert, you do not have to say anything, but it may harm your defence if you do not mention when questioned something which you later rely on in court. Anything you do say may be given in evidence. Do you understand?"

"Aye. I heard it at Cat's flat. And every time you hauled me in here as a kid."

Sinclair ignores my dig. "You're entitled to free and independent legal advice. Would you like a solicitor present?"

"Don't need one. I didn't do anything wrong."

"This interview is being recorded as evidence," Muir chimes in, her voice crisp, professional. "Do you understand that?"

I nod.

"Verbal response for the recording, please," she prompts.

"Aye, I understand."

"Would you like anything to drink before we begin?" Sinclair says. "Water? Tea?"

"I'm good. Let's just get on with it."

He nods and folds his hands on the table. "We're here to discuss the thefts at the Glen Garve Resort. Three incidents in all. A watch, valued at approximately twenty-five thousand pounds, vanished from one room. Then there was the pair of diamond earrings. And finally, a signet ring was taken, along with two thousand pounds in cash."

"Look, this is all a misunderstanding. I think Samantha Drummond—"

Sinclair holds up a hand. "I'll be asking the questions here, Robbie."

I clench my jaw. Didn't he say I'd get to tell my side of the story at the station? And yet here we are, at the station, and I'm still not being given the chance to speak. When exactly will my chance come?

"Let's start with your employment at the resort," Sinclair continues. "You worked in maintenance, correct?"

"Aye."

"And that gave you access to guest rooms?"

"When necessary. For repairs."

"According to the keycard logs, you accessed room 118 on the fourth of August at sixteen thirty-seven. Can you explain why?"

I straighten. "I didn't. I wasn't in that room on that day."

Sinclair raises an eyebrow. "The logs show your keycard was used to enter the room. They also show your keycard was used to access room 207 on August the twelfth and room 203 on August the fourteenth. The guests in each room reported items missing shortly afterwards."

The walls seem to press in slightly. I've been in here enough times to know how these interviews go, but unlike the younger version of me—cocky, defiant, not giving a shit—I care about the outcome this time.

"I'm telling you, it wasn't me," I insist. "Someone must have taken my keycard, or—"

"Are you suggesting," Muir cuts in, "that someone took your keycard, used it, returned it without you noticing, then took it again for the second theft, returned it again, and then took it a third time?"

I can hear how daft that sounds. Can almost see my younger self sitting here, spinning wild tales to explain away whatever trouble I'd landed in. The difference is, this time I'm telling the truth.

"No, that's ridiculous, obviously. More likely they cloned my card somehow, or tampered with the logs to make it *look* like it was me."

The silence in the room is heavy, thick with doubt, and I know they both think I'm talking shite.

"Let's move on," Sinclair says, sliding a photograph across the table. "Do you recognise this?"

It's a signet ring. Gold with a crest on it. The same one that fell out of my locker. The same one I begged Johnny to claim he found elsewhere. But I can't tell these two that.

"No," I say. "Never seen it before."

"Never?" Sinclair probes. "You're certain about that?"

"That's what I said."

"So you've never held this ring in your hand? Never touched it?"

Something cold slides down my spine. I suspect this is a trap, but what am I supposed to do? Change my story? Oh aye, because that's famously something innocent people do.

"No," I say, but my voice lacks conviction now.

Sinclair exchanges a glance with Muir. "That's interesting, because we found your fingerprints on this ring, Robbie."

Fuck.

Of course they did. When it fell from my locker, I picked it up. Held it in my bare hand before I gave it to Johnny.

"I don't—" I begin, but my throat dries up. I rub my palms against my jeans under the table.

"Your fingerprints are still on file from your previous convictions," Sinclair explains. "The match is conclusive."

A dull ache starts behind my eyes. "It's not what you think. Okay, I *did* touch that ring, but I found it in my locker. Someone planted it there."

"And who would that be?" Muir asks.

"Samantha Drummond. The head of housekeeping."

"That's quite an accusation." Sinclair leans back. "Do you have any evidence to support it?"

And there's the rub. There's Cat's photos of the overdue bills, but explaining how we got those would mean admitting she and David broke into Samantha's office. And anyway, those only prove that Samantha's been having money troubles, not that she stole anything.

Still, I try to sound confident. "She's recently divorced and struggling financially. She's been spending beyond her means. And she's had it in for me for years."

"That's motive, perhaps," Sinclair acknowledges, "but not evidence. Nothing that explains how your keycard was used or how the ring ended up in your locker. And what did you do with the ring after you found it?"

"I handed it over," I say carefully.

"To who?"

I hesitate, knowing I'm walking into dangerous territory. But I've already lied about the ring once. I can't lie again. So I say, "To Johnny."

Sinclair and Muir share a look.

"That's interesting," Sinclair says after a pause, "because according to the statement your brother gave us, he came across the ring while walking through the resort grounds. Always seemed a little convenient, if you ask me."

"Johnny had nothing to do with this. He was just—"

"Covering for you?" Sinclair suggests.

"Look." I lay my hands flat on the table. "I found that ring in my locker. Someone planted it there—Samantha, I'm sure of it. I panicked and asked Johnny to help. That was my mistake, not his."

"When you say you asked your brother to *help*," Muir says, "you mean you asked him to lie for you, is that right?"

Fuck. I never wanted to get Johnny into trouble.

"I put him in an impossible position. He shouldn't be punished for that."

Sinclair sighs. "You know what disappoints me about all of this, Robbie? For years, you were in and out of this station. Vandalism. Fighting. Shoplifting. But then things changed. You seemed to settle down. I actually thought to myself, *MacDonald's finally grown up.*"

His words shouldn't sting, but they do. Not because I particularly care what Sinclair thinks of me, but because he's echoing what everyone in Bannock has always thought—that I'll never amount to anything but trouble. That's what my da believes. And it's what my maw believed when she walked out.

"I *have* grown up. That's why I'm sitting here telling you I didn't do this. I'm not the same arsehole I was in my teens."

"Let me lay this out for you, Robbie," Sinclair says. "We have keycard logs showing you entered rooms from which items were later reported missing. We have no maintenance records to explain why you were in those rooms. We have your fingerprints on one of the stolen items. And we have a fabricated story from your brother about how that item was found."

Put like that, it sounds bad. Really bad.

"I didn't steal anything," I insist, but the words sound hollow even to my own ears.

Sinclair shakes his head. "Robert MacDonald, you are being charged with theft from the Glen Garve Resort. You will be detained pending a court appearance where you can apply for bail."

The words hit me like a physical blow. This is really happening.

"Do you understand the charge against you?" Muir asks.

I nod numbly.

"Remember, a verbal response for the recording, please."

"Aye," I manage. "I understand."

"Interview terminated at twenty-two oh-three." Sinclair

reaches to stop the recording, and the red light on the device blinks off.

I stare at the scratched surface of the table, trying to process what's just happened. Seven years ago, I knocked a guy out cold in an underground fight. An hour or so after that, I found the McIntyres' car wrapped around a tree. That night changed me. Made me walk away from fighting, from the rush of violence. Made me try to be better.

And now here I am, back in this bloody interview room, about to be locked up for something I didn't even do.

The irony would be funny if it wasn't my life falling apart.

CHAPTER TWENTY-SEVEN

ROBBIE

The cell is six paces long and four wide. I know because I spent most of the night pacing it like a caged animal. The thin mattress might as well be concrete, and the light overhead, which stayed on all night, casts everything in a sickly glow. Between the two, sleep was nearly impossible. I managed maybe two hours before giving up.

Not that I can blame it all on the cell. My head wouldn't shut up, just kept looping the same thoughts over and over, trying to figure out how the fuck I'm going to get out of this mess.

I sit on the bed, roll my stiff shoulders, and wince. My mouth tastes like I've been chewing on an old sock, and yesterday's clothes have taken on the stink of sweat and frustration. Christ, I'd kill for a shower. Even a toothbrush. But all I've got is the toilet in the corner, offering about as much privacy as a shop window.

Earlier this morning, I was taken to court for my bail hearing. The sheriff granted bail with a surety, a hefty one at that. Now I'm back in this cell, waiting—*hoping*—for it to be paid. If not, I'll be shipped off to a proper prison to await trial.

The thought sends a cold shiver down my spine. This cell is bad enough, but at least it's temporary. A real prison cell? Months behind bars, counting the days until it's my turn in the dock? And if I'm found guilty? Years. For something I didn't even do.

Fuck me.

My thoughts drift to Cat. The way she yelled out that I was innocent when I was led to the police car. The fire in her eyes as she stood up for me. I didn't even get to say a proper goodbye to her.

Did *she* sleep well last night? Somehow I don't think so. It's oddly comforting to know she cares, even though I hate the idea of her worrying on my account.

The sound of footsteps approaching pulls me from my thoughts. Keys jangle, then the cell door swings open to reveal PC Muir.

"MacDonald," she says, all business. "The surety's been paid. You're being released on bail."

I stare at her for a moment while my brain catches up. Then, "Who paid it?"

"Your father."

Of course.

"Right." I nod, relief mixing with a twisting in my gut at the thought of being in my da's debt. Again.

Muir gestures for me to follow her out into the corridor, and I stand, my legs stiff as fence posts. She leads me to a desk littered with forms and plastic trays, where she runs through my bail conditions. "You're to report to the station every Monday at ten a.m. Your second hearing is set for next Tuesday at nine. Make sure you show up or you'll be back here before you know it."

I nod, trying to fix it all in memory despite my brain feeling like porridge.

"One more thing," she adds. "You're not allowed near the Glen Garve Resort, and you're to stay away from this Samantha Drummond. Don't interfere with our investigation. Understood?"

"Crystal clear," I mutter. Though that's going to make proving my innocence bloody difficult.

She slides over my property bag—the essentials of my life whittled down to wallet, keys, phone—and hands me a pen for some paperwork. I scribble my signature where she points.

She then walks me through to the reception area, where my da is waiting. He stands with his back straight and arms crossed, looking like he'd rather be anywhere else. His hair is neatly combed, his clothes pressed and proper as always. The general manager of the Glen Garve Resort, every inch of him.

Muir confirms with him that he understands the terms of the surety—essentially that he's on the hook if I skip bail—then leaves us to it. Da doesn't say a word, just turns and strides towards the exit. I follow him out into the bright morning light, squinting against the sudden glare.

A few locals are milling about outside the station. They stop their conversations to stare, so I scowl back at them, which probably doesn't help my case, but fuck it. I'm not in the mood to play nice.

Da walks briskly towards his car. "Get in," he says without looking at me.

"I'll make my own way home. Besides, I parked my bike on Main Street."

"I didn't just put up several thousand pounds to bail you out so you could wander off and get yourself into more trouble. Get in the car. We need to talk."

"I didn't ask you to bail me out," I reply coldly.

"No, you didn't. But who else was going to do it?"

I glare at him but say nothing. After a tense standoff, I relent and get into the passenger seat. Da starts the engine and pulls away from the police station, the air between us thick with unspoken words.

We drive in silence for several minutes, leaving Bannock behind and heading out into the countryside. The familiar landscape rolls past: green hills, patches of forest, the occasional farmhouse.

"Are you taking me somewhere specific or are we just here to talk?" I say finally. "Because if we're just here to talk, you might want to, you know, talk."

Da keeps his eyes fixed on the road ahead, his knuckles white on the steering wheel. "Do you have any idea what this is doing to the resort's reputation?"

Of course that's his first concern. Not how I'm doing after a night in a cell. Not whether I'm guilty or innocent. Just the fucking resort.

"I didn't steal anything," I say through gritted teeth.

"Hmm." The scepticism in that sound makes my blood boil.

"Why won't you believe me?"

"Because you've given me no reason to. You think I don't remember all the times I had to drag you out of trouble when you were younger? The fights, the shoplifting, the underage drinking? And now this, stealing from guests. It's . . . beyond shameful."

His words cut deep, not because they're particularly harsh—I've heard worse—but because they drive home how little faith he has in me. Seven years I've been on the straight and narrow, for Christ's sake! Well, mostly straight. Hooking up with the occasional hotel guest? Sure. But I haven't been in a fight, haven't got on the wrong side of the law, haven't given him any reason to doubt me for seven bloody years.

"Aye, well, maybe if you'd been around instead of burying yourself in work all the time, things would have turned out differently," I say bitterly.

Da grips the steering wheel even tighter, and silence once again stretches between us. Then he exhales—a shaky, weary sound.

"I'll admit I could have done a better job, but I wasn't expecting your mother to walk out on us—wasn't expecting to become a single parent. And I couldn't give up my work. I needed to keep money coming in."

"Aye, so you had enough in savings to bail out your eldest son one day, right?"

Even as I say it, I wince inside. I meant it as a wry sort of joke—something to break the tension—but it lands flat. Maybe a bit cruel. There's an awkward pause before Da lets out another heavy sigh then falls quiet again.

The countryside continues to roll past outside the window. Hills and sheep and old dry-stone walls, so bloody normal you'd hardly think anything had happened. I drum my fingers on my knee, restless.

"You look tired." The comment comes out of nowhere, Da's voice a touch softer than before.

I glance at him. "Aye, well, I didn't get much sleep last night."

He nods, and for a moment—just a moment—I think he might, you know, ask how I'm doing. But then he says, "Johnny wanted to come with me to the station. He's been worried sick about you."

My wee brother, always caught in the middle of the shitstorm between me and Da.

"Let me guess, you told him it didn't take two people to collect me? Said he needed to work his shift at the resort?"

He doesn't respond to this.

"I've not spoken to Johnny in a while, seeing as you asked him to keep his distance. How's he doing?"

"Stressed. Upset." A pause. "He believes you're innocent, you know."

"At least someone in the family does."

Da opens his mouth, hesitates, then shuts it again and shakes his head, apparently thinking better of whatever he was about to say. What comes out instead is: "You should meet with my solicitor. Discuss your options. I'll cover the costs."

"You don't have to—"

"I want to," he interrupts. "Whatever has happened between us, you're still my son."

It's not exactly a heartfelt breakthrough, but I suppose it's better than nothing.

We don't talk much more until Da drives back into Bannock and pulls up on Main Street by my motorcycle, which is still parked outside Cat's flat. A couple of locals walk past and peer through the window at us. Da shifts uncomfortably in his seat.

"Reminds me of when you were younger," he says quietly. "The stares. The whispers."

I don't reply. What is there to say?

"Don't make me regret paying the surety, Robbie. Show up at the police station every week, as you were told, and stay out of trouble."

"Aye. Will do." I get out of the car. He drives off without any further words.

Is this what family is supposed to feel like? Because it just feels exhausting.

I glance up at Cat's flat, but I don't try her door. She'll be at school now, teaching. Besides, I'm not fit company for anyone at the moment—not until I've had a shower and changed my clothes.

I swing my leg over my bike and start her up, the engine's low growl vibrating up through me like an old friend. The ride home is short but cathartic, the road blurring beneath my wheels, the engine drowning out things I don't want to think about. For a little while, I can almost forget about the cell, the handcuffs, the accusing stares as I was led to the police car. Almost.

Outside my cottage, I dismount and head for the door. Just inside, on the hall floor, a white envelope waits for me—one of those grim official ones with my name printed in bold type. The logo in the corner tells me exactly what it is.

"You've got to be fucking kidding me," I mutter, shaking my head at the universe's idea of a joke.

CHAPTER TWENTY-EIGHT

CAT

The final bell rings, and I practically sprint from my classroom. I've been sneaking not-so-subtle glances at my phone since lunch, when David texted to say Robbie had been released. My S3 class definitely noticed my distraction during our discussion of *Romeo and Juliet*. Somewhat ironic, given my own romantic drama unfolding.

I drive to Robbie's cottage, my stomach in knots. I tried to see him at the police station last night, but they wouldn't let me in. After that, I couldn't sleep, just kept seeing him being led away in handcuffs and feeling the weight of everyone's judgemental eyes boring into me.

Pulling up beside Robbie's motorcycle, I take a deep breath then get out my car. The cottage looks peaceful against the backdrop of Bannock Woods. Hard to believe its owner's life is imploding.

I knock, but there's no answer. So I try again, louder this time.

"It's open," Robbie calls, his tone weary.

I head in then go through to the kitchen, where sunlight

streams through the French windows, catching the dust motes in the air. Robbie sits at the table, hunched over a mug of something I suspect has long since gone cold. He looks up as I enter, dark circles under his eyes, and for the briefest moment, he looks almost lost. Then his expression shutters closed.

"Hey," I say, dropping into the chair opposite him and putting my bag on the one beside me.

"Hi. How was school?" The question, which would be perfectly ordinary any other day, seems ridiculous today.

"Not bad, but I had trouble focusing. Romeo wasn't the only troubled hero on my mind."

He attempts a smile. "Och, I hope you weren't worrying about me. I'm fine."

I reach across the table and place a hand on his. "Are you, though?"

He shrugs. "Well . . . honestly? I've been better. But my da paid my bail, so that's something, I suppose."

Robbie briefly fills me in on what happened, including that his second hearing is next Tuesday. My knowledge of the justice system is sketchy at best, and most of what I do know comes from TV, which isn't much help since in Scotland we do things differently than in England or the US. But apparently, his second hearing is when he enters his plea.

"Well, you'll be saying not guilty, obviously."

The fingers of his free hand tap restlessly against his mug.

"I'm not sure it's that simple. Da wants me to chat with his solicitor, and I will—maybe I'll have a clearer plan of action after that. But at court this morning, I got five minutes with the duty lawyer before my bail hearing. He said if I plead not guilty and get found guilty anyway, I'm probably looking at three to five years.

But if I hold my hands up from the start . . . one or two years maybe, less with good behaviour."

"Jesus, Robbie. You can't plead guilty to something you didn't do!"

"Aye, but what if I fight it, lose anyway, and spend even longer locked up?"

"We'll find evidence to clear your name," I insist. "We just need—"

"A confession from Samantha? CCTV footage that doesn't exist? Some kind of miracle?" His mouth twists in a wry smile. "Besides, my bail conditions include staying away from the resort and from Samantha. Break my conditions and I'll be remanded in custody until my trial. Makes proving my innocence a bit difficult, doesn't it?"

"I can keep investigating. I'm not bound by your bail conditions."

"No. You've done enough already." He gently pulls his hand away from mine. "This town has a long memory, Cat. If they decide you're trouble, they'll hold it against you forever. Trust me, I know. I don't want to bring you down with me."

"I don't care what people think about me," I say, though that's not entirely true. I heard the whispers at school today, saw the way some of the other teachers looked at me. Word of my rather vocal defence of Robbie last night has, of course, already made its way around town. It doesn't sting yet, but I know how these things work. Gossip has a way of wearing you down over time.

"You *should* care. You're new to your position at Bannock High. You've got your whole career ahead of you. Standing by me . . . it'll turn folk against you."

The fact he's worrying about *my* future when his own is

dangling by a thread . . . well, it just about breaks me. The town might see Robbie as trouble, but I know the truth.

"I'm not abandoning you. We're in this together."

Robbie just shakes his head, like I'm a naive child who doesn't understand how the world works. And maybe I am. But I'd rather be naive than give up on someone I care about.

My eyes catch on an official-looking envelope on the table. I reach for it before Robbie can stop me.

"Cat—" he starts, but I'm already pulling out the letter.

It's a fixed penalty notice from the Scottish Safety Camera Programme. The details jump out at me: Robbie was caught doing seventy-eight on a road with a sixty limit. Hundred pound fine. Three points on his licence.

"Talk about kicking me when I'm down, eh?" Robbie says with a hint of his usual dry humour. "Remember I said I thought I might've been caught by one of those mobile speed vans?"

I do remember, and this couldn't have come at a worse time. We're trying to prove he's a changed man, and while a speeding ticket isn't theft, it doesn't scream model citizen either.

"A hundred pounds?" I scoff. "Please. I happen to know what your day rate is, and that's hardly going to bankrupt you. Besides, if necessary, I'll just break something else in my flat for you to fix."

A ghost of a smile touches his lips.

"Seriously, Robbie, forget the speeding ticket—that's nothing. And as for the theft charge, listen to me: you are not going to jail for something you didn't do. I won't let that happen."

"Oh, aye? Are you going to flash your teacher badge at the judge and give me detention instead of prison?"

I set the letter down and move around the table, taking the chair next to him instead. Robbie watches me warily, like he's not sure what I'm up to.

"You know what I think?" I slide my hand onto his thigh.

"I'm guessing you're about to tell me."

"I think you need a distraction." My hand inches higher. "Something to take your mind off all this, even if it's just for a wee while."

Robbie catches my wandering hand before it reaches his crotch. "Cat, I appreciate what you're trying to do, but I'm not exactly in the mood."

I lean in and press a soft kiss to the stubble along his jaw. "Are you sure? Because I can be very persuasive."

"I'm sure." He gently pushes me back. "This isn't something we can just shag away, and believe me, I wish it were. If sex solved everything, my troubles would have buggered off years ago."

I sigh dramatically and flop back in my chair. "Fine. But in that case, I've got another idea."

"God help me."

"Let's go riding."

"Oh. Aye, that's fine. We can hit the road, and—"

"No, not on your bike, silly."

He raises an eyebrow. "Wait, do you mean on a horse?"

"No, a unicorn. Of course a horse! I went on your bike, now it's your turn to try something new."

"Absolutely not."

"Come on! It'll be good for you. The smell of the stables, the way a horse seems to know what you're thinking before you do . . ."

"The broken neck when I inevitably fall off?"

Laughing, I loop my arm through his and give his biceps a wee squeeze. "I won't let that happen. I promise."

"Cat, I've never been on a horse in my life."

"And today we're going to fix that." I give his arm another

squeeze then rise from my chair and try to haul him up with me. He doesn't so much as budge, no matter how hard I tug. "Please? For me?"

"No."

"Pretty please?"

"Still no."

I let go of his arm and put both hands on my hips, fixing him with what I hope is my most intimidating teacher glare. "I'm not leaving until you say yes."

"Then you'll be here a long time."

"That's fine. I've got nowhere else to be." I plonk myself back down and fold my arms.

Robbie holds out for nearly half a minute before letting out a resigned sigh and shaking his head. "Fine. One ride. But if I break something, it's on you."

I smile, victorious. "Deal!"

◆ ◆ ◆

Twenty minutes later, we're at Bannock Stables. Janice waves from behind a wheelbarrow piled high with straw, then her mouth forms a perfect "o" when she catches sight of Robbie trailing behind me. Just like everyone else in Bannock, she's no doubt heard about the arrest.

"Cat!" She schools her features. "Didn't expect to see you today."

"Thought I'd introduce my friend to the joys of horse riding," I reply cheerfully.

She shoots another glance at Robbie. Then, to my relief, she smiles. Maybe the repair job he did on her fence has put him in her good graces. "Well, you know where everything is. Bracken's free if you want her."

"Perfect! And maybe Thor for Robbie?"

Robbie throws me a look. "*Thor?*"

"Don't worry, he's a gentle giant."

We head to the tack room, where I grab my trusty helmet then peer at the shelves for something that might fit Robbie. I pluck a large one and plonk it on him, but it barely covers his ears. After a bit of rummaging, and coughing through a cloud of dust, I finally spot a gigantic one lurking right at the back. It looks like it hasn't seen daylight for years. I brush off a few cobwebs and offer it to Robbie with a flourish.

"This should fit your massive noggin," I tease.

He manages to wrestle it on, then we head to the stalls, where Bracken is dozing contentedly. Three doors down, Thor is impossible to miss: his massive head pokes out over the stable door. He's doing his best statue impression, the only giveaway the gentle twitch of one ear.

"Wait, *that's* Thor?" Robbie says. "Christ almighty. That's not a horse, that's a double-decker bus on legs. Can't I start with something smaller?"

"You're six foot five, Robbie. If we tried putting you on Bracken, she'd lodge a health and safety complaint. Besides, this guy is as lazy as a Sunday morning. Perfect for a beginner."

I demonstrate how to approach Thor then gesture for Robbie to give it a try. "Go on, hold your hand out flat so he can smell you."

Robbie edges forwards with the same enthusiasm most folk save for tax returns or dental work. When Thor reaches to snuffle at his palm, Robbie stiffens, but he doesn't bolt.

"You see? He likes you. Trust me, tough guy, if you can handle a motorcycle, you can handle Thor."

After saddling both horses, I walk Robbie through the basics of mounting. "Take it step by step: reins in your left hand, foot in the stirrup, then swing your leg over, nice and smooth."

Robbie huffs but manages it without major incident, though up on Thor, he looks about as relaxed as someone sitting on a time bomb.

"Piece of cake," he deadpans. Even Thor seems unconvinced.

I show Robbie how to hold the reins, then I get up on Bracken and we set off round the paddock at a walk. Soon I notice Robbie shifting in the saddle like he's sitting on a hedgehog.

"Is this supposed to be quite so sore on my balls?" he asks bluntly.

"Sit up straight!" I order, half giggling. "Keep your heels down, but don't grip the saddle for dear life—you'll just bounce more. Move *with* Thor, not against him. Unless you want to end up singing soprano, of course."

Robbie mutters something about medieval torture, but he follows my instructions, and soon the thundercloud on his face softens. "That *is* better," he admits grudgingly.

"See? It's not just English I can teach."

"Don't let it go to your head, McIntyre."

When I'm satisfied Robbie isn't about to go flying off Thor's back—or make a gelding of himself—I lead us out of the paddock and towards Bannock Woods. The trees create a dappled canopy overhead, and the air is cooler among the foliage.

"This is actually quite nice," Robbie admits, his posture noticeably more relaxed. He looks around, taking in the filtered sunlight and ancient trees. "I know these woods well, but it's a different perspective from up here."

We ride on for a bit, allowing a silence to settle—the kind that's warm and companionable rather than awkward. The only sounds are the rhythmic clip-clop of hooves on the dirt path and occasional birdsong. Thor plods along, steady as a stubborn old tractor, seemingly aware of just how much faith is being placed in him today.

"You know," I say eventually, "riding a horse isn't so different from being on a motorcycle. It's that same feeling of freedom, of connection to the world around you, but with the added bonus of bonding with another living being."

Robbie smirks. "I'll stick to my bike for speed, thanks."

"But you can't do *this* with your bike." I lean forwards and stroke Bracken's neck. She flicks her ears at me like she knows she's the star of the show.

"No, but my bike doesn't need to have its shit shovelled."

"Fair point," I laugh.

We continue along the path until we reach a small clearing. Sunlight streams through the gap in the trees, illuminating a patch of wildflowers swaying lazily in the breeze. I draw Bracken to a halt and gesture for Robbie to do the same.

"This is one of my favourite spots," I tell him.

Robbie looks around, taking in the peaceful scene. For once, he doesn't have a sarcastic retort. He just nods appreciatively.

Then Thor shifts his weight and spreads his back legs. Robbie tenses. "What's he doing? Am I about to be thrown?"

"No, he's just having a pee! Stand up in your stirrups for a sec."

"You've got to be joking," Robbie mutters, but he rises, and Thor relieves himself with what seems like endless volume.

"Jesus," Robbie says, staring down in disbelief. "It's like a bloody waterfall."

When Thor finally finishes, Robbie settles back into the saddle. "You didn't warn me that might happen."

"Consider it part of the authentic experience," I say with a grin. "Anyway . . . I've got to ask, Robbie. How are you doing? Really?"

He weighs his reply before speaking. "I don't know. It's like no matter what I do, folk round here will always see the teenage eejit I used to be."

I reach over and touch his forearm. "Well, you know what? I won't stop until everyone in Bannock sees you the way I do."

"Oh, aye? And how's that? Tattooed, irresistible, and with a few interesting piercings?"

I snort. "Okay, maybe they shouldn't see you *exactly* how I see you. But you know what I mean."

He winks at me. Then, more seriously, he says, "Like I said back at the house, you don't have to stick by me, Cat. Most people would've walked away by now."

"Well, I'm not most people, and you better get used to that."

Robbie chuckles. "You certainly are . . . unique."

For a while longer, I listen to the birdsong and the gentle sound of Bracken munching on grass. I try to freeze this perfect wee moment in my memory. Then I say, "All right, we should probably make tracks before Thor decides this is nap time instead of adventure hour."

Robbie nods, and we turn our horses and head back to the stables, together.

CHAPTER TWENTY-NINE

ROBBIE

Cat brings her car to a halt outside the Bannock Hotel, and I frown, suspicion prickling at the back of my neck.

"Why are we stopping here?"

We managed to scrub off the worst of the horse smell at the stables, but I'm not in the mood for a social call, especially not at the Bannock Hotel. This is McIntyre territory, and I'm about as welcome here as a fox in a henhouse.

Cat grins, her hazel eyes sparkling with that unmistakable look, the one that's got trouble written all over it. "Trust me on this. Come on."

I don't move. My fingers drum the door handle. "I'm not sure this is a good idea. Lewis runs this place, and while he doesn't hate me as much as Ally does, he's not my biggest fan either."

"Please?" She turns to face me fully, head tipped just so, giving me her best pleading stare. "For me?"

Damn it, Cat McIntyre could probably convince a nun to rob a bank.

"Fine! But if Ally throws me out on my arse, I'm blaming you."

She grins triumphantly and hops out of the car. I lumber after her with considerably less enthusiasm. Warm lights glow in the stone building's windows. To anyone else, I'm sure the place would look welcoming. Just not to me.

Cat pushes open the door and strides in like she owns the place—which, I suppose, in a way she does. I trail behind her, feeling oversized and out of place in my leather jacket and boots. She leads me through to the hotel's small restaurant, and I stop dead in my tracks.

It seems the restaurant is closed to the public tonight. Instead, a long table has been set up in the middle, and it's crowded with people. The McIntyre brothers are all here with their partners. Elspeth Stewart, her cheeks flushed the same colour as her wine, is chatting away with Bryce from the Pheasant. Aidan Stewart sits with Grace—his girlfriend and David's twin sister—while their toddler does laps around the table. Even the dog is here, curled up on the floor, blissfully snoozing through all the noise.

It's a fucking family dinner, and Cat's dragged me right into the middle of it.

"Cat!" Elspeth calls out, spotting her. "I was wondering where you'd got to." Her eyes flick to me, and her smile wavers for a moment before returning, polite but uncertain. "Oh! Robbie!"

Conversations stutter to a halt, and suddenly the whole room is staring at us—well, at *me*. Ally glares at me from across the table like he's weighing up which window would be easiest to toss me through.

I'm about to back out when Jamie stands, walks over, and extends his hand to me.

236

"How are you doing, Robbie?" he asks, as if my presence here isn't completely bizarre. "Take a seat. Join us."

I shake his hand, too surprised to do anything else.

"I'm not sure that's a good idea." Ally sets his glass down hard enough to make it—and a few plates—rattle. "Robbie was arrested just yesterday, and there are children present. Impressionable ears and all that."

"Ally," Emily murmurs soothingly, resting a hand on his shoulder, baby Ciaran nestled in the crook of her other arm.

Before anyone else can protest—or before I can make my escape—a tiny figure darts straight at me. It's Aidan's wee lass. Without a hint of the wariness the adults are showing, she ducks between my legs then peeks out from behind me, giggling. From across the table, wee Ru watches her with wide-eyed fascination.

I freeze, unsure what to do, then glance down at her with a raised eyebrow. "Er . . . hello there."

She giggles some more.

Cat smirks at Ally. "Looks like Jamie and Callie don't mind Robbie joining us."

Just then, the dog gets up and ambles over, his tail wagging. Cat gives him an affectionate scratch behind the ear, then he noses at my leg and gives me one of those soulful looks Labradors specialise in. I hold out my hand, and he gives it a cautious sniff, followed by an approving lick.

"Bruce doesn't seem bothered either," Cat observes. "What about the rest of you?"

A few forced smiles appear around the table, but the atmosphere remains strained.

"Look, I should probably go—"

"No," Cat interrupts firmly. She slips her arm around my waist, and even with all these eyes on me, I can't help but relax a little at her touch. "Look, Ally, you've got your partner here, Emily. And Lewis has Iona. And Jamie has Maisie. Aidan has Grace, and Elspeth has Bryce. So it's only right that I've got my boyfriend, Robbie."

Boyfriend? I nearly choke. When the hell did that happen?

Iona actually does choke, sputtering into her wine glass. "Your *what*?"

"Boyfriend," Cat repeats sweetly but firmly, squeezing my waist as if daring me to contradict her.

I don't. Partly because I'm too stunned, and partly because . . . well, she does mean more to me than just someone I've been sleeping with. She's had my back through all this shit. She's been growing on me, creeping into places in my head I thought were locked up tight.

"When I bumped into you two the other day," Ally says, "you assured me, Cat, that Robbie hadn't so much as laid a finger on you."

"And he hadn't," Cat says smoothly. "At that point. But things change, Ally. Get with the times." She turns to Maisie, who's next to an empty seat—Cat's spot, apparently. "Mind budging up a bit so I can squeeze in an extra chair and Robbie and I can sit together? Elspeth, is there enough food for Robbie too?"

Elspeth, clearly relieved to have something practical to focus on, brightens. "Of course! You know me, I always make enough for seconds. Let me go serve you both a plate. Lewis, could you grab some cutlery for Robbie, please? And pour him a glass of wine while you're at it."

Lewis just shrugs, gives me a sort of "well, here we are" smile—more resigned than hostile—and heads off to fetch cutlery. Maisie shuffles over to make room, and before I can come up with a convincing excuse, Cat is herding me into a seat at the table.

"So, Robbie," Maisie says, leaning in with a gleam in her eye that reminds me of Cat, "how long have you and Cat been official?"

Christ. If I had to choose between another police interrogation and this, I'd take my chances with the police.

"Er . . ." I glance at Cat, who's watching me with a little too much amusement. "It's . . . recent."

"Very recent," Cat adds. "But we're happy. Aren't we, Robbie?"

I do my best not to look like a man cornered by wild animals. "Aye."

Iona, sitting across from us, flashes a sympathetic smile. "Don't mind us. We're just surprised. Cat mentioned she was interested in you, but we didn't realise things had progressed quite so fast."

"You told your friends you were interested in me?" I ask Cat, raising an eyebrow.

She has the grace to blush slightly. "Maybe."

"She called it Project Bang a Bad Boy," Maisie whispers.

"Maisie!" Cat hisses, her cheeks now flaming red. She glances around to make sure no one else at the table overheard, but they're holding their own conversations, thankfully.

A chuckle escapes me despite the awkwardness of the situation. "Project Bang a Bad Boy, eh?"

Cat looks mortified. "That was before I got to know you. It sounds terrible now."

"It does," I agree, but I can't help smiling at her discomfort. Serves her right for ambushing me with this dinner.

Elspeth returns with two plates of beef stew with mountains

239

of mashed potatoes and veg. The smell alone just about undoes me. She sets them down with a warm smile. "Eat up while it's hot!"

I mumble my thanks and wonder again why the hell Cat brought me here. I'd rather be back on that bloody horse than sitting at this table with every McIntyre and Stewart staring at me like I'm a bomb about to go off. But then I remember how I felt earlier, alone in my cottage, the weight of everything crushing down on me. Maybe Cat knows exactly what she's doing. Maybe some company is what I need, even if it's awkward as hell.

I take my first taste, and God, it's delicious. Suddenly realising how hungry I am, I gobble up some more.

After a few hearty mouthfuls, I glance around the table. The strained silence that fell when Cat and I arrived is long gone. These people are finishing each other's sentences and sharing inside jokes. Elbows bump, everyone comfortable in one another's space. It's a language I've never learnt to speak. After Maw left, dinners between me, Da, and Johnny . . . well, they weren't like this. Not even close.

Cat gives my thigh a light squeeze under the table and shoots me a reassuring smile. I return it. Even if I'm still not too sure about being here at a McIntyre and Stewart family dinner, I can't deny that the food is good.

"You know, Robbie," Elspeth says from further down the table, "it's long past time we had you over for a meal. We've never said an official thank you for what you did all those years ago, saving Jamie's life."

The chatter hushes again—not tense this time, but thoughtful.

I clear my throat, uncomfortable with everyone turning their attention back to me. "I just did what anyone would have done."

"Maybe so," Elspeth says, "but we're grateful for it all the same. I lost my best friend that night—Mairi was like a sister to me—and we lost her wonderful husband, Angus, too. But thanks to you, Jamie is still with us."

"And look at me now," Jamie says with a grin, clearly trying to lighten the mood, "healthy enough that I won a hill race recently."

"Aye, but daft enough that you ditched your kilt before the finish line and flashed half the town," Lewis adds drily.

"Only thanks to your poor sportsmanship, Lewis! Seriously, grabbing a hold of my kilt because you couldn't face not being first?"

Cat shudders dramatically. "Enough! I'm still traumatised by that particular memory. Please let's not talk about it anymore."

Despite it being a sensitive topic for Cat—I can't imagine she much appreciated her brother bearing all—smiles break out along both sides of the table. Jamie grins too, apparently perfectly happy being the butt of the joke, so to speak.

But then Ally says, "Speaking of traumatic experiences . . . being arrested must have been quite the ordeal, Robbie. Especially for something you claim you didn't do."

And just like that, the tension is back.

"Ally!" Cat warns.

"What?" He raises his hands in exaggerated innocence. "I'm just making conversation."

I take a sip of wine and weigh my response. "Let's just say the hospitality at the police station leaves a lot to be desired. But I didn't steal those items, and I'll be pleading not guilty."

Ally gives a noncommittal "hmm", but Cat's had enough. She turns so sharply towards him her chair lets out a squeak.

"Seriously? You're going to sit there and interrogate Robbie at a family dinner? I know you think you're protecting me, but maybe try trusting me for once. Robbie *is* innocent. He's been framed, and instead of judging him, you could try supporting him—or at the very least, supporting me."

It's as if someone has hit pause. Forks hover halfway to mouths, everyone waiting to see where this will go next.

Cat takes a deep breath, her eyes softening as she looks around at her family. "I know I haven't always been the easiest wee sister. I went a bit wild in my student days, and I might've begged you, Ally, for cash more times than I care to admit. It was Robbie who pointed out to me how lucky I am to have three big brothers who've always watched out for me. So . . . for what it's worth, thank you."

Ally, Lewis, and Jamie exchange surprised glances, clearly not used to such gratitude from their sister.

Cat takes a shaky breath. "I think part of the reason I enjoyed partying so much was because it was an escape from grief. But now I'm interested in moving forward to a new stage in my life." Her hand finds mine under the table. "Robbie's been doing great work in my flat. When it's all finished, I'll have you all round to see it. It might be a tight fit, but we can have fizz and cakes and a bit of fun. And maybe"—she shoots Ally a sidelong glance—"a night without any arguments?"

I look around at the faces watching Cat, some surprised, some touched, all attentive. She commands people's attention in a way I've never been able to, with an openness I've never mastered.

Something loosens inside me—a knot I didn't realise was there—and before I can talk myself out of it, I'm speaking.

"Look, Ally . . ." My voice is gruffer than I mean it to be. "I owe you an apology for . . . well, for being a bit of a dick when I was younger." I glance at Aidan. "I owe you one too."

Ally blinks as if he's not sure he heard me right.

"I was angry, a stupid kid with too much attitude and not enough sense." My mouth twists ruefully. "That doesn't excuse anything I said or did, of course. But . . . aye. Sorry."

Cat squeezes my hand so tightly it almost hurts.

"And just to be clear, aye, I've made my fair share of mistakes over the years, but the thefts at the Glen Garve Resort? Not me."

Ally doesn't jump straight in with another barb or accusation. He just stares at me like I've sprouted antlers. Then he gives his head a bewildered shake and manages, "Right. Well." He clears his throat awkwardly and glances down at his plate as if hoping for some guidance from the mashed potatoes. "That . . . er . . . that's appreciated."

But then, recovering his composure, he jabs his fork in my direction so hard a few peas fly off his plate. "But if you break my sister's heart—if you so much as make her cry—you'll answer to me, MacDonald."

"Ally!" Cat and Emily exclaim in unison.

"What? I'm just making sure we understand each other."

I almost smile. This, at least, is familiar territory. "Understood."

The meal continues, Aidan launching into an animated tale about a rafting trip he and Ally organised for a stag party today. It feels like he's working up to a punchline, but before he can reach it, the restaurant door swings open.

"Sorry we're late!" David announces. "Bit of a last-minute dash, but we got here as fast as we could."

Heads whip towards the doorway, where David stands grinning, Johnny smiling shyly behind him. Judging by the stunned expressions around the table, I'm not the only one who wasn't expecting these two to crash dinner.

"Johnny?" I blurt. "David?"

I push my chair back, but before I can stand up properly, Johnny strides over and pulls me into a hug so tight it nearly knocks me off balance.

"Robbie! I've been so worried about you. I hated not being able to speak to you."

I pat his back awkwardly, acutely aware of everyone watching us. Ally, in particular, is surprised by this display of affection between Johnny and me. I suppose he's never seen this side of me before—the protective older brother rather than the troublemaker.

"I missed you too," I tell Johnny, keeping my voice low. "It's good to see you, but is it okay that you're here?"

"Aye." Johnny releases me. "Da said it's fine now the police have completed their investigation. I can't believe they charged you. I'm so sorry."

David, who's already given his sister a squeeze, now scoops Callie up. "And here she is, the princess of Bannock!" Callie squeals with delight as he spins her around.

"So, er . . ." Jamie gestures between Johnny and David with his fork. "Great to see you guys, but what's going on here? Do we need two more chairs?"

"I can explain." All eyes turn to Cat, who smiles sheepishly. "I thought it'd be a nice surprise for Robbie to have his wee brother here, and David's practically part of the family anyway. So . . . I fired off a quick text to David before Robbie and I got here. Hope it's all right that I invited them, and aye, we're going to need a couple more chairs." She turns hopeful eyes to Elspeth. "You were able to rustle up an extra plate for Robbie . . . any chance of two more?"

CHAPTER THIRTY

ROBBIE

As Cat drives us back to my cottage, the setting sun paints the sky in streaks of orange and pink.

I can't stop looking at her. The delicate curve of her chin, the slight upturn of her nose with that wee stud that glints in the fading light, the way her lips curl into a smile when she catches me staring.

"What?" she asks, her eyes returning to the road.

"Nothing. Just . . . that unexpected dinner turned out not too bad in the end."

She laughs, the sound light and musical.

Before long, we come to the dirt track that leads to my cottage, and she turns onto it, the trees casting long shadows. After everything that's happened recently, I should probably be focused on clearing my name, on figuring out how to prove my innocence. But right now, all I can think about is Cat.

She parks and kills the engine. For a wee while, we just sit there, the quiet settling around us like a blanket.

"Thank you," I say finally. "For . . . getting me out of my own head today. And for standing up for me."

She turns to me, her expression soft. "Anytime, MacDonald."

We head inside, and I shrug off my jacket. Cat sits on the wee bench by the door to slip off her trainers, then she peels off her jacket and hangs it neatly on a peg beside mine. It's such a small, ordinary thing, but watching her make herself at home in my space hits me hard. Something shifts deep inside me.

I slip one hand around her waist and draw her in. With the other, I tip her chin up, cradling it between my thumb and forefinger. Her skin is soft and warm, and her eyes lift to meet mine. Wide, searching, expectant.

I lower my mouth to hers—not gentle, but hungry, like I've been starving for the taste of her. She lets out a quiet, surprised sound against my lips, but then she's pressing closer, her hands fisting in my shirt.

Eventually—because we do actually need to breathe—I draw back, but I don't let go of her, just brush my thumb along her jaw. "You called me your boyfriend."

Her cheeks are already flushed from the kiss, but now the blush blooms even brighter. "Aye. I did."

"Did you mean it?"

"Yes." No games. No teasing. Just honesty.

My heart thudding, I press my forehead to hers. "You're mine now."

She shivers.

"Say it."

"I'm yours," she whispers, and the words send a jolt of possessiveness through me.

I pin her against the hallway wall, claiming her mouth again, rougher this time, tasting her gasp on my tongue. My hand slips under the waistband of her jodhpurs, my fingertips skimming over bare skin until I find her—hot and slick, ready for me.

She trembles, arching into my touch, and I press my mouth to her neck, letting my teeth skim the delicate skin as I breathe in her sweet, floral scent. She lets out a breathy moan when I slide two fingers inside her, her nails digging into my shoulders with delicious urgency.

"Tell me what you want, Cat."

She doesn't hesitate. "You. All of you."

I remove my fingers and scoop her up in my arms—bridal style because there's no other way to do this, not tonight—then carry her upstairs to my bedroom.

She takes in the simple decor, her eyes roving over the paperbacks on my shelves before finally landing on the large bed with its oak frame. I lay her gently on it then switch on the bedside lamp, a warm glow spilling across the room. I take her in—Cat, on my bed, cheeks tinged pink, auburn hair spread across my pillow, hazel eyes gazing up at me.

"You're beautiful."

I lie down beside her, intent on drawing this out and savouring every second, but Cat's always full of surprises. Quick as a flash, she swings a leg over and straddles me, her warmth sinking into me, even through my jeans. Her hands make quick work of her top, tugging it over her head while I just lie and watch, mesmerised—starving for her, utterly under her spell. She shoots me a devilish grin, unhooks her bra, then tosses it aside.

At the sight of her full pert breasts, whatever remaining control I have dissolves. I shuffle back until I'm slouched against the headboard, pulling her with me so her gorgeous tits are right in front of my eyes.

"Bloody hell, Catriona, you're gorgeous." I let my fingers roam over the trail of freckles dusted across her skin, then I press a kiss to each one, feeling her shiver against my lips.

I cradle her breasts—just the right fit for my hands—and she bows towards me with a shaky moan that sparks fire in my veins. I draw one tight nipple into my mouth, swirling my tongue around it while her hands tangle in my hair.

Her hips roll against my erection as I lick and tease her with my tongue. Every little sound she makes has me aching for more—her groans, the way she breathes out "Robbie" like it's a prayer, the heat and need burning between us. Right now, nothing else matters but her.

Cat's hips pick up speed, grinding against me with greedy intent. It's a work of art, seeing her move like this, still wearing those caramel-coloured jodhpurs that cling to her as if they were made just for her.

I grip her arse, giving it a firm squeeze that draws a gasp from her lips. "Cat, are you trying to get yourself off on me?"

She nods, biting down sexily on her lower lip.

"Let me help you with that." I flip us over, pinning her beneath me.

I take my time easing those jodhpurs down—slowly, deliberately, because she's the sort of woman who should be unwrapped like a gift. She arches her hips, making it easy for me to slide them off, along with her knickers, baring all that glorious skin.

For several heartbeats, all I can do is look at her—drinking in her lean legs and delicious curves. And then I'm leaning over her and whispering into her ear, "I'm going to make you come on my tongue."

She swallows audibly, then I get to work, trailing kisses down her neck, over those gorgeous breasts, across her belly, marking every inch with my lips. When I reach her thighs, she opens them for me.

"Good girl," I murmur, my thumbs parting her folds so I can look at her: glistening, swollen, pink. Fucking perfect.

I lower my head, and Cat lets out this desperate, breathless little moan. My nose nudges her most sensitive spot as my tongue explores, savouring her unique scent and taste.

"Robbie!" she whimpers.

I lap and tease until her whole body trembles with the telltale signs of an orgasm brewing. To heighten things for her, I seal my lips around her clit and give a purposeful hungry suck. That's all it takes. She shatters, calling out my name, her thighs squeezing my head as I feast on every gorgeous sound she makes.

The salty-sweet tang of her climax sends a fresh rush of heat to my cock. It's straining against the rough denim of my jeans, the piercing pressing almost torturously against the fabric.

When the last tremors of her orgasm subside, Cat goes boneless, her legs floppy. I press a slow, lingering kiss to her pussy then glance up. One arm drapes across her face, her chest lifting and falling, those gorgeous pink nipples stiff and begging for my mouth all over again.

"How was that?"

She peels her arm away, blinking at me like she's still floating somewhere above the bed. A lazy smile tugs at her lips. "It was . . . unbelievable."

"Want more?" I trace my thumb across her hot cheek.

She nods, and I strip off my shirt then make quick work of my jeans and boxers. I slide between her thighs, plant a quick kiss on her mouth, then line myself up and ease in, slow as you like, revelling in the way her hot, slick heat grips me, inch by glorious inch.

Her eyes flutter shut, and she lets out a moan, a sound that hits me somewhere deep and primitive.

"Look at me," I demand, and when she does, I push in deeper. This time, we both groan.

"Do you have any idea," I growl, rolling my hips, "what you do to me, Catriona McIntyre? How good you feel around my cock?"

In response, Cat wraps her arms around my neck and her legs around my hips, pulling me in even deeper, as if she can't bear a single millimetre of distance between us. Christ, it's like nothing else, like coming home, only I never knew what that felt like until now.

Cat undulates beneath me with this natural, instinctive rhythm that drives me wild, matching me thrust for thrust, rolling her body up into mine every time I sink deeper, greedy for every bit of friction we can make together.

The connection between us is electric—hot, frantic, desperate—but underneath it there's something softer too. The way she clings to me. The way our mouths find each other between gasps and moans.

Before long, our skin grows slick with sweat and we're both panting with effort. When Cat's walls flutter around me, I know she's close.

"That's it," I murmur as she looks up at me like I'm responsible for the stars in the sky. "Let go for me!"

She falls apart beneath me, and I follow her over the edge with a guttural groan, pouring every bit of myself into her as we come undone together.

Afterwards, I don't pull away. Instead, I gather her close, pressing my damp forehead to hers as we catch our breath. I want to tell her she means more than anyone ever has, but I don't know how.

Eventually, I manage, "Cat, this . . . isn't just a bit of fun for me." It's not nearly enough, but it's all I've got.

"I know. And you're not just a bad boy to me."

I pull out and lie down beside her, wrapping my arms around her and letting her settle against me with her head nestled beneath my chin. The things I can't find words for hang quietly in the air, but I hope she hears them in the way I hold her close.

After a while, the sweat on our skin cools. Cat stretches, blissed out and deliciously sleepy. I get up and drape a woollen throw over her. "Just going for a shower."

She lets out a lazy, satisfied wee sigh and curls herself into the pillow.

When I return five minutes later, a towel slung low around my hips, I'm fully expecting to find her asleep. Instead, she's sprawled naked atop the sheets, propped up on her elbows and eyeing the cork board, which she insisted I take after her and David's undercover mission at the resort. Her phone is awake beside her.

"Looking very relaxed there," I say, admiring her perfect arse. I can't resist sauntering round the bed for a better view, my gaze dropping shamelessly between her thighs.

Cat doesn't even glance up. "Oi! Stop ogling my bits. I'm conducting serious detective work here."

"Sorry, but can you blame me? You're an absolute vision. Also, detective work in the nude?"

She grins at me then returns her focus to the board. "Incoming English teacher fact: Ernest Hemingway wrote naked. Victor Hugo too. Others, I'm sure. It must be good for inspiration, and I need inspiration because I'm going to clear your name. I'm looking back through the photos I took in Samantha's office, and the records Johnny gathered for us, just in case I missed something."

Suddenly she frowns and shifts onto all fours (which only gives me an even better view) then crawls closer to squint at something pinned near the bottom of the board.

"Talking of which . . . oh shit, I . . . I think I may actually have something!"

She twists around, her eyes alight with excitement, and it takes true effort to tear my gaze away from everything else on display.

"I think I can prove you didn't nick anything. Just . . . give me a minute!"

And before I can ask what she means, Cat leaps off the bed and dashes stark naked from the room. I watch her go, torn between feeling like my luck might finally be turning and wondering how the hell my cock's already hard again. Seriously, I'm pitching a tent in my towel here.

CHAPTER THIRTY-ONE

CAT

My heart hammers as DS Sinclair leads our unusual procession through the Glen Garve Resort's staff corridor and towards Craig's office. This is it, our one shot to clear Robbie's name. Since my breakthrough last night, I've rehearsed my points, gathered our evidence, and now I just need to make everyone listen.

Robbie walks beside me, his jaw set in that determined way I've come to recognise. His hand finds mine and gives it a quick squeeze.

"Ready?" I whisper.

He nods once. "As I'll ever be."

I shoot a quick glance over my shoulder at PC Muir, who's taking up the rear. Her expression is professionally neutral.

Ahead, Sinclair stops at Craig's office door, knocks twice, then opens it without waiting for a response. Robbie, Muir, and I file in after him.

Craig sits behind his desk, looking more tired than imposing. Johnny hovers by the window, and then there's Samantha, perched on a chair with perfect posture, her appearance flawless and her uniform so crisp I'm surprised it doesn't crackle when she moves. The tight bun at the nape of her neck doesn't have a single hair out of place, but I don't miss how her fingers clench around her handbag when she spots Robbie.

"What's *he* doing here?" she demands. "I thought he was banned from the premises."

"Mr MacDonald is here with our permission," Sinclair explains. "As part of our investigation."

Samantha's perfectly shaped eyebrows rise. "I thought you had concluded your investigation?"

"We've been advised that new evidence has come to light." Sinclair glances at me and Robbie. "Apparently, all will become clear shortly."

I take this as our cue. "It will." I step into the centre of the room and give Robbie a quick tug so he moves with me. All eyes turn to us. "Robbie, care to kick things off?"

He clears his throat. "Sure. Let's start with what we know. Items were stolen from three different guest rooms. My keycard was used to access each room around the time the items were taken. And my fingerprints were found on Mr Harrington's signet ring.

"About the ring, I've already admitted to DS Sinclair and PC Muir that I did touch it. I panicked and lied at first—stupid, I know—but I thought the truth would make me look guilty. What happened is this. When I cleared out my locker, the ring just . . . fell out of it. Johnny was there—he can tell you how shocked I was."

Johnny nods emphatically. "He really was! Besides, if Robbie had put the ring there himself, he wouldn't have let it clatter to the floor the way it did. No, he'd have quietly slipped it into his pocket, right? I know my brother, and he was as surprised by the ring as I was."

Samantha snorts. "Is this why this meeting was called? So Robbie's own wee brother can swear he's innocent?" She flips her gaze to Sinclair and Muir. "I'm sure you'll forgive me for saying he doesn't exactly scream 'reliable witness'. And besides, as Robbie himself said, the keycard logs show he went into the rooms."

"They do," I agree. "Pretty incriminating, right? Except . . . there's something we should really clear up. Specifically, the claim that Robbie's keycard was used to access Ms Laurent's room on the day her diamond earrings went missing, an allegation he denies. Officers, could one of you please confirm for us all the date and time that Robbie supposedly entered Ms Laurent's room?"

Muir consults her notes. "Monday the twelfth of August at fourteen fifteen."

"Thank you. But in that case . . . how do you explain this?" With a flourish worthy of Sherlock Holmes himself, I produce a letter and hold it out to Muir. "For the benefit of everyone else, could you tell us what this is?"

Puzzled, Muir takes the letter from me. Her confusion only deepens as she scans it. "It's . . . a speeding ticket. Addressed to Mr MacDonald. There's a photograph of him here on his motorcycle."

"And the timestamp?" I prompt.

She blinks. "Fourteen seventeen . . . on Monday the twelfth of August."

"Just two minutes after he allegedly entered Ms Laurent's room," I point out. "And yet here he is, nine miles away from the resort. Meaning it couldn't possibly have been Robbie who went into Ms Laurent's room."

Sinclair walks over and grabs a hold of the letter. "Let me have a look at that." A few moments later, he lets out a low whistle. "Bloody hell."

"I went to pick up some washers for a repair," Robbie explains. "Fairly routine. I didn't remember it until Cat noticed the time on the speeding ticket was too close to the time in the keycard records."

The room falls silent as the implications sink in. Sinclair studies the letter more carefully.

"I'll need to verify this," he says, "but if it's legitimate . . ."

"It is," I assure him. "And it proves someone else used Robbie's keycard—or made it appear that way in the system. Someone who knew his routines, who had access to the resort's security system, and who had a motive to frame him."

Samantha shifts in her seat, a bead of sweat visible at her temple despite the room's air conditioning.

"Someone with financial problems, perhaps?" I suggest. "Someone who recently received final notices on several bills? Someone who, despite these money troubles, still bought a nine-hundred-pound handbag last month?"

Samantha's face drains of colour before flushing a deep red. "How did you . . . ? That's private information!"

"But it's true?" I press.

She stands abruptly, smoothing her skirt with a trembling hand. "My personal finances are none of your business. And they have nothing to do with these thefts!"

"Don't they?" I tilt my head. "Because it seems to me that someone with mounting debts might be desperate enough to steal valuable items from guests."

"This is ridiculous! And who are you to question me anyway? You're not staff, nor are you the police." Samantha turns to Craig. "You're not seriously listening to this, are you? I've worked here for fifteen years without incident. Meanwhile, *he*"—she jabs a finger towards Robbie—"has been trouble since day one."

Craig's expression is unreadable as he looks between Samantha and his son.

"People aren't always what they seem," Robbie says. "For example, Samantha likes to present herself as a stickler for the rules, but she's not above breaking them when it suits her."

Samantha's lips press into a thin line. "I have no idea what you're talking about."

"No?" Robbie raises an eyebrow. "So you've told my da about your relationship with Drew? Because I'm pretty sure resort policy says you have to disclose something like that, especially when there's a power imbalance."

The silence that follows is thick enough to chew on.

"You and Drew?" Craig says, leaning forwards, clearly stunned.

Samantha's composure crumbles further. She sinks back into her chair, eyes darting between Craig and the door as if calculating an escape route. "I . . . that's . . . it's relatively new," she stammers. "I was going to mention it."

"Were you really?" I fold my arms. "Or were you keeping it quiet because there are other things you're hiding too?"

"This is outrageous!" Samantha's voice rises. "So I'm seeing Drew and I forgot to fill out a form. That doesn't make me a criminal!"

"No," I agree. "But it does show you're willing to break rules when it suits you. And who's to say where you draw the line when it comes to secrets?"

I glance at Craig. "By the way, while we're on the subject of disclosure, I'm dating Robbie."

Robbie chokes on a laugh and shoots me a look that says, *Really? Now?*

I shrug, giving him a small smile before turning back to Samantha. "Now, about your trip to Inverness on the nineteenth—the one you were strangely secretive about, keeping details even from Drew. What was that for? Nipping off to flog the stolen goods, perhaps?"

"Of course not! And what I do in my free time is none of your business." Her carefully constructed facade is unravelling. She's cornered and desperate, and I can see the gears turning like mad behind those wild eyes.

Johnny's phone buzzes. He checks it then, without a word, walks over to the door and opens it.

Drew stands in the doorway, looking confused and a bit wary. His eyes widen when he spots Robbie. "Sorry, am I interrupting something?"

"Not at all." Johnny gestures for him to enter. "In fact, your timing is perfect. Thanks for coming."

Drew hesitates before stepping inside. The room feels smaller with another person in it, and I notice how his eyes dart from Robbie to Samantha, who's gone very still.

"Welcome, Drew," I say. "We were just talking with Samantha about the thefts around the resort—and the secret sexual relationship she's been having with you."

Drew's cheeks redden.

"Samantha was about to explain to us why she made a trip into Inverness on the nineteenth," I add. "A trip she's been oddly secretive about."

"I don't have to tell you my personal business!" Samantha objects. "What is this, an interrogation?" She glances at the officers.

"No, you don't have to tell us what you were up to," I agree. "But your refusal to talk is sure making you look guilty."

"All right, fine! You want to know what I was doing? I was selling my grandmother's brooch to pay bills. Happy now? Yes, I'm in debt!" She glares at me. "But that doesn't make me a thief."

"No, but framing Robbie does."

"I didn't frame anyone!" Her voice rises an octave. "If anything, you're the one trying to pin this on me!"

Drew shifts uncomfortably, and I turn my attention to him.

"Drew, we know Robbie couldn't have taken Ms Laurent's earrings. He was miles away when his keycard was used. Someone else went into that room but made it look like it was Robbie."

Drew's eyes flick to Samantha then away again. It's brief, but I catch it.

"Someone who knew the resort systems," I continue. "Someone who knew when Robbie would be off-site. Someone who might have been passed over for promotion in favour of Robbie."

Drew's face flushes. "That's . . . you can't just . . ."

"You're right!" Samantha shrieks suddenly. She stabs a finger at Drew. "It could have been him! *I* wouldn't have the first clue how to break into a guest's safe or anything like that. But someone in maintenance would. They know all the tricks!"

"Samantha, what are you talking about?" Drew's voice is strained. "I-I haven't done anything!"

"You've always been jealous of Robbie," Samantha insists. "You've moaned about him to me countless times. Maybe you framed him to get his job!"

For a moment Drew just stares at Samantha, speechless, then his confusion morphs into anger. "You're not fucking pinning this on me. It was your idea! You're the one who said you needed money for your debts. You're the one who suggested taking Mr Ashford's watch because 'the old fool wouldn't even notice'."

"And we'd have got away with it if we'd stopped there! But once you started pinching things, you couldn't stop, could you? The money from selling the watch would have been enough to solve my problems. I didn't need the other stuff!"

They glare at each other, the air between them crackling with tension and betrayal. Then, as if simultaneously realising what they've just admitted to, they fall quiet, their faces paling.

"I . . ." Drew starts, faltering. "I didn't—"

"I think we've heard enough," Sinclair says, his mouth set in a grim line.

"Fucking hell, Drew," Robbie mutters. "So you *were* in on it. I thought we were mates."

Drew scowls. "Mates? You were promoted over me, even though I've been here longer. And why? Because your daddy runs the place."

"Excuse me?" Craig stands, his chair scraping across the floor. "Robbie was promoted because he was the better candidate. No other reason."

Robbie looks at his father in surprise, clearly not expecting this defence.

"Better candidate?" Drew scoffs. "He's only here because of nepotism. Everyone knows it."

"That's just not true," Craig says firmly. "Robbie has a natural talent for the work. He can fix things I've seen others struggle with for hours. He earned that promotion."

Something shifts in Robbie's expression—a softening, a realisation that perhaps his father has seen and valued his skills all along.

"Well, it doesn't matter now, does it?" I interject, unable to resist a moment of triumph. "Game over, you two. Looks like you're not as clever as you thought."

"This is your fault," Drew snarls, his eyes fixing on me. "We'd have got away with it if it wasn't for you!"

He lunges forwards so suddenly I barely have time to flinch. But before he can reach me, there's a solid *thud*, then he stumbles back, blood streaming from his nose. Robbie stands between us, his right hand clenched into a fist, his chest rising and falling with controlled breaths.

My heart stutters. Even in the chaos of the moment, the significance of what just happened hits me. Robbie, who swore off violence seven years ago, just broke that vow. For me.

"That's assault!" Samantha shrieks, pointing at Robbie. "You all saw it! Officers, arrest him! He can't just punch people!"

"It was clearly self-defence," Craig says. "Drew was going for Catriona. Right, sergeant?"

Sinclair clears his throat. "Er . . . aye, that's right, Craig. Self-defence." He glances at Muir, who nods in agreement.

"But there *are* two people here who need to be arrested," Craig adds.

The officers move forwards, handcuffs at the ready.

"Samantha Drummond, Drew Miller, you are under arrest on suspicion of theft and attempting to pervert the course of justice," Sinclair says. "You do not have to say anything, but it may harm your defence if you do not mention when questioned something which you later rely on in court. Anything you do say may be given in evidence."

As the cuffs click around their wrists, Robbie remains positioned protectively in front of me, his broad shoulders creating a barrier. I peer around him, watching as Samantha turns on Drew, her face contorted with fury.

"This is all your fault!" she hisses. "If you'd just been satisfied with the watch, we wouldn't be here. But no, you had to get greedy!"

"Me? You're the one who came up with the plan in the first place!" Drew retorts, blood still trickling from his nose.

They're led away, bickering and blaming each other. Sinclair pauses at the door. "Robbie, your bail conditions are lifted. We'll need to take a statement from you—for the record—but we'll get these two to the station first." He hesitates then adds gruffly, "I owe you an apology. We were wrong about you."

He closes the door behind him, leaving just Johnny, Craig, Robbie, and me in the suddenly quiet office.

Robbie turns to me with a look of disbelief. "You did it."

Before I can reply, Johnny bounds over and pulls Robbie into a hug. "I'm so happy!" He hugs me next. "Thanks for helping my brother when I couldn't."

Craig rounds his desk and comes over too. "Yes, thank you, Catriona." He glances between Robbie and me. "You said something about being Robbie's . . . girlfriend?"

"Aye, that's right." I squeeze Robbie's hand.

Craig nods. "We'll need to talk more later, then. But first, Robbie, you and I need to talk, man to man. Johnny, Catriona, could I ask you to step outside for a few minutes?"

CHAPTER THIRTY-TWO

ROBBIE

The door clicks shut behind Cat and Johnny, leaving me alone with my da in his office. Silence stretches between us like a physical thing. Not the usual tense quiet we've perfected over the years, but something different. Uncertain.

Da settles into the seat behind his desk and gestures to the chair across from him. "Sit down, Robbie."

I lower myself into it, half expecting him to launch into a lecture about the impact this whole mess has had on the resort's reputation. But he just sits there, hands folded on the desk, looking at me with an expression I can't quite read.

"It seems I owe you an apology," he says finally. "I was too quick to believe you were responsible for the thefts."

I shift in my chair, unsure how to respond. Da isn't a man who apologises easily—or at all, really.

"Aye, well, you stumped up for my bail, at least."

"I did, but I should have done more." His eyes drop to his hands for a moment before meeting mine again. "Robbie, the relationship we have . . . it isn't as strong as I'd like. It never has been."

Something tugs at my heart, a feeling I immediately try to push down. I've spent too many years building walls around myself to let them crumble at the first sign of fatherly concern.

"I'd like to work on that," he continues, each word sounding like it costs him something. "For you and I to become closer. First off, of course, I'd like to offer you your job back at the resort."

I consider it. The Glen Garve Resort is the only place I've ever worked for any length of time. But these past two weeks, being my own boss, using skills I rarely got to practise at the resort . . . there's been something freeing about it. Something that's felt . . . right.

"I'm going to have to turn down that offer, Da."

His eyebrows rise in surprise.

"I appreciate it," I add. "I mean it. But . . . now that I've set up as self-employed, I want to try to see that through. See if I can't build a successful business of my own."

Da nods. "I can understand that." His lips lift in what might almost be a smile. "Just know that if ever you change your mind, there will always be a place for you here."

"Thanks, Da. Anyway, if that's everything . . ."

"No." He gestures for me to stay. "There's more. I think . . . I've never truly understood you, Robbie. And that's my failing." He runs a hand over his face, suddenly looking every one of his fifty-eight years. "Your maw . . . well, I think we can both agree she wasn't the best mother to you. Far from it. But . . . I could have been a better father."

The words hang in the air between us. How long have I waited to hear him say that? To acknowledge that maybe, just maybe, not everything was my fault? And yet now that he's finally turning the lens on himself, I can't help but stick up for him.

"At least you stayed."

"Aye, but I owed you more than just that. I think the worst thing your mother did was make me believe you were the problematic one, when that wasn't the case. I should have seen that so much sooner."

I swallow hard, unprepared for the emotions his words trigger.

"I . . . wish I'd done a lot of things differently," he continues. "Even just these last few weeks . . . you've been through hell, Robbie, and you shouldn't have had to go through it alone. I should have had your back."

"You didn't want to interfere with the police investigation. I get it."

He grimaces. "Maybe. But I'm sorry for leaving you to shoulder everything on your own."

I think of Cat's relentless optimism and that cork board covered in notes and string. "To be fair, I wasn't entirely on my own."

"Aye. Catriona McIntyre, eh? She's quite something. A good catch, I reckon." Da's lips twitch. "Considering you and Ally never got along, it's funny you've ended up with his wee sister."

"Aye, life sure takes some unexpected turns."

"That it does." Da stands and I follow suit. He extends his hand across the desk. "I'm proud of you, son. For standing your ground when everything was against you, and for forging your own path."

I reach out for a shake, but he clasps my hand in both of his—a clumsy, awkward gesture that somehow means even more than his words.

Something shifts between us. It's not forgiveness, exactly—

there's too much history for that—but it's a start. A foundation we can build on.

My throat tightens. "Thanks, Da."

◆ ◆ ◆

Johnny and Cat are waiting outside the office, and the moment I step through the door, Johnny launches himself at me—again—for another hug.

"You're free!" His voice is muffled against my shoulder. "I knew you'd clear your name. I just knew it."

I pat his back. "Aye, well, it was mostly Cat's doing."

Cat grins, and as soon as Johnny releases me, she wraps me up in a hug of her own. "Team effort," she corrects.

"So?" Johnny says. "What did Da want to talk to you about? Did he offer you your job back?"

"He did. But I turned him down."

Johnny's face falls. "But I thought . . . I mean, I was looking forward to working with you again."

"Relax, Johnny. I'll see you all the time outside of work. I just want to try this self-employed thing. See where it takes me."

"Oh." He considers this. "Actually, that makes sense. I can see you enjoying being your own boss. And based on what Cat's told me about the work you've done in her flat, you'll have no trouble finding clients."

"Exactly," Cat agrees. "Robbie's got real talent. He's going to do great."

Johnny nods then nudges me with his elbow. "Never thought I'd see the day, but you seem to be smitten, Robbie."

I roll my eyes but don't deny it. What's the point? It's written all over my face whenever I look at Cat.

"Thanks so much again, Cat," Johnny says. "For keeping him company, as well as for clearing his name."

He gives her a quick squeeze—lots of hugging going on today—then turns to me. "Actually, Robbie, while I've got you, there's something I've been wanting to run by you. See, I've had some plans for a wee while now, but I put them on hold because I couldn't even think about them while there was a risk of you going to prison. But now . . ."

He leans in so close I can feel his breath on my ear and mutters something quietly.

For a split second, I'm stunned. Then a slow grin spreads across my face and I clap his shoulder, hard enough that he winces and tries to shove me away with half-hearted indignation.

Cat narrows her eyes at us suspiciously. "What are you two plotting?"

"Nothing," Johnny and I say in perfect unison, both trying—and failing—to look innocent.

She snorts but lets it go.

We chat for a few more minutes, Johnny keen to know *everything* about me and Cat, but eventually it's time to say goodbye. Johnny has to get back to work, and I'm eager to put as much distance between myself and the Glen Garve Resort as possible, at least for today. I'll be back, though. Besides, Da mentioned he wanted to have a chat with Cat, but that can wait until another day.

We part ways with Johnny, then Cat and I step out into the sunshine, and I take a deep breath of fresh Highland air. For the first time in a fortnight, it feels like I can actually fill my lungs properly.

"Freedom suits you," Cat observes, slipping her arm through mine as we cross the car park towards my bike.

"Aye, it does. Thanks for believing in me. For fighting for me when I was ready to give up."

"That's what girlfriends do," she says with a cheeky smile. "And it turns out wishes really do come true. Remember the clootie well? This is what I asked for: your name being cleared."

"Is that right?"

"Mm-hmm. Anyway"—she leans in conspiratorially—"I had a vested interest in keeping you out of prison."

"Oh aye? And what was that?"

"The sex, of course." She winks. "Talking of which, we proved your innocence, and that calls for a special celebration—a bedroom one. Take me back to your place. Or mine. I'm not fussy, so long as we end up naked together."

I laugh, feeling lighter than I have in weeks, maybe years. "Your wish is my command."

We reach my Triumph Bonneville Speedmaster, the sunlight bouncing off its sleek black and chrome curves. I run my hand over the seat, remembering all the times this bike has been my only escape, my only freedom. But now I've got Cat too.

I hand Cat her helmet then pull on my own. She climbs on behind me, wrapping her arms securely around my waist, pressing her body against mine. I fire up the engine.

"Mind your speed, Robbie!" Cat calls. "The last ticket may have turned out to be a blessing in disguise, but I don't want you getting any more, all right?"

"Understood!"

I twist the throttle and we roll away from the resort, past the manicured lawns, past the carefully cultivated flowerbeds, and onto the open road.

The Highlands unfold around us: emerald hills, untamed

forest, fields scattered with sheep. The wind whips past, carrying the scent of sun-warmed heather and pine. But for once, I'm not riding to escape. I'm riding towards something. Towards a future that suddenly seems full of possibilities.

EPILOGUE
CAT

I step back to admire my handiwork. The cheese and crackers are artfully arranged on one plate, with a selection of treats from Morag's Bakery on another. Morag insisted on throwing in a few extras for free after Robbie fixed her leaking roof last week.

"You know," she'd said, lowering her voice as she handed over the box, "I always thought that MacDonald lad was nothing but trouble. Shows what I know! He's a proper gent."

I smile at the memory. Bannock's opinion of Robbie has been shifting, and I know it means more to him than he lets on.

But speaking of Robbie . . . I check the time on my phone and let out a frustrated huff. Where is he? He promised he'd be here to help me set up for my flat-warming party. The first guests are due to arrive any minute.

I've barely finished the thought when the front door opens.

"I'm back!" Robbie calls.

"Where have you been?" I march through to the hall to confront him. "I've been running around like a headless chicken trying to get everything ready!"

"Sorry," he says, not looking particularly apologetic. "Had something important to take care of."

I give his chest a playful smack, only for him to flinch. "Ow!"

My annoyance vanishes in an instant. "Oh my God, what's wrong? Are you hurt?"

"Well . . ." There's a mischievous glint in his eye. "Depends on how you look at it." He takes a hold of my hand and pulls me towards the bedroom, away from the door where guests might arrive any minute.

"Robbie MacDonald, if you think we have time for—"

"Not that," he interrupts with a smirk. "Though I like where your mind went." With no shame whatsoever, he grabs the hem of his T-shirt and lifts it up.

My breath catches, not just at the sight of him (old habits die hard, and apparently so does ogling), but because something new catches my eye—a glint of cling film stretched over his chest. Two patches, actually.

"What's this?"

"A surprise. Here, look."

He gestures to one of the patches. Beneath it is his chain tattoo, only it's changed. The broken link that once symbolised his fractured relationship with his father has been repaired. The lines are fresh, and the skin around them pink and tender.

"Da and I still have a way to go, but we're on the right path now. I didn't want to keep carrying that broken link anymore."

I swallow hard. "That's . . . beautiful, Robbie. I can't believe you did that."

"And then there's this one . . ." He indicates the second patch of cling film, just over his heart. A small black cat is curled there now—elegant and mischievous and perfectly drawn.

"For me?" I whisper.

"Aye. For my Cat."

Every molecule in my body wants to fling myself at him, but his poor chest looks sore enough as it is. So I settle for going up on my tiptoes, cupping his jaw, and pressing a gentle kiss to his lips. "I love it. And I love you."

"I love you too," he murmurs back.

A knock at the door interrupts us.

"Later," I promise, my eyes telling him exactly what I mean.

The corner of his mouth lifts. "I'll hold you to that."

Within half an hour, my living room is filled with all the people I love most. My brothers and their partners have taken over the sofa and armchairs, while Elspeth and Bryce chat with Johnny and David near the window. Bruce has found a sunny spot on the floor and is snoozing contentedly. Aidan and Grace sit beside him, watching wee Ru toddle after Callie, who won't stay still for a moment. Emily cradles baby Ciaran—he's somehow sleeping peacefully despite the noise.

I'm buzzing around like a hostess possessed, making sure everyone has a drink and that no one dares set a glass directly on my new coffee table.

"Coaster!" I reprimand, sliding one under Jamie's beer bottle.

He raises an eyebrow. "Who are you, and what have you done with my sister?"

"Very funny," I retort, but I catch Robbie watching me with amusement from across the room. Maybe I am being a bit . . . particular. But hey, I'm proud of this place, as I think I have every right to be.

"The flat looks fantastic, Cat," Lewis says, glancing around appreciatively.

"It's gorgeous," Iona agrees. "You've really made it your own."

I beam. "Thanks. Robbie did a great job, didn't he?"

"Oh, I can't take all the credit," Robbie says. "See that shelf over there? The one that's very slightly wonky? All Cat."

I roll my eyes, but there's laughter—from my brothers especially—and Jamie claps his hands together. "Robbie can be funny! Who knew?"

"*Anyway*," I say, "as much as I love what we've done with the place, I'm sure it won't be long before Robbie invites me to move in with him. So in a way, all this work was for nothing."

A hush falls, and everyone looks back and forth between me and Robbie. I half expect someone to whip out a bag of popcorn.

"Oh, you're *sure* I'll be inviting you to move in, are you?"

"No doubt about it. After all, you did just get a new tattoo . . . of a cat. To represent me."

Emily's eyes light up. "Can we see it?"

"Er . . ."

"Aye, show us!" Maisie chimes in.

With a martyred sigh—like he's being forced into hard labour rather than a minor striptease—Robbie pulls his T-shirt up. He tries for a scowl, but there's a glint in his eye that says he secretly enjoys the fuss (even if he'd never admit it).

The women immediately swarm him like seagulls on a dropped chip. Grace gasps, and Emily fans herself with a napkin. Maisie leans in for a closer inspection, while Iona strokes her chin like an art critic at the Tate. Even Elspeth gives him a once-over so thorough I half expect her to hold up a score card.

Ally—who's been passed Ciaran—groans loudly. "Really? Is this appropriate?"

"Oh, hush," Emily admonishes. "It's sweet."

David, who moments previously chased Callie out of the room, returns only to fling an arm over his eyes in mock agony. "Not again! Johnny, save me! Before I do something scandalous." He blindly gropes for his boyfriend's hand.

Johnny, chuckling, entwines his fingers with David's. "Think it's time we told them?"

"I think we must." David lowers his arm from his face and clears his throat. "If I could have everyone's attention, please! And Robbie, if you could *please* pull your top back down? Thank you. All right, I'd like to take this opportunity to let you all know that I am officially off the market. Johnny and I are engaged!"

The room erupts in cheers and applause. Johnny gives a shy grin, his face flushed pink.

"But there's more," David continues once the initial excitement dies down. "There's been a cancellation at the resort, so . . . we're getting married next month!"

At this, Iona's smile becomes noticeably strained.

"Oh! Sorry, Iona!" David says hurriedly. "I hope you don't feel like we're skipping the queue."

"Not at all. I'm happy for you!"

Jamie snorts. "Maybe tell your face that." This earns him a thump on the arm from Lewis.

"Really, it's great news," Iona insists. "Just feels strange, that's all. Lewis and I haven't even set a date yet."

Lewis slips an arm around her waist. "Don't worry, we will soon. I promise."

Jamie nods sagely. "I wouldn't worry about it, Iona. At least you're one step ahead of Aidan and Grace. They have a wee girl, and they're not even engaged yet."

"Oi!" Aidan shoots him a warning look. "Careful!"

"Jamie McIntyre!" Elspeth tuts. "Maisie, I thought you'd reined this one in?"

Maisie shrugs. "I tried my best, but you know what he's like."

"We do," I say, giving Jamie my best teacherly glare, which he ignores. "But we're getting off track. I'm pretty sure David wants to lap up being the centre of attention for a wee bit longer."

"I absolutely do," he confirms.

"And Johnny too, of course," I add quickly. "So . . . a toast! To Johnny and David!"

"To Johnny and David!" comes the chorus as glasses are raised.

The evening continues, laughter bouncing off the walls, and Bruce and Ciaran somehow both snoozing through everything.

Robbie manages to claim a chair, and I slip onto the arm of it, letting myself soak in the scene—my family, my friends, all gathered here together. Across the room, Ally catches my eye and gives me a nod, which I take as his way of saying that he approves. Of everything. Of Robbie, of me, of the cheese selection.

Leaning down, I whisper in Robbie's ear, "I think you've won over your toughest critic."

Robbie glances at Ally. "Aye? Well, let's see how he reacts to this." Before I can so much as blink, he tugs me down onto his lap, his arms winding round my waist.

Ally's jaw twitches—just for a second—but then wee Ru throws himself at his da's knees with a giggle. Ally scoops his son up and tosses him into the air, everything else forgotten.

I twist round to look at Robbie, taking in the sharp angles of his face, the pierced eyebrow, the blue eyes that used to seem so cold but are now warm whenever they land on me.

Six weeks ago, I was the party girl who'd moved back to her hometown, buying a rundown flat she had no idea how to fix.

Now I'm hosting a gathering in a place I've made my own, sitting on the lap of a man I was warned to stay away from but who turned out to be exactly what I needed.

Maybe I'm not the wild child anymore. Maybe I've grown up a bit. But looking at Robbie—my tattooed, motorcycle-riding bad boy who's not really bad at all—I know one thing for certain: life with him will never be boring.

I wouldn't have it any other way.

A NOTE FROM THE AUTHORS

Want to say one last goodbye to the characters of the *True Scotsman* series? Subscribers to our free email newsletter can download a bonus epilogue set during David and Johnny's wedding.

Craving more Scottish romance? Meet a grumpy ferry captain and the sunshiny nanny who turns his world upside down in *Captain of My Heart*, book one in our *Scottish Single Dads* series.

For more information, visit amymcgavin.com.

Bonus Epilogue

Captain of My Heart

Captain of
My Heart

AMY McGAVIN